THE SKIRMISHERS

Mick Green

Publisher: Inspiring Publishers,
P.O. Box 159, Calwell, ACT Australia 2905
Email: publishaspg@gmail.com
http://www.inspiringpublishers.com

A catalogue record for this book is available from the National Library of Australia

National Library of Australia The Prepublication Data Service

Author: Mick Green
Title: The Skirmishers
Genre: Fiction

Paperback ISBN: 978-1-923087-87-3
ePub2 ISBN: 978-1-923087-86-6
PDF eBook ISBN: 978-1-923087-85-9

To my family and everyone who has supported me over the years,
to all our service personnel,
and to those who have made the ultimate sacrifice:
this work is dedicated to you.

The military units depicted in this book are, at times, fictional or representations of disbanded regiments. However, references to active regiments and military units are intentional. I have specifically chosen to mention those that have profoundly impacted my life and military career.

PROLOGUE

Boom!

Major Mike Sharpe sensed rather than saw the blinding flash, and his reaction was to immediately shut his eyes and hit the ground. The explosion's shock wave passed through his body, resulting in a feeling like his soul was falling out of him. Just when the positive wave—an effect of the explosion—had passed through him, making him feel he would never be one with his body again, the inevitable negative shock wave reversed the cycle, bringing him back to his senses.

He opened his eyes, cleared the dust from his goggles, and began to survey the situation around him—one he had become all too familiar with over the last few years in both Iraq and Afghanistan. It wasn't just the common sight of dust, debris, and the inevitable crater; he was also deeply in tune with his sense of smell, noticing the mixture of dust and explosives that penetrated his cotton kaffiyeh face covering.

The blast was incredibly close, but the radio burst from the JTAC—the American Joint Terminal Attack Controller— moments before the explosion gave them precious few seconds to take cover. Their state-of-the-art ballistic hearing protection had saved their eardrums from the blast and enabled him to quickly gather situational awareness without too much disorientation. He spoke assertively but barely above a whisper to his team through the radio. The throat mic picked up every word he said.

"Sierra Kilo, Alpha: Check in. Over."

The radio immediately crackled in his earpiece as his team, in turn, answered. They'd been very lucky: no injuries.

Okay, that's the closest blue-on-blue I've experienced, he thought. The immediate need was to get the team out of there. "All call signs to checkpoint Bravo," he messaged, directing his team to the extraction point.

He picked himself up as the sun began to shine through the quickly dissipating dust cloud that had been produced by the explosion. There was plenty of cover in their location, and the route to the checkpoint had been well planned. Even though they had survived the blast, there was little danger of any enemy combatants remaining in the area after an explosion of that magnitude. The Skirmishers operated in pairs, and on this mission, he had partnered with one of his corporals, Stephanie Holgate. She flashed him a knowing glance, conveying both bewilderment at the explosion's proximity and gratitude for their survival.

"Major Sharpe," she said meaningfully.

"I know," he replied.

"Fucking outrageous, Sharpie." He detected the disdain in her voice as she reverted to his nickname, which wasn't unusual.

"At least we got a warning," he retorted sarcastically.

She smiled; the dark humor was already kicking in.

They quickly set off. As they made their way back, he studied her. At that moment, Corporal Stephanie Holgate, the twentysomething supermodel, was currently covered in half the desert, her impeccable white teeth shining through the remnants of the dust cloud. She was probably one of the most ferocious members of his fighting team and was also a beacon for trouble. While referring to her as a "supermodel" might sound derogatory in normal circumstances, her appearance was undeniably striking. Behind those blue eyes, though, was a born fighter, brought up in the north of England but with a bizarre Home Counties accent, which had probably developed after spending a good part of her formative years traveling.

He remained alert, patrolling the rear, while Steph took point. He reflected on the endless nights out in which he would watch Steph inevitability face multiple attempts by various guys to get her to take notice of them, hoping for an all-night liaison. It was like a sadistic comedy, as she would clearly be giving off a *not a chance* signal, but the guys, emboldened by alcohol, would keep trying and subsequently look all the more stupid for it. Whenever the line was crossed, he watched as grown men crumpled into a heap. They'd either said the wrong thing to her or, once they'd heard she was in a frontline army unit, challenged her on whether she was up to the job. Often, she'd smash a head into a pool table or break the nose of some guy who probably deserved it. So many memories, so many nights—and it all seemed to be coming to an end.

He wouldn't miss the endless admin that inevitably followed such wild nights, as he tried to talk various fellow officers down from making an example of his team. In the last year or so, they had all matured; the violence they faced every day on the battlefield made them yearn for the quieter life back home.

Major Mike Sharpe and Corporal Stephanie Holgate were the last back to the checkpoint, and he was genuinely pleased to see eight other smiling faces, all talking about the near miss.

"What was that all about, sir?" asked Paul Johnson, the unit sergeant.

"That was the RAF getting a little bit too close," Mike replied.

"We didn't call the air strike."

"I'm guessing it came from a unit nearby," Mike said.

"Clearly, they had no idea we were there. Lucky we got the JTAC call," Johnson added.

"And we may well have the RAF to thank for that."

After checking in with each member of the team and ensuring the extraction point was secure, Major Mike Sharpe had a few moments to reflect. This was the last tour of duty for the Skirmishers, and it was arguably the most successful. They had been used on multiple missions to disrupt and confuse the enemy prior to wider coalition engagement. Most importantly, he was bringing them all home—no injuries, no fatalities.

He looked at his team. Over the years he'd put together a group of misfits that other leaders in the regular army would have rejected, but ultimately, he regarded them as probably the most professional fighters in the army. The idea for the creation of the Skirmishers had come from his own predicament as a misfit within the officer corps. Mike had been lucky to meet Tom Sawyer, who understood that combat had a place for freethinking mavericks, given the right time and circumstances. Over the years, the Skirmishers' skills had been honed to disrupt the enemy in any way possible. At times, they had caused so much disarray and confusion that the opposing force had simply surrendered. Their disruptive tactics had made them the go-to squadron of choice before the execution of larger, more difficult missions. They were sent in ahead of other troops to create diversions—or, as one of his team often said, "Create a storm." Their tasking frequently came from the very top, and the Skirmishers had earned the respect of all who worked with them. Their accomplishments would become legendary, their stories likely embellished as they were retold in officer, senior, and junior rank messes.

As the heat bore down on him, sipping water from his canteen, his thoughts turned to their current predicament. It was all about getting extracted back to the forward operating base and getting his team home. More significantly, this wasn't just the last mission of the tour; it marked the end of the road for the Skirmishers as the British Army began its final redeployment home.

It was inevitable that all ten of them had decided to leave the army, despite his efforts and those of Colonel Tom Sawyer, to persuade them otherwise. On operations, they were revered, but in a peacetime army, it was hard for any of them to see how they would actually fit in. Colonel Tom had not been able to get a Skirmishers squadron approved with the directorate of Special Forces, and none of them had the desire to go through Special Forces selection. Leaving the army was exactly what they wanted. For Mike, as the end of the tour got closer, he just couldn't see himself being a staff officer or jumping on the promotion elevator. Like the rest of his team, the regular army in peacetime wasn't ready for him or him for it, and that was why he was a major, leading a team without a junior officer.

"Alpha, this is Sierra 4. Blue Force approaching," came the familiar voice of Jon Apolosi, one of his Fijian soldiers, into his earpiece.

"Roger. Out."

A minute later, there came a roar from a loud, crisp, well-spoken voice: "Who the hell are you lot?"

Mike looked up and smiled as a slightly agitated army captain approached him. He stood up, which stopped the captain in his tracks. He looked Sharpe up and down, probably trying to formulate who was in front of him.

Major Mike Sharpe, affectionately called "Sharpie" by some—a nod to the famous Bernard Cornwell character—stood around six feet tall, with mousy brown-blond hair, piercing blue eyes, and an indistinct accent. He possessed the type of personality that would normally light up any room he walked into, and it often worked in his favor, especially when conversing with senior officers' wives. Mike would often receive an element of gratitude after the wives told their husbands what a fantastic human he was. However, the reality was that the army wasn't ready for him. Part of his problem stemmed from his disinterest in the rank system and his preference for spending downtime with his team, which often drew the disapproval of fellow officers. This had been highly detrimental to his career, until he met Colonel Tom, who'd chosen him to create and command the Skirmishers. Despite his approachability, personality, and overall demeanor, he was a ferocious fighter. He had fought his way up through the system all his life and was a natural leader for this group of individuals.

Here we go again, he thought as he stood before the captain. Although Mike was a higher rank, he decided, for the entertainment of his team, that he'd have a bit of fun with the captain. It was funny, though, as he thought to himself how the Skirmishers must look from the outside. They were often mistaken for Special Forces teams because of the way they appeared. All had different personalities, styles, and backgrounds—an Aussie woman, an Englishwoman, two Scotsmen, two Fijians, and four Englishmen, including himself. None of them really looked like a regular soldier.

"And who are you?" Mike asked with an air of authority.

"I'm Captain Stevens of the Third Cambridge Regiment. And you can refer to me as *sir*," said Stevens, trying to reinforce his authority.

"Was that you who called the air strike?" Mike asked.

"We called it in. Too much enemy contact on the ground." Stevens now seemed agitated that Mike hadn't addressed him as *sir*.

"I assume you noticed that they were firing on someone in that contact? Did you think to check whether there were any friendly soldiers operating in those coordinates?" asked Mike, half sarcastically.

There were a couple of guffaws from the Skirmishers and a few more from the five Cambridge regiment men who stood next to their captain.

"Maybe mission planning could be improved?" continued Mike.

It slowly began to dawn on Stevens that the man in front of him was mocking him.

"Good work in giving us that departing present; make sure you thank the RAF." Sharpe noticed a vein starting to bulge on the side of Stevens's neck and on his temple.

Mike knew Stevens was getting more and more agitated, so he decided that it was probably wiser to defuse the situation before it escalated.

"Sir, chopper inbound," called a distant voice.

Mike heard the all-too-familiar *waka waka* sound of a Chinook helicopter as it neared the extraction point.

"We'll finish this discussion later," said Stevens, belatedly realizing that the *sir* had been directed at Sharpe.

"I guess so," Sharpe responded half-heartedly, walking away with his team.

"Thought you were going to have more fun, sir?" Sergeant Johnson teased, laughing.

A wry smile crossed Major Sharpe's face.

The flight time back to the forward operating base was less than fifteen minutes. The Skirmishers gathered their remaining gear and reboarded the Chinook for Camp Bastian, accompanied by the Cambridge regiment who had just completed their tour of duty.

Mike felt uneasy knowing Captain Stevens would be at Bastian with him. He glanced at his team and the Cambridge regiment— young soldiers with weathered faces showing the strain of their tour. He knew that once those faces looked fresh again, possibly with a couple of extra stress lines, the real problem would likely lurk behind their eyes. What they had seen and done could not be explained to someone who had not lived and breathed it. He contemplated what all this would really mean in the long term and how soon, with time, it would all be forgotten by the grateful public. He snapped out of it when the aircrew announced two minutes to landing and the relative safety that landing would bring.

When they arrived at Bastian, Major Troy Hannigan greeted them. He informed Major Sharpe and Captain Stevens that the colonel wished to see them after they cleaned up. The colonel also wanted to express his gratitude to both the regiment and the Skirmishers for the day's operation.

The Skirmishers, thought Captain Stevens. *Great!* There was more to Mike Sharpe than he had realized.

Wonderful! thought Sharpe. *It never goes well when you put the Skirmishers on parade.* No doubt there was more trouble ahead before he left the army. He all but forgot about the fun he was having with Captain Stevens.

As professional soldiers, the Skirmishers cleaned their equipment meticulously, got ready for the parade, and went out to a makeshift area set up for the colonel to do his briefing. "Who's in charge here?" the Cambridge regiment sergeant major roared.

"I guess that's me," replied Sergeant Johnson.

"What the hell is this in front of me, Sergeant?" he asked as he looked at the strangest bunch of soldiers he'd probably ever seen in his life.

"These are the Skirmishers," replied Johnson.

"I don't really give a shit, Sergeant. Where's your officer?"

"He'll be out in a minute, if you wanna have a chat with him. He doesn't say too much, so you'll probably get very little from him," said Johnson, stretching the truth but reducing the aggravation for his boss.

Sergeant Johnson knew the RSM must have heard about the Skirmishers, because he walked away. This was unusual for an RSM, but he was grateful nevertheless.

Major Sharpe and Captain Stevens were in front of the colonel in his makeshift office in the joint operations center. By the welcome Mike had received from the colonel, it immediately dawned on Stevens that Sharpe and Sawyer were very close. "I see you and Stevens bumped into each other, Sharpe. Hope everything was friendly," said the colonel knowingly.

"All good, sir." Mike realized Stevens had probably already spoken with the colonel. "Stevens sent the team his best wishes just before the extraction."

Stevens blushed.

"Good man," Sawyer said to Stevens. "You can learn a lot from the major."

Nothing more needed to be said. The colonel had guessed Mike had been playing Stevens along, and it was good for Stevens to receive a little humility.

"Let's see the troops, shall we, gentlemen? We can debrief over a drink later, Sharpie. We have much to discuss," Sawyer said.

On the way out to the parade, Stevens quietly said to Mike, "I apologize, Major."

"For what?" said Mike.

"For calling in the close air strike near your position."

"Felt like it was *on* our position," Mike said with a smile.

"I didn't realize you were a major."

"Oh yeah, the rank thing," said Mike. He'd finished having his fun. "Seriously, your team did some great work out there; you should be proud of your regiment."

"Thanks," said Stevens. He felt oddly chuffed that he'd received a compliment from someone he strangely liked. The Mike Sharpe effect!

On parade, the contrast between the two groups of soldiers was stark: the Cambridge regiment lined up in an orderly fashion, battle weary but extremely dutiful, as the colonel spoke with them. The Skirmishers formed a semicircle, showing respect but without the same formality. Although the Cambridge soldiers swelled with pride when Sawyer awarded them a unit citation, they watched in astonishment as the colonel approached each Skirmisher and embraced them.

Colonel Tom Sawyer addressed the Skirmishers: "We created you. We trained you. Some had their doubts, but I am certain that without you, the army and the coalition would have faltered. Remember your origins, how you were chosen for the Skirmishers, and what you've become. The time has come to reintegrate into civilian life. If you ever need support, you know where to find it."

Throughout his career, Sawyer understood that different soldiers were motivated in varied ways — some through grand speeches, others by simple words of encouragement. His experiences spanned both the intelligence community and the Special Forces. He held immense pride for the Skirmishers and recognized that for them, brevity carried weight. Nothing pretentious or overly elaborate; the less said, the better.

The next day, as they awaited their departure in the VIP facility—facilitated by the UKMAMS, whom they'd met earlier in their tour—Mike felt the time was right to address his team. Before boarding the RAF Voyager bound for RAF Brize Norton, he called them together. "As you know, we'll skip the decompression in Cyprus and handle it once we're home. We have three months of resettlement—or 'holiday', as some of you cheekily put it—before venturing into civilian life.

"We'll get together when we arrive home; we'll say our goodbyes in the same manner that this team bonded. We'll always be there for each other, as brothers- and sisters-in-arms. Never be a stranger to one another, and always stay on the right side of the line. If we ever get into trouble, we still have each other. What we've done on countless tours has changed the future—hopefully for the better—for the people of this country, but now they face their own path, like you. The path will not be easy, and you will at times have to make decisions that might not work out for you. Remember to learn from these decisions. If you're ever in a situation where there appears to be no way forward, or if you're ever in trouble, don't be afraid to call the number. Now go and take on the world!"

1

Tommy Stewart was in his element as he walked purposefully through the streets of London. Although he loved his hometown of Edinburgh, he found the vibe of London intoxicating, making it his go-to location whenever he had time off. He wasn't familiar with Shoreditch, but a friend had told him it was a tough part of London to grow up in during the 1980s and early 1990s. Over the years, urban regeneration had transformed the area as young professionals, technology companies, trendy bars, and restaurants moved in. Tommy was always amazed by the number of black London cabs, moving like a giant snake, only breaking for passengers. He was also intrigued by the number of red buses, the lifeblood of the city, taking people to thousands of stops across London. Meanwhile, millions traveled on the subway system below. He found the whole operation fascinating and mind-blowing.

It was a pleasant day for the time of year, so Tommy decided to walk the final nine hundred meters or so to his destination. He wore his usual jeans, a smart collared shirt left untucked, and trail shoe-like trainers. He was meeting Rachel, a girl he found on an app, swiped right, exchanged text messages, and had a quick chat with.

They agreed to meet at 1:00 p.m. Arriving thirty minutes early would allow him to have one or two pints to loosen up. Not too many, though, as he hoped the rest of the afternoon would involve him getting his rocks off.

As he walked past a café, he noticed a couple people-watching as they enjoyed their coffee. He wondered idly if they knew his plans and hopes for the day. If they were really observing him, they would see he was one of the few people walking purposefully without distraction. He couldn't understand how people could be so oblivious and lack situational awareness. It was concerning that these people seemed naïve to the fact they were potential targets for muggers or pickpockets—either that or they didn't view the world in the same way he did. He walked past a Pret a Manger, the Bull in a China Shop bar, and Shoreditch House; then realized he was near the meeting place, The Eagle.

The Eagle was a pub on a corner of a very narrow street. It seemed out of place, considering the area's reputation, and honestly, it wasn't the type of establishment he'd expected. Rachel had warned him it was more of a local pub, not her regular bar, but it wasn't far from where she lived. That was all he'd needed to hear—*not far from where she lived.* He liked the sound of that!

As he entered the pub, he was immediately taken aback by the smell of stale beer. He did a quick scan before making his way to the bar. There were a couple of guys at the table nearest to the front door and three or four people at the bar, all of whom were probably regulars who inevitably sat in the same seat every time they drank there. At the side of the bar was a large table with ten to twelve men sitting around it, playing cards and clearly enjoying an afternoon drinking session.

The pub itself was typically English; it had a historic feel about it and the traditional pride of place dark-wood bar with matching furniture throughout. The carpet probably hadn't been changed since the eighties, but attempts had evidently been made to steam wash it a thousand times to try to clean up the many spilled pints.

The two guys at the table acknowledged him, and he nodded back as he made his way to the bar. He ordered a pint of lager, and then, much to his embarrassment, the barman asked him for ID. He reached into his wallet and, for the first time, pulled out his driver's license instead of his army ID card. The barman handed it back. There were a couple of laughs at the large table, but Tommy didn't imagine they were aimed at him. As he returned the driver's license to his wallet, he could just make out the black imprint on the plastic cover that had been left behind by his army ID.

He'd left the army just three weeks earlier. He watched as the barman pulled the pint, staring at the amber liquid that filled the glass. The bubbles began to rise to form the bright-white head of the beer. *If only you knew,* he thought, looking at the barman. Asking for his ID after all the things that Tommy had seen and done in his short life.

Three months' holiday and three weeks out of the army, he thought as he took the first mouthful of beer. It had been three weeks since he'd had his last drink—well, *drinks.* He smiled. The last night of the Skirmishers. It had been great seeing them all again, although he had gone on holiday beforehand with Lisa "Skippy" Carter and Jon Apolosi and Jon's family. He liked Skippy a lot but had too much respect for her and not enough courage to ask her out on a date. Besides, he'd convinced himself, it would ruin their friendship in the long run.

What a night it had been, though, that last gathering of the Skirmishers. It had also been the toughest night of his life, as he'd said a final goodbye to his friends and his unit. Despite the promises to get together again, he was never really sure it would happen. *No, of course it will happen,* he told himself. He knew that as long as Mike Sharpe was motivated to organize something, there would be future opportunities for a reunion.

"You want another one?" asked the barman.

Tommy glanced down at the glass, which he had emptied in what seemed like no time at all. He looked at his watch. Fifteen minutes had passed since he'd lost himself in his thoughts.

"Aye, please," said Tommy in his soft Scottish tone.

The barman placed another pint in front of him. Tommy heard a noise from the large table that sounded like a poor imitation of a Scottish accent from a very pissed-up Cockney. He decided to ignore it but was annoyed with himself that he had chosen to sit at the bar rather than in a seat that would allow him to have his back to the wall and full view of the pub.

He took another couple of mouthfuls and began entering the same trancelike state as before. His thoughts turned to the first time he'd met Mike Sharpe. He smiled as he remembered that he had been in deep shit at the time for striking a corporal. He recalled Mike walking into the room where he was being held, kicking all the SNCOs out with an air of charm that meant they all did as he said, without hesitation.

"You like fighting, Tommy?" Mike had asked, barely above a whisper. It was the strangest question an officer had ever asked him.

"No, sir," Tommy had replied.

"You're no good to me, then." Mike's tone had sounded rather sarcastic.

"Er . . . yes, sir?" Tommy had said, trying to give the correct response.

"You're still no good to me," Mike had replied.

Tommy remembered being annoyed and thinking that this officer was playing with him. *What the fuck do you want, sir?* They were both silent for what had seemed like forever. Tommy had hesitated, then spoke when the pregnant pause in the conversation had gotten to be too much for him to handle—but on Mike's part, it had been a clever ploy.

"Look, sir," Tommy had said with a hint of aggression, "I'm not sure what you're doing here, but that corporal deserved everything he got. He's a bully, and he overstepped the mark. We were just having a quiet drink when he came over and started taking the piss out of my mate. Then he pushed him; I told him to stop, and he told me to fuck off, calling me Ginge and telling me to take a shower because he said I stunk of piss. Then he pushed me, so I hit him. But only once."

"Only once?" Mike had asked.

"Yes."

Mike had smiled. "Did you stink of piss?"

Tommy had been bewildered. *Who the fuck is this?* he'd thought.

"Tommy, a few home truths, my friend," Mike had said, having guessed what Tommy was thinking. "You were the best recruit in basic training?"

"Yes."

"You were the best rifleman?"

"Yes."

"You broke your unit record on the assault course?"

"Yes."

"You've already had four charges against you: three for fighting, one for insubordination?"

"Yes…" Tommy had said sheepishly.

"Tommy, this is the last-chance saloon for you," Mike had said. "I can get you away from all this if you like."

"How?"

"By joining my team."

"Your team?"

"Have you heard of the Skirmishers?"

"No."

Tommy remembered how Mike's blue eyes had seemed to pierce through his body as he spent twenty minutes talking to him about the unit he was putting together, why he was doing it, and how he thought Tommy would fit into it. Mike's final words really stuck with him: *"I want to create a family, Tommy. One where everyone is prepared to have one another's back. One where your teammates would fall on a grenade for you. One that will look past people's backgrounds and see only the importance of them being on the team."* Mike's speech had been so intoxicating that Tommy would have signed away his life there and then.

"Do you need time to think about it?" Mike had asked.

Tommy had responded, "No, sir!"

"Good," Mike had said. "In the interest of diversity in the army, I needed a ginger."

"Oi! Ginge!"

Tommy suddenly snapped out of his trance and saw the pissed-up Cockney lad from the big table standing over his barstool.

"Wake up, Jimmy!" he said to Tommy while trying to imitate a poor Scottish accent, using *Jimmy* as a derogatory term for a Scotsman. "You're a long way from home. Are you lost?" The Cockney lad was clearly drunk but more aggressive.

Tommy was annoyed with himself; he had completely lost situational awareness and had not seen the guy approach. His first thought was to laugh it off.

"Yeah, something like that," said Tommy.

"Aye," the guy said, still trying to put on a Scottish accent.

Tommy turned around a little farther on the barstool to look at the lad but kept his eye contact to a minimum. The guy was around five seven, with a medium build, and obviously liked a pint, as he sported a small potbelly under his T-shirt. Tommy guessed he was probably the youngest of the group—maybe even his age—and was trying to impress a few of the older lads, especially the guys wearing designer suits. He had some tattoos on his forearms, but Tommy didn't look long enough to make them out; they weren't that good, though. He noticed out of the corner of his eye that some of the locals had gotten up and left. Had he missed that, or had they left because they'd seen the situation that was brewing? He quickly glanced at his watch. Rachel would be there in five minutes; he decided that he should leave and meet her outside instead.

"Waiting for someone, Ginge?" said the Cockney lad.

"Been stood up," replied Tommy, trying to defuse the situation further.

This brought an almighty roar of laughter from the large table.

"Don't worry, Ginge, you'll lose your virginity one day," said one of the older guys.

"Hope so," said Tommy.

Again, the table roared with laughter.

"You're okay, Ginge," said another one of the older guys.

The Cockney lad walked away begrudgingly; he had something to prove, maybe. Tommy looked at his phone and saw that he had missed a text message from Rachel: Sorry, hon, will be five minutes late. Tommy made up his mind to leave and meet her outside. He hoped that was the end of it.

"Where are you going, Ginge?" said the Cockney lad.

"Home," said Tommy.

"'Home'? Or did you just call me a homo?"

Shit, thought Tommy. *This wanker is trying to prove something to the other guys at the table.* He decided to ignore it and walked toward the door. He felt a shove on his back—enough to make him stumble but not fall. Tommy straightened up. Could he outrun the man, reach the door, and escape into the relative safety of the high street?

Tommy quickly realized it would be a close call. It was worth a try, though. And of course, what would happen if Rachel walked in right now? However, the decision was about to be made for him. The Cockney lad attempted a blow to the head; Tommy instinctively blocked it and drove his open hand into the guy's face, instantly breaking his nose. The lad fell to the floor.

"Oi, you fucking Scottish cunt!" someone yelled from the table. Tommy knew he needed to get out of there fast. As the first two men got up from the table, he noticed their muscular upper bodies stretching out their immaculate designer shirts. Hopefully, all that muscle would slow them down. *Two quick hits, and then run,* he thought.

Tommy sensed that something else wasn't right—someone was behind him. It was too late. He caught a glimpse, in the dusty reflection of the mirror that doubled as a beer advertisement, of the silhouettes of the two guys who had been seated at the table when he'd first walked into the pub. He felt a sucker punch strike him on the side of the head. His brain shorted out, confusing him as he fell to the ground. *IED, explosion, I'm hit, I'm hit, man down, man down, contact!* His mind raced; he thought he was in Afghanistan. Blows rained down on him as the onslaught began. He faded in and out of consciousness, instinctively curling into a ball to protect his head and vital organs before passing out. For a moment, as he returned to consciousness, he felt the sensation of flying. Had there been another explosion? Then he felt a rush of fresh air mixed with the sense of glass breaking, heard sirens in the distance, and then—nothing.

Mike Sharpe sat on the balcony of his London apartment, overlooking the River Thames. It had been an unusually warm day for this time of year, but the evening was starting to feel a little colder now that the sun had gone down. He was drinking coffee, reading a copy of *The Times*, and enjoying a well-earned rest day from his grueling fitness regimen. He knew he was lucky to have an apartment like this, one he could never have afforded on an army officer's wage and one that a boy with a working-class background could have only dreamed about. When he first joined the army, he met a cavalry officer, Ian Fleming, whose family had built an empire in real estate. Ian had told Mike that money in bricks and mortar was always a good investment and that his family was putting up a new apartment building overlooking the Thames. Mike had little to invest except for some money a wealthy aunt had left him through his mum. Ian convinced him, arranged the deposit, finance, and even a tenant, to ensure Mike could be part of the venture. Ian's suggested approach worked, although Mike still had a hefty mortgage, and now he was living there with no rent coming in. But Ian had been right: Mike had paid off a good chunk of the mortgage through the tenant, and the apartment was worth three times the value he'd paid for it. Ian's advice, in hindsight, had been the best anyone had given him in terms of making money outside of the military. The building itself had a twenty-four-hour concierge, a gym, and many restaurants on the ground floor. It was all still a complete novelty to Mike, as it was the first time he had ever lived in it. Ian had even helped him move in.

The ambience of the evening was suddenly broken as his cell phone vibrated with an incoming call. Although it was on silent, the lit screen was bright enough to attract a curious passing insect that had probably ventured out from the warmth of its home because of the unseasonably good weather. There was no number listed on the caller ID, but he answered it anyway.

"Mike Sharpe."

"Um, is this Major Mike Sharpe?"

"I guess, yes," Mike responded, feeling strange that someone used his rank.

"I'm Detective Sergeant Bec Reed of the Metropolitan Police."

"How can I help?"

"We think one of your soldiers is in the London University Hospital."

"Who, Detective Sergeant?" replied Mike.

"You can call me Bec. We think his name is Tommy Stewart; he had dog tags on his key ring."

Mike's brain scrambled. He had only left the army unit he'd been assigned to a week ago—he was still technically in the military, as he was on terminal leave. He found it ironic that the last six months of his service were almost entirely spent on courses and taking leave.

"Is he okay?"

"Badly beaten; he was set on in a pub. Doctors think he'll be okay, but we can't find any next of kin. Luckily, you were his emergency contact number. This is why we're calling. We're also trying to call the army compassionate cell to inform them."

"He left the army a couple of weeks ago," Mike replied.

"Look, we can send a car to pick you up, if you like," Bec offered.

"That would be good. I'm in the Spear Tower, apartment 718."

The journey in the police car was uneventful, as was the passage through the hospital to a high dependency ward. Before going to Tommy, Mike was taken to an interview room and introduced to DS Bec Reed. She was around five foot seven, with brown hair pulled back into a ponytail. She looked extremely athletic, but it was hard to tell in her made-to-measure suit. Mike had already clocked the fact that the suit was designed to carry a weapon in a holster.

For the next thirty minutes, DS Reed briefed Mike on what had happened to Tommy. She explained that there had been an eyewitness who had called the police and an ambulance just before the attack happened. He was lucky, as the sirens had spooked the attackers, and they decided to throw him through a plate glass window to get him out of the pub. By the time help had arrived, he was already being attended to by a paramedic. "He's a strong boy. He was curled in a ball when they found him."

"How bad are his injuries?" asked Mike.

Bec opened her notebook. "Two cracked ribs, a broken nose, a chipped tooth, cuts, bruising and abrasions almost everywhere. No brain injury, though, and his vital organs seem okay. After an attack like that, he is very, very lucky."

"And you got the bastards?"

Bec hesitated. "Nobody saw who did it."

"But you said there was an eyewitness."

"Er, yes . . . and no."

Bec looked at Mike, mesmerized by how blue his eyes were—and there was something else there, too, as all of a sudden she felt as if a laser had passed through her body as he gazed back at her. She noticed he had quickly become deadly focused. She wondered what those eyes had seen.

She snapped out of it. "The witness gave us a statement and then retracted it. Look, Mike, I wouldn't normally give this information out, but I'm with the Organized Crime Division. Tommy ran into some nasty criminals today, all connected to organized crime in London. They own that part of Shoreditch. People are intimidated by them and therefore will not break the code by talking to us."

"*Jesus!*" said Mike. "So nothing happens?"

Bec was keen to change the subject. "Why don't you go see Tommy? He's on some strong drugs, but he'll know you're here."

Mike controlled his anger—he was here for Tommy, after all. But to hear that perpetrators had set upon him like a pack of dogs in an unprovoked attack, with no consequences, got under his skin. *Compartmentalize and box it; we'll open that one on another day,* he thought. As though it had been orchestrated, a doctor and nurse knocked politely on the door. The doctor introduced himself and gestured for Mike to follow him to Tommy's room.

The hospital corridors were fairly quiet and slightly eerie as Mike walked alongside them. Usually, the route to anywhere in a hospital would benefit from a map and compass, but in this case, Tommy's room was just a few doors from where he had just been briefed. As he walked into the private room and looked at the bed, he saw Tommy Stewart's unmistakable red hair; other than that, his face was so swollen and his eyes were so blackened that it would be impossible to recognize him even if you had a photo. Tommy was wired up to several machines. Still, Mike had expected much worse than what he saw.

"Lucky boy," remarked the doctor.

"Doesn't look like it," Mike responded.

"Trust me, with the beating he took and the potential for the attack to have carried on a lot longer, it could have been much worse. Had someone not called the police, he would have undoubtedly suffered a head injury. We'll continue to monitor him just in case his brain does swell, but at this stage, he's come out of it remarkably well. He's lucky to be alive."

For some reason, those last words affected Mike more than they should have: *lucky to be alive*. Tommy had done multiple tours in two different theaters of operation, and he could have lost his life to some scum in London. Mike felt his anger rising but controlled himself once more.

"Hey, Doc, thanks for all you're doing for him. He's a great lad and didn't deserve this."

"No one deserves this. We see it all too often, though."

"When will I be able to speak with him?" Mike asked.

"He's on very strong drugs, but we'll slowly start weaning him off them tomorrow morning. He'll be able to hear us now but won't remember anything."

The doctor's pager went off; he made his apologies and said he would see Mike in the morning.

Mike looked at the nurse. She must have been as old as Tommy, but she appeared to be exhausted from what he guessed was a long shift. She took a seat next to her patient and diligently began to fill in his medical chart.

"I see he was in the army."

"Yes, he was."

"My brother was too."

"Oh yeah? What regiment?"

"The Royal Anglians."

"What's he doing now?"

"Oh, um . . ." She hesitated. "He was killed in an IED explosion in Helmand."

Mike's stomach sank. He held back his emotions and tried to keep himself together. "I'm sorry for your loss."

"He loved the army, everything about it, including going with his mates on operations. He was so full of life—but somehow, we always knew something would happen to him. Really strange . . ."

Her mind seemed to wander off. "Oh, sorry." She perked up. "We're having trouble contacting his next of kin. Can you help?"

At that moment, DS Reed walked in. "We're having no luck finding any details either."

"The information should be in his army records. I'll get them tomorrow," Mike said. "Tommy wouldn't want us to contact his parents, anyway—not until he could talk with them himself and let them know he's all right."

"Okay," said Reed. "By the way, we're posting a couple of constables on his room tonight."

Mike was puzzled. "Why would you do that? Is he at risk?"

"Like I said, organized crime—and he's now a chief witness."

Mike was annoyed with himself. He should have known that.

"I can offer you a lift home, Mike," said Bec. "No point in you staying here; we'll look after him."

At first, Mike protested, but then he reluctantly agreed. He needed sleep and to be there when Tommy woke up in the morning.

"Did you have any luck with the other number?" Bec said to the nurse.

"No. No one answered it. Sounded like a fax machine or a data line," she answered.

"What number?" Mike asked.

"Interestingly enough," the nurse said, "there was another number under his emergency contact. It was thirteen digits long. Really bizarre."

"And you dialed it? What phone did you use?" said Mike.

"Oh, we used the hospital exchange phone."

"Okay," said Mike. "I know what that number is; it won't work from any phone other than Tommy's. It's an old encrypted response number that will send a distress call if a code isn't entered when that data tone is heard."

It was unusual that Colonel Tom Sawyer had insisted the team be given access to this secure messaging system for at least a year after they'd left the military. It really was a small ingenious application, but the fact that the team still had access to it created a lot of speculation.

Bec looked flustered. "Um, we dialed it," she said. "From his phone. What does that mean?"

At that exact moment, Mike remembered his own phone in his pocket, still silenced. He tentatively pulled it out. He knew what to expect but was hoping somehow that it wasn't going to happen.

On the locked screen of his phone was a bubble showing nine text messages received. He opened the first, which was automated and directed to him:

1800Z distress call Sierra Kilo 3. This is recall notice, open app for location.

He then opened one of the texts that was sent directly to him:

Alpha/Sierra Kilo 1 co-ords received ETA 0900 entire team. Sierra Kilo 1 was Sergeant Johnson.

Mike's face must have said it all.

"What exactly does dialing that number mean?" Bec asked again.

"Trouble!"

2

The water from the shower hit Mike's body like a rhythmic beat from a bygone era of soul music, relaxing and invigorating the muscles he had just worked. Over the years, he had modified the regimented regime of the army to ensure that he didn't follow the institutionalized program. However, today was different—he was following it almost to the letter. Up early, he'd hit the gym that morning for a "beasting"—or rather, a beating—with his Krav Maga instructor. He'd dabbled in martial arts for years but was introduced to the Israeli fighting style through an Israeli army exchange officer. Once he had realized its effectiveness in hand-to-hand combat, he insisted that it form part of the training given to the Skirmishers. Krav Maga was easy to learn and extremely effective when practiced. He was now enjoying that post-workout euphoria and was glad he had managed to fit it in before his day began.

Mike's bathroom was designed to be a wet room, allowing him to easily move from shower to sink. He grabbed a towel on the way and patted himself down. Then, with the precision of a man used to this routine, he applied shaving cream to his face without thought. The mirror had some sort of gadget that prevented it from steaming up; he often wondered how it worked but quickly forgot about it once his morning rituals were complete. As he held the razor, Mike thought about the evening before. He had been dropped off at home by DS Bec Reed, and almost as soon as he'd walked through his front door, he'd received a call from his former sergeant, Paul Johnson.

Paul was a lynchpin for Mike, a plain-speaking guy who had the ability to take complicated issues and break them down into bite-sized chunks that everyone understood. He didn't suffer fools, which probably came from his Scottish Highlands background. Mike regularly pointed out to Paul that nobody would know from his accent that he was Scottish, but as Paul saw himself as a Scot, Mike knew not to push it too far. They'd clicked the moment they met; Paul should have been a warrant officer 1 in the regular army, but his plain way of speaking had often offended those who would make the promotion decisions. The Skirmishers were not the most disciplined soldiers, but Paul managed to bring them together, keep them in line, and got them to genuinely care about the most important thing of all: one another. Despite his size— he was just five feet six inches—the team gravitated to him, respected him, and looked to him whenever they needed help. He was also extremely tough; Mike winced as he thought about the countless times he'd been paired with Paul during Krav Maga training. Although Mike never tried to show it, during the toughest sessions, Paul had regularly inflicted on him the sort of force that would hurt for days afterward. It didn't worry Mike, as he knew the mantra *Train hard, fight easy* was at play.

Despite not getting the promotion, Paul had been lucky, as he had the ear of those who mattered, and it had served him well as the senior noncommissioned officer, or SNCO, in the Skirmishers. Ultimately, he had turned down another promotion to stay with the team. At the very end, and with weeks of service left, Colonel Tom Sawyer had pulled a masterstroke and had somehow gotten Paul cleared to receive promotion to WO1 and an immediate pension. The argument was that Paul should be treated like a Special Forces soldier and, on paper, effectively lost rank to join the Skirmishers. Mike shook his head as he thought about the influence Sawyer seemed to have at every level of the establishment.

Mike was really pleased to hear Paul's voice on the phone and relieved that Paul had managed to delay the team RV until 0900 today. Paul not only had realized that something bad had happened to Tommy when he'd received the alert but also had phoned the hospital and managed to extract enough information to know nothing was life threatening. He had then sent an encrypted message to the team to try to slow them down. He knew he wouldn't be able to prevent them from coming to London, even though they were no longer a unit; they were all too close for that. They had seen and done too much together, and besides, someone had used the encrypted emergency number. They may have been out of the military, but they were going to respond.

Mike spent about twenty minutes explaining the events of the day, and as usual, Paul listened, only occasionally interjecting a *hmm* or *yes* to reassure Mike that he was still on the line.

Once Mike had finished, Paul chose his words carefully. "The team will have a lot of issues with what you just told me, and it may escalate very quickly, but let's cross that bridge when we come to it, boss. First and foremost, I'll get them to focus on Tommy. Make sure you arrive at the hospital at 0920. That will give me time to get them on board and aligned."

"Thanks, Paul."

"Always here for you, sir," replied Paul. And he was.

Paul and his wife, Sarah, had taken Mike in from day one and treated him as part of the family. Paul had two older boys, both mad about the army. Paul had often remarked that it ran in the family—his dad had served, as did his grandad. In the years he had been in the Skirmishers, Paul realized Mike had the weight of the world on his shoulders. The army either loved what the Skirmishers were doing or hated it, and it made time at home a political minefield for Mike. Paul had often shared his thoughts with Tom Sawyer, but the colonel had reminded him that Mike was a resilient bastard, or he would not have stuck with the regular army for so long. Paul used to laugh when Sawyer always finished that sentence with "Or the regular army wouldn't have put up with him."

After finishing his shave, Mike threw on some jeans and a T-shirt and was just doing the lace up on his boot when the intercom system burst into life.

"Hi, Mike, it's Bec. I have coffee and a lift waiting for you."

"Ha, thanks," he said. "Be right down." Maybe he had forgotten she'd offered him a ride?

Mike spotted DS Reed's car right in front of the entrance to the foyer. He got in, and she handed him the beverage. "Thanks," he said.

"I'm sorry, Mike. I couldn't remember whether I said I would pick you up at nine this morning, so I thought I'd come by anyway."

Mike was grateful; a car had been something he had lived without for some time. The constant deployments meant it would sit in a garage, gathering dust.

"Thought a coffee was in order, as I figured you wouldn't have slept well," Bec smiled.

"I actually slept really well," said Mike. "Spoke to a friend, and it cleared my head."

As he raised the brew to his lips, she looked at him. She had an eye for detail, which was not unusual for someone in the Organized Crime Division. Yesterday she'd noticed his biceps, forearms, and shoulders. He obviously worked out. She glanced at his thighs now, noting the way his jeans fit him perfectly. *He's very fit,* she thought. She saw that his knuckles looked red and slightly swollen. *Has he been fighting?* she wondered. Finally, she pondered how Mike had come to live in that apartment building. It wasn't that he looked out of place, but she was pretty sure from his background that he wouldn't have been able to afford it.

"Have you been in a fight, Mike?" Bec asked.

Mike nearly spat out his coffee. "What?"

"Your knuckles—they look red and swollen."

"I worked out this morning."

"Jesus, what kind of workout is that?"

"A tough one."

"How did you fit that in this morning?"

"Just a routine."

"What about your partner?"

Mike looked at her. "Are you interrogating me, Detective Sergeant?"

"N-no," she stuttered. "Um, goes with the job, I guess."

Oh God, she thought. *Why did I ask that?* She could feel his blue eyes like lasers on the side of her head. They were like the blue Canadian lakes shown on tourist posters—so clear that you could practically jump straight into them and enjoy a swim.

"No," said Mike.

"No?"

"No partner," he clarified.

She didn't know why, but she felt like a teenage girl again. Was she attracted to him? No . . . well, maybe but not like that, surely. What was it about him that made her feel this way? She couldn't put her finger on it.

She pulled up to the front of the hospital in a space reserved for Emergency Services. They climbed out of the vehicle and walked through the main entrance. The hospital was busy, presumably with day patients and those visiting loved ones. Bec had explained to Mike that Tommy no longer needed the support of a high dependency team and had been moved overnight to a ward that was in a more secluded part of the hospital, one that was easy for her team to monitor. It took a few minutes for Bec and Mike to walk to the lift that would take them to the ward. While waiting for the elevator, Mike discarded the coffee cup in the bin and took some minty-fresh gum out of his pocket.

Bec looked at him again. There was something about the way he talked, the way he moved; he had a confidence and self-assurance that was becoming rare in men.

He offered some gum to Bec as they stepped into the lift and watched the car count up through the floors. Nothing was said in the silence, that strange psychology where all conversations seem to stop in a small, confined space. That silence was broken as soon as the doors opened. *Here we go,* Mike thought as he looked over at the group of Skirmishers congregated on the opposite side of the reception area. The team had not stayed in the main foyer as planned but had made their way to the ward. So much for security; first Paul and now the team had managed to track down the ward Tommy was in. Luckily, Paul was with them.

Bec seemed a little agitated as she looked at the group. "What the fuck?" she whispered under her breath.

"It's okay," said Mike in a calm voice.

At that moment, Jon Apolosi looked up and saw Mike. *"Boss!"* he said, trying to keep his voice down but booming the word out anyway. He rushed over with the others, and Mike could hardly make an introduction to Bec, as the group swamped him with hugs and questions.

"Give the boss some space," said Paul Johnson. Mike and Paul hugged. "They're not letting us in," said Paul. He winked at Mike.

"Paul, team—this is Detective Sergeant Bec Reed."

Pleasantries were exchanged, and Bec was inundated with lots of names.

Wow, she thought. *Tommy is a popular guy.* At that moment, she got an indication of what Mike meant to them all. But Bec was soon distracted—no, annoyed—when she looked over at her two constables who were guarding the ward. Standing in front of them were two women, one taller than the other, who were clearly flirting—or were they trying to distract the officers? Bec went from annoyed to alarmed. She was just about to act when she felt a strong hand grab her wrist. She looked up and saw that it was Mike.

"It's okay," he said. "Those two are mine as well." A classic distraction plan was taking place, and neither woman was diverted from their immediate objective by their boss's arrival.

"Skippy, Steph—stand down," said Mike.

They both turned around immediately and came over, leaving two rather disappointed-looking constables. Bec looked them up and down as they walked toward her. *Holy shit,* she thought. The one on the left looked like she had stepped off the cover of a men's magazine. The one on the right had short black hair, an athletic build, and an innocent-looking face that disguised the fact that she looked very much like she could handle herself. *Soldiers? No way,* Bec thought. Then she was annoyed with herself for even thinking that.

Steph and Skippy walked up to Mike and gave him a hug, and Steph whispered almost seductively in his ear, "Five more minutes, and we'd have been in."

"Security around here is piss-poor," said Skippy.

Mike sheepishly looked at Bec. "Steph, Skippy—this is Detective Sergeant Bec Reed."

"Call me Bec."

"No offense," Skippy immediately offered.

Bec smoothed things over by saying, "You guys will have to tell me how you managed to find out that Tommy was in this ward."

"Oh, you need to speak to Andy," said Steph. "He handles intel, among other things."

Andy added, "And you're with the OCD, DS Reed." It was a statement more than a question.

"What the fuck?" replied Bec.

"Andy, not now," Paul responded.

Bec explained to the team that Tommy had awakened multiple times during the night, and each time he'd seemed stronger, so they'd moved him to this ward. Even with her powers of persuasion, she would need to limit the number of visitors, all on doctor's orders. That said, she would allow a group of five to go in first and then the other four.

Paul looked at Mike. "You go in, boss, and take Steph, Skippy, Andy, and Jon. The rest of us will wait."

Mike sensed Paul wanted a private word.

"Bec, can we have a moment before we go in?" Mike asked.

"Sure," she said. "I need to check with the nurse first, anyway."

Bec walked toward the entrance of the ward.

"What's up?" Mike asked Paul, subtly guiding him away from the team. "It's unlike you to not rush in to see him."

"I already did," said Paul, beaming from ear to ear.

Mike was astonished. "How the fuck did you manage that?"

"I met Nurse Blair in the canteen this morning."

"Nurse Blaire?"

"Brother was killed in Afghanistan—sad, really. She and I had a lot in common."

Mike remembered her from the night before.

"You know her?"

"No," said Paul. "Andy got the intel on the medical team, and I happened to bump into her." He was still beaming.

At that moment, Bec exited the ward with Nurse Blaire. The nurse shared a knowing smile at Paul, seemingly unaware that she had caused a potential security lapse. Mike pondered how Paul got past the two cops, but did he really want to know?

Five team members went into Tommy's room to find him asleep.

They sharply inhaled upon seeing Tommy's battered face—a bruised jaw and eyes darkened by a broken nose.

The nurse advised letting him wake naturally, which had been occurring every half hour. They'd likely wait another ten minutes.

The group settled in, chatting lightly as they waited. Bec took a seat among them.

"Are you wearing a bra under that?" Skippy looked at Steph with a mischievous grin.

"No," said Steph. "What the fuck has that got to do with anything?"

"Showing off your perfect nipples again, Steph?" asked Skippy.

Bec was confused. *What sort of conversation is this, when their mate is lying in a hospital bed a few feet away?*

Skippy was right: the long-sleeved T-shirt accentuated Steph's upper body and hugged her in a way that made you want to unwrap it to see if perfection really did exist underneath. Skippy and Steph had shared rooms, tents, foxholes, and hotels together over the years. Skippy had once remarked that if she ever got sick of men, then Steph had to promise to hook up with her. Over the years, though, Skippy had learned that for all the looks and charm Steph had, very few men would ever talk to her on the level; they were usually too intimidated or too pissed. Steph had once asked Skippy, genuinely, how she seemed to hook up with men whenever she wanted to.

"Skippy, what the fuck?" Steph responded, but like a giggling sister, she quickly realized that Skippy was starting to scheme. Her confusion suddenly turned into a very naughty smile.

"Fancy giving Tommy something to remember when he wakes up?"

"Oh yes, I like that idea," said Steph.

Mike looked at Bec. How was he ever going to explain the logic behind what the girls were about to do? He had seen them pull these stunts many times before.

Tommy started to stir.

Skippy and Steph walked silently but quickly over to him.

They positioned themselves on either side of the bed.

Tommy opened his eyes and blinked . . .

Oh shit, he thought as he squinted through his blackened eyes. Were they deceiving him? In front of him was just the most perfect view—he must be dreaming. To his right, it looked as if God himself had decided to create the most perfect breasts. He marveled at the shape of them and the fact that each breast seemed to point up to the ceiling as Steph's chest raised and lowered with every breath. Tommy's eyes slowly moved to the left. He noticed Skippy's slender, athletic shape; his gaze traveled from her stomach to the bottom curve of her breast, and then he imagined that the nipples were erect because she was in a state of arousal in front of him. *Fuck, I must have died,* he thought as he continued to gawk.

Both girls leaned over and gently kissed Tommy on the cheek and, in the most seductive manner possible, said, "Glad you're awake, dickhead."

Tommy smiled. A tear formed in the corner of his eye, which didn't go unnoticed by either girl. It made their stunt worth it.

"Steph, Skippy," he said. "If that's the last thing I'm ever going to see, I'll die happy." He meant it.

At that moment, Bec began to understand the bond among this group of misfits. She should have been horrified by what had just happened, but she was somehow choked up. To make the situation worse, she watched as Tommy tried to sit up despite some discomfort; he had seen his boss. Mike hugged him carefully.

Bec snapped out of it as Mike caught her off guard with an immediate and probing question to Tommy. It was almost like Mike was trying to keep Tommy from sinking into self-pity.

"You know what happened to you, Tommy?" he asked.

"Yes," said Tommy. "The DS explained it to me."

"No, not her report. Do *you* know what happened?" Mike didn't want to hear another police report; he just wanted any gaps filled in.

DS Reed had held off going anywhere near that question. She'd not been sure that Tommy was ready. Her ears pricked. She then watched as the one named Andy, the intel guy who seemed to have known she was in the OCD, walked over and took out a notebook. She also noticed that a switch seemed to turn on in Tommy, like someone had put a starter battery on his wrist and fired him up.

As Tommy explained the buildup to the attack, it was clear his memory was fine. He moved through the attack itself and relayed what he'd seen. To Bec's amazement and utter annoyance, because it was clearly a police matter, Andy began filling in the gaps.

"I stood up to leave," said Tommy. "The Cockney lad pushed me in the back."

"Nick Clover," Andy said, businesslike. "Younger brother of Liam and Karl Clover. They run a small firm responsible for a defined area of Shoreditch. They got lucky, as their father muscled in on the region before it regenerated. That pub and a nightclub, which is actually pretty famous, are where they hang out."

Tommy continued, "I took out Nick, the Cockney lad, and weighed up the options. I had planned to take out two more guys; both looked like they could handle themselves. Then I was going to turn and run as soon as those guys hit the deck. I didn't get to execute the plan, though—it was at that point when I saw in a mirror the reflections of the two guys who had been sitting in the front of the pub. They were behind me." He looked at Mike. "Sorry, boss. I fucked up. I completely lost my SA," he said, referring to their acronym for situational awareness.

"Tommy, you were in a pub in London, not Afghanistan," Mike replied reassuringly.

"Did you get a look at them?" said Andy.

"Not really. Oh wait—one was bald."

"That's Terry Patrick, a long-term enforcer for their firm. He has form," Andy said, reading from his notes.

"And that's it, boss. I remember the feeling of flying and fresh air, and then I heard sirens."

"The girl you were meeting saved your life, Tommy," Andy added.

"I never got to meet her."

"Andy, that's all for today," Mike said. "Make sure you brief the rest of the team."

"Wait," said Bec, her face reddening. "This is a police matter. What the hell do you think you're doing? You could put lives at risk with the information you've acquired."

Andy, not quite knowing when to stop talking, tried to explain. "Not really. Most of this information is open source; anyone who frequents that pub would know this."

Mike could see Reed was fuming and moved to calm the situation. "Andy, team—let's look after Tommy and let the police do their job."

Bec was genuinely concerned. If the firm got wind that someone was looking into them, it could jeopardize the work of the OCD. Why were they checking them out, anyway? She knew she needed to get Mike alone.

"Am I at risk, boss?" Tommy asked. "I saw the cops escort me last night to the ward."

"You could be, Tommy," said Bec.

"I'm not sure, Tommy," Andy interjected.

Everyone turned to look at Andy, who glanced at Mike. "Go ahead, Andy," Mike said reassuringly.

"They have little interest in Tommy; it was the girl you were meeting who was the greatest risk, and she never completed her statement."

"They paid her off?" said Tommy.

"No. It's a long story, but they let it be known that if anyone grassed, an accident might happen."

"Tommy was a witness," said Bec. "That puts him at risk."

"Not really. He can't remember much, and no witnesses will talk. No CCTV footage . . . the case looks flimsy at the moment," said Andy. "Why would they send someone here and stack the odds back in the CPS's favor if it went that far?"

As usual, Andy was well ahead of everyone.

"You practically told me these guys are untouchable, Bec," said Mike.

Bec couldn't argue. She had seen it all play out before.

"Tommy, we'll send in the rest of the team, and then you get some sleep," Mike said, with concern in his voice. "Hopefully, you'll be out of here in a few days. Oh, and we've extended your stay in London by a couple of weeks." Mike looked at Bec. "The police will foot the bill."

Mike's words added to the tension Bec was already feeling.

"Key witness or something," Mike said.

They were just about to turn and depart when Tommy asked for a favor.

"What is it?" Mike asked.

"Can you thank Colonel Sawyer for visiting me in the middle of the night?"

"Tommy, he wasn't here," said Mike.

"I'm sure he was—I wasn't dreaming," said Tommy.

Tom Sawyer, what the hell are you up to? thought Mike.

DS Bec Reed had heard enough and stormed off.

As they passed in the corridor, Mike told Paul to keep the visit time with Tommy to a minimum. "Once you're finished, get the team together outside the hospital. I noticed a picnic area at the side of this wing. Have them grab some lunch and gather for a meeting," said Mike.

"Roger that."

Ninety minutes later, Mike and the team were sitting around a large picnic bench in one of the areas set aside for patients and visitors. They had spent the previous thirty minutes going over the events of the last twenty-four hours, and Andy seemed to have had most of the gaps in information covered. Paul, with meticulous attention to detail, was gathering information, breaking it down and then testing assumptions. Mike waited quietly. He knew the question would come, but he just didn't know when or how he would answer. It took another ten minutes before Skippy finally asked.

"So this is all well and good, but what the fuck are we going to do with this information, and when are we going to teach those bastards a lesson?"

Mike stood up, and the team immediately turned toward him, like they had done many times before when he was about to start a mission brief.

Tommy walked back to his bed after his shower. It had been bliss. Although it had been forty-eight hours since the attack, he was now well enough to have his first shower, and it reminded him of the countless times he had stood in the refreshing flow of water after spending days in the field on exercise or operation. He was starting to feel like his old self, despite the way his body looked. He climbed into the freshly made hospital bed. There was a knock on the door, and in walked Bec Reed with a blonde woman alongside her.

"Tommy," said Bec. "I have a visitor for you, vetted and checked."

Tommy was looking at a familiar face. "Rachel?" he said.

The girl he'd been going to meet at The Eagle—the one who had saved his life.

"I'll leave you two alone," said Bec. "Thirty minutes only, Rachel."

Rachel looked at Tommy. He was battered, but she was pleased to see him smiling and coherent.

"It's all my fault," she said. "I am so sorry, Tommy. If I hadn't been late, you wouldn't be in here."

"No," he replied. "If you had turned up on time, I might not be here."

Rachel looked puzzled.

"What happened was going to happen," said Tommy. "If you had been in the pub, you wouldn't have been able to call the police. You would have been caught up in it."

"But I should have tried to stop them. I was scared," said Rachel. "I stood like an idiot outside the pub, frozen to the spot, and could see you were going to be in trouble."

"But you phoned the police and got an ambulance straightaway. Those sirens saved my life." Tommy was sincere but firm. "Other people would also have frozen, not been able to think. We see it all the time in the military. But you did think, though."

Rachel let out a huge sigh, like a weight had been lifted from her.

She looked at him again. "I withdrew being a witness."

"I know."

"Tommy, you have to realize, I live around the corner from that pub—and then yesterday, I received a warning through someone I care about."

"Who?"

Tommy could see the guilt in her eyes. "My husband."

"Fuck, you have a husband?"

"I know how it looks, but he's in jail doing time—six years. He gave me permission to see other men, as long as I waited for him."

"Fuck," said Tommy. "So they threatened him, I guess."

"Yes, he got a warning in prison that they would kill him unless I disappeared as a witness. They told him that if he convinced me to keep quiet, his last two years will be easy. I had to agree, Tommy. I still love him, even after four years. After I agreed, he received notice late last night that he'll be moved to an open prison. He goes tomorrow."

"Shit, they have that sort of power and can use it that quickly?" Tommy was genuinely astonished.

"On the inside and the outside," said Rachel. "I've never seen them before, but Ray—my husband—said that they have everyone in the bag."

Tommy shook his head. Rachel looked at her watch. "Look, I better go soon," she said.

Tommy let out a huge sigh and then laughed.

"What?" Rachel asked, pleased that he seemed to be taking all this in stride. She liked him, she decided, despite everything she had said. She felt he had lifted a huge burden from her shoulders.

"What?" she repeated, now laughing with him.

"That morning, I was walking toward the pub thinking I was going to meet this gorgeous blonde girl, have a drink, and spend the afternoon in bed with her. Didn't work out quite the way I thought it would."

They both laughed louder.

Rachel looked over at the door and saw that the corridor was empty.

"Well," she said. "I understand you just got out of the shower."

"Yes."

"Did you clean everything?" said Rachel, looking at Tommy suggestively.

She moved her hand under the cover of the crisp clean hospital sheet and brushed it over Tommy's leg. She made her way up until she came in contact with what she was looking for. He was already semi-erect.

"Hmm, too long in the field, soldier?"

Tommy gulped.

"Well, let's give you a clean."

She lifted back the sheet, quickly glanced at the door, and then let her lips gently caress the top of Tommy's now erect penis. *Oh wow,* he thought. *What a couple of days this has been. First Steph and Skippy show me their tits, and now Rachel has my cock in her mouth.*

Going to that pub had almost been worth it, after all!

Rachel left the hospital feeling very pleased with herself. She liked the man she had just met and enjoyed giving him something to remember her by. She was also pleased her husband would serve an easy two years in an open prison. She was lost in thought as she walked back to the London underground station and did not hear the car pull up beside her. The window lowered, and a man called her name.

"It's Rachel, isn't it?"

"Yes," she replied.

"Weren't you told to keep your mouth shut?"

"I just went to visit him to see that he was okay."

"Sure, you did."

Two silenced percussion blasts echoed in the street. Rachel collapsed.

3

Mike leaned back in his chair, gazing across the River Thames toward the Palace of Westminster and Big Ben. He could discern the throngs of tourists beneath the London Eye, all keen to experience the iconic Ferris wheel and mark another item off their bucket lists. Turning back, he faced his leadership team seated around the table he'd relocated from the dining room to the balcony. The weather was so good for this time of year that it had become an item worthy of national media attention. The balcony was a perfect spot: not overlooked by anyone and secluded enough for them not to be heard by other residents unless someone raised their voice.

Inviting the team into his personal space had initially been a cause for concern for Mike. Yet, ever since DS Reed's dramatic exit from the hospital room, it was clear that her heightened suspicions meant subtlety was paramount. Beyond the team's initial reactions to the luxury of Mike's apartment—and the teasing about his upscale residence—they promptly turned their attention to the matter at hand.

The Skirmishers' leadership team would normally comprise Sergeant Paul Johnson, Corporals Steph Holgate and Andy Thomas, and Lance Corporals Jon Apolosi and Mark Jackson. Mike had spoken at length with Paul about limiting the actual distribution of information to a very small group, and they had both concluded that it would be discussed with a select few only. Although it wasn't completely unusual to exclude the lance corporals from these meetings, it still didn't sit well with Mike; he valued their input. He knew it would come, though, when the time was right.

As Mike looked at Paul, Steph, and Andy, he knew they weren't getting from him what they wanted. Their meeting yesterday had gone from a situational representation brief (sitrep) from Andy to a pretty tense thirty minutes of interrogating Mike on what they were going to do next. At the initial hospital meeting, Mike hadn't really answered Skippy's question of what they were going to do to pay back these bastards. He'd tried to divert the answer by getting them to focus on Tommy and his well-being. He realized, though, that there was going to be a fine line between stalling and one of the team deciding to take matters into their own hands. The problem that was weighing on Mike's mind was that this was not some operation in a war-torn country—this was London. No rules of engagement here, and the law of the land was on their back. Any action they took would have consequences.

After yesterday's meeting, Mike had had lunch with DS Reed to try to clear the air. To be fair to Bec, she could have given Mike a lot worse than he was expecting, but she was very quick to establish authority. She had essentially warned him off. "Should you or your team meddle in police affairs, I'll have you arrested."

Attempting to shift the dynamics, Mike had ventured, "Bec, may I pose a question?" The weariness in his voice had caught her off guard.

"Of course." She had almost instantly changed her tone from authoritarian to surprisingly open.

"How long does it normally take the police to get a conviction—not on just anyone but someone of significance within the London gang communities?"

"You mean, within the actual leadership?"

"Yep, but beyond a small firm like the Clover family in Shoreditch. I mean the bosses, those at the top."

"Almost never, Mike. It's the reason why when it happens, it makes national news."

"Frustrating."

"Very." Bec had been uncertain whether Mike's comment was a pointed remark or genuine empathy. However, she felt she had accomplished her objective for the lunch. "Have your team stand down and cease gathering intel," she instructed, her authoritative tone returning. To her frustration, he did not respond right away.

"Tommy comes out of hospital in a couple of days."

"Yes."

"Will he have protection?" Mike pressed.

"No," Bec replied. "We're sure he's not really at risk." She'd looked down, slightly tense. "No case for them to answer."

Mike observed Bec closely. She'd averted her eyes to the left when saying Tommy wasn't in danger. It might have been a natural glance—or maybe she was holding something back.

"You think he might be at risk, don't you?" Mike inquired, his tone firm yet courteous.

Bec paused before answering. "Our intel says he's not, but there's always the unexpected. We can never be one hundred percent sure."

Seeing an opportunity, Mike decided to raise a point. "The woman who was shot and reported on the news—it was Rachel, wasn't it?"

Bec paled but remained composed. "Yes. Yes, it was." She tried to curb her rising panic. What started as a successful lunch was now derailing.

"We made a big mistake, Mike. We underestimated them and their connections. Rachel wanted to see Tommy, and we allowed it to happen. We had no idea that the gang would do something like that, with the potential to expose themselves to more scrutiny. We quickly realized that it was possibly an unauthorized action."

"'Unauthorized'?"

"Done without leadership sanction." Bec halted. "I've said too much."

"Let me guess, there's no evidence linking back to them?" Mike had grown frustrated but didn't show it.

"No." Bec was annoyed by how she felt.

"Seems Andy Thomas was right. Untouchable—isn't that what you said?"

It was now Bec's turn to stay silent. *Bastard,* she'd thought. *He set me up for that.*

During yesterday's meeting, Mike had asked the leadership team to speak to each of the Skirmishers individually, including Tommy. He wanted to know what they were genuinely thinking and feeling. This was left to Andy and Steph, as Paul and Mike had agreed that Paul had so much influence on the team that they may try to second-guess why they were being asked.

"Okay," said Paul. "How is the team? What did you get from them?"

Andy had spoken to Jon, Timi, and Mark.

"The feedback wasn't that surprising. I know you said to talk to them separately, but I wasn't going to try to separate Jon and Timi!"

They all laughed. The two Fijians had been recruited to the British Army as rugby players—well, officially as soldiers, but they spent more time representing the army at rugby. Both were as tall as they were wide—not fat, all muscle. Their families were very close, and they did everything together. They were like twin brothers. Mike was unsure why Colonel Tom had recommended them for the Skirmishers, but they were both among the initial group to go through training. Whatever the reason Sawyer had to recommend them, it was made clear to Mike not to ask. He'd been pretty pissed about that, as they were the only two members of the team about whom he didn't have an inkling as to why they were selected.

Timi was the junior soldier and Jon was more senior. Jon had an extensive logistics background and thus also acted as the squadron quartermaster, or QM.

"Timi and Jon are really angry about what happened to Tommy, but they both said they weren't sure what they can do. I explained to them that if we do anything, there could be consequences. They knew that, and aside from being worried about what that meant for their families, they compared it to being on operations."

"Nothing else?" asked Paul.

"They were confused about why the police couldn't just arrest the perpetrators. That took some explaining," said Andy. They all nodded in appreciation.

"And Mark?" said Paul.

"Mark was as sharp as usual; broke it all down and even offered up an attack plan."

"We could have probably brought him into this," said Mike to Paul.

"Don't worry," said Andy. "He gets that as well."

Mike pondered awhile. Mark was the quietest and most well-mannered person on the team, but his calling for some combative action immediately gave an insight into his thoughts.

"That's it," said Andy. "Mark's a man of few words but finished with 'Just let me know when.'"

"Steph?" said Paul.

Steph explained she'd spoken first with Steve Kenny, the youngest member of the team. He had joined later than the rest, was a bit of a lad, and had a problem with listening too much to his other brain than his real brain. He considered himself a ladies' man and for some reason seemed to have a reasonable amount of success. That said, Steph and Skippy bantered with him mercilessly when he got to be too much for everyone. Steph had explained that she'd taken Steve for a coffee, which he'd been very pleased with, as that had never happened before when they were home. "I think he thought I might be interested," said Steph with a smile on her face.

"Steve's ego hasn't changed much," joked Andy.

"Much worse than that," explained Steph. "He was pissed off at me."

"Why?" the three others said in unison.

"Tommy told him about what Skippy and I did when he first woke up in hospital. He was so upset that he missed out on the view!"

That was the real icebreaker; they all laughed out loud.

Steph brought them back to reality fairly quickly. "Steve isn't doing well, boss. Behind that bravado, he's not coping that well with being outside the army. He shouldn't have left."

"He was my biggest concern, but he wouldn't stay in without the rest of us," Mike said. "From this point forward, we need to be there for him; he'll spiral otherwise."

"That's it, though," Steph said sincerely. "I decided not to talk about this situation with him. He was opening up about all his other problems. To be honest, it was like chatting with a younger brother. I actually liked the fact he talked without the usual front."

"He needs this group and a sense of purpose," Paul said.

Mike knew that was aimed at him. *A sense of purpose.*

"What about Skippy?" Mike asked, trying to move things on quickly.

"You know she and Tommy have an attraction, Mike, right?" said Steph. "They're just too fucking stupid to realize it."

Mike nodded. "I saw the way he looked at her in the hospital."

Steph smiled. "Thought you had."

Paul and Andy were confused. "What? No way."

Mike decided to explain things to his two friends.

He looked at Steph, who had already predicted what he was about to say. She smiled at him, as she knew these were the key moments that caused Mike to stand out from other leaders—he noticed little personal things. In the whole team, when it came down to people, only she and Mike picked up on the smallest details. Andy was a machine when it came to observing the tiniest characteristic in everything apart from intimacy. Paul was almost the same, but his brain would click quickly when it was explained or pointed out.

"When Steph and Skippy"—Mike cleared his throat—"had their breasts out, it was written in poor Tommy Stewart's swollen eyes. He couldn't hide it."

Paul and Andy still looked confused.

Mike was hoping he wouldn't need to explain it, but he did anyway.

"Skippy is a beautiful woman: athletic, superb figure, fantastically well proportioned, innocent face, and a vivacious personality."

Steph was staring intently at Mike, her blue eyes glistening slightly. Mike realized the awkwardness of what he was about to say next.

"If you were to describe your ultimate fantasy woman, it would be Steph," said Mike. "Her traits are the same as Skippy's but on another level. She's drop-dead gorgeous in many guys'—and I guess girls'—eyes. She has the same personality as Skippy, but Tommy didn't look at her the same way."

Andy genuinely didn't understand and said as much; he was keen to learn about what he had missed. Paul was beginning to cotton on.

"When Tommy gazed at Steph"—Mike was now looking at Steph—"he saw everything he wanted in a woman, and he said as much. When he looked at Skippy, he didn't look straight at her breasts. He started lower and worked his way up. He was . . ." Mike stopped, looking for the words. "Drinking her in. He looked at her with love."

Steph felt flushed. She appreciated the way her boss had described her but appreciated even more the way he had described the interaction between Skippy and Tommy. She felt her nipples harden, and she became a little turned on, which left her confused, as it was an involuntary response.

"Wow," said Andy. "I can pick up the smallest detail or nuance of almost everything, but I didn't see that."

"Don't worry, Andy," said Paul. "Maybe we were distracted."

"So you're saying Skippy wants in?" asked Paul.

"Yes," said Steph. "Skippy and I had a heart-to-heart about Tommy last night. I think I've left Skippy confused—or rather, I've woken her up to the fact they have an attraction. This could become problematic. We've never had a relationship in the team. I don't want to get ahead of myself, but this could be new territory." Steph hesitated. "That's why she volunteered to pick him up from hospital."

Mike looked at Paul for assurance. "It's not a problem, Steph."

"What about Tommy?" Paul realized that whatever Steph was about to say in response to his question, it would carry the greatest weight in any decision Mike would make. Steph realized this as well.

"He was fairly circumspect to start. Like all of us, he couldn't believe that the police were finding it so hard to do anything, especially considering the beating he took. I think if they'd been able to do something, he would have told us to let it go. He asked me what you thought, Mike."

Mike looked up. He trusted Steph with his life, but he knew that question would be difficult to answer. "What did you tell him?"

"The truth, as always. I told him we were exploring options and trying to work through the cause and effect. He got that."

"Well done, Steph," said Paul.

Steph looked at Mike. He was staring at her but not looking at her; he seemed far away. She knew, once again, that the weight of the world was on his shoulders.

Almost on cue, he refocused and looked her in the eye. "You're holding back something." It was a statement of fact; he wasn't asking for a defensive answer.

Steph had been in this position before. Little got past Mike, and now he wanted to know what else was on Tommy's mind.

"It's the guy who sucker-punched him."

"Terry Patrick." The one they called the enforcer. Mike didn't need to remind them; his picture was on a whiteboard in Mike's apartment.

"Tommy was pissed that he lost his SA, Mike, and it's eating him up. He's having nightmares about it already. He told me he's had combat dreams from operations but never a nightmare."

"PTSD?" said Andy.

"No, I'm sure it's not," said Steph.

"Then what's going on in his head, Steph?"

She hesitated. "Tommy looked me in the eye, boss, and said he must extinguish the nightmare."

"'Extinguish'? Kill?" asked Mike.

"Not sure. He had the look of Terry Patrick being on his radar, whether it's with us or without us."

"Did you tell Tommy about the speculation on the girl?"

"I mentioned it in passing that it might be connected but that we don't know. He said nothing, boss, just gave a hundred-mile stare."

"Thanks, Steph." Mike appreciated the direct response.

Leadership can be lonely, but this time Mike was going to do something he had rarely done before. "You're all part of the leadership team, but I can't ask anything of you out of uniform. I want a *go, no go* on conducting an op. Paul?"

"I want to know the full extent, particularly the cause and effect of anything we do. This is an environment we're not used to—but, boss, to be honest, I'm surprised we didn't act a couple of days ago when we speculated about the girl. I think we might be growing up! It's a go from me."

"Steph?"

"Go." Steph never minced words. He noticed her blue eyes ice over, like her brain had suddenly clicked into a different mode.

"Andy?"

"To answer Paul's question—and it is a good question—the cause and effect is complex. If we take them out, it leaves a void. The problem for the locals is that void could be filled by a more vicious firm. Surprisingly, for the area, the people paying the Clover firm for protection expect protection. They're really suppressed, boss. Protection for them is the quiet life, until they fail to pay. I know that sounds weird, but it's the law of the street. We need to think about that some more, but it's a go from me. The question remaining is when and how hard?" Andy paused, regained his thoughts, then looked at Mike. "As long as you sanction it, boss."

"Andy, can you arrange for my apartment to be swept?"

"It's already done."

Mike wasn't surprised by Andy's answer. "Can you arrange tac comms?"

"Yes. Easy."

"Andy, I need the police off our backs and no evidence left behind of anything we do."

"Okay, on it."

"Any evidence of planning needs to disappear."

"Assuming this is the only place we plan, it should be a simple matter of destroying the paper trail. Nothing online, boss?" Andy meant it partly as a question and partly as a statement.

"Nothing aside from initial internet searches into organized crime in London and the Clover brothers. Other than that, nothing else."

"Can I look at your browsing history? I won't pry or talk about anything else I find. I want to ensure you've not overstepped the mark, but I also want there to be a trail or it will smack of a cover-up. It would have been expected that you would have searched for some elements relating to the incident."

"Okay, Andy, no worries. Anything else?"

Andy was direct. "What do you know about that girl, boss? Rachel?"

It was the question Mike had been expecting.

"It was her." Mike said nothing else.

Everyone on the team sighed.

Mike tried to stay calm. "The police still can't do anything—no connection. I didn't tell you I had found out it was her, as I preferred taking the speculative approach with the team."

There was silence for a moment, and then Andy brought everyone back to attention. "We need to update you on team logistics; Steph can do it later."

Steph glanced at Andy. *Bastard,* she thought. There was part of that jigsaw that affected Mike.

"How are the scenarios going?" Mike asked Paul and Steph. He often delegated options to them so as not to influence their thoughts with his own.

Paul responded, "We've outlined several options for you to look at, but the simplest and easiest to execute is recreating the situation Tommy found himself in. Same day, same time, same pub."

"Why is that your preferred option?"

"We looked at the nightclub, Red Zone. It's exclusive, full of famous people and VIPs. It's difficult for the general public to get into, except if they look the part or are wealthy. It's their crown jewel, and it's where their main revenue comes from. Doing it there would certainly give us an element of surprise, but security would be all over us like a rash, as would the police. Logistically, we wouldn't be able to get the team in anyway. We still have three options for you to look over for the club, and we also recommend a recce there. It's where the Clover brothers' father spends most of his time. He still runs the whole operation. We know a lot about the club's security but little about the VIP area, which is actually called the Red Zone. You need to be an

A-list celebrity or a millionaire to get into the Red Zone VIP area. If you apply, you're pre-vetted; if you're a celebrity, you're normally invited."

"But wouldn't we stand out?" said Mike.

"Oh, it's not intimate in any way, boss. It's huge. You would just be a guest of another millionaire. They don't ask questions once you're inside, for obvious reasons," said Andy.

"Wait a minute. How on earth will we do a recce? Do we know a millionaire? Don't tell me Jon has managed to get us in?" Mike asked.

"Not this time, boss, although he was working it," said Andy.

Paul glanced at Steph. "You're looking at the person who sorted that."

Steph was annoyed. She tried often—but in her opinion, not very well—to hide her background. "Okay, so I know a few millionaires who are members of that club."

Mike frequently forgot that Steph's father was a self-made businessman. He knew she came from a wealthy background, but she didn't make a big deal of it. Mike had pushed her to get a commission in the army, but she was having none of it. *How many female officers are leading combat teams, Mike?* she would often say. *You could be the first,* he would respond. The truth was that if she had commissioned, Mike would have tried to get her to come back into the Skirmishers and help him establish the unit within the Special Forces. Of course, it didn't happen.

"I'd like to see the Red Zone," said Mike. "It will also give me a chance to look at what we're up against. It may show us the missing parts of the jigsaw—the questions around their strength, what the command and control is like, and answer Andy's question on cause and effect."

"Already arranged," said Paul. "You're Steph's date."

"Do we need an IRT on standby, boss?" asked Andy.

"No immediate reaction team necessary. We need to be the coolest VIPs in there—in for forty-five minutes, max, and then out. We can't afford to be dicked. Especially with the way the actual op might work."

"I'll plan some intel objectives for you both," said Andy.

"Sarge, would you mind checking them?"

"Andy, call me Paul—and no problem. We need to get the team to try to lose the rank thing, boss."

"Agreed. Work on it."

"So it's the pub for the actual op?" confirmed Mike.

"By far the easiest option. They have the same routine every Tuesday, and the afternoon is always quiet. The problem is, that's all I have," said Andy. "Tommy went in at the only time of the week they're there. The pub is a front; it gets busy on Fridays and Saturdays, but I reckon they launder money through it."

"Flesh it out further and report tomorrow. Other business?" said Mike.

"Logistics, boss." Andy looked at Steph.

"Okay." Mike looked slightly confused.

"Well, Mike . . ." She took a sharp intake of breath. "As you know from yesterday's brief, the team is finding it tough extending their accommodations in London with the associated costs. The all-ranks club in Waterloo is fairly priced, but the expenses are adding up the longer they stay. So we've got a solution, but it affects all of us. Tommy is sorted and will move back into the hotel. We managed to bag an adjoining room for his caretaker, who will be Skippy." Steph winked. "No extra cost, and the police are paying."

Mike shook his head, smiling.

"Paul here is sorted; he's at a mate's place. Mysterious Andy is also sorted, staying with a friend. Not sure who." She playfully punched Andy in the arm. "Jon and Timi are fine; they're on some sort of holiday deal. I'm sure Jon had blagged something. By the way, he also blagged the adjoining hotel room for Skippy. So I'm staying in a two-bedroom shoebox, and I've given that up to Mark and Steve."

"Cool. So we're sorted, then? Good work," said Mike.

"No," said Steph. "Just me who has the problem."

"Where are you going to stay?" Mike asked, already noting the mischievous look on her face.

"I don't know, boss." She smiled.

Andy added, "We need to prep for the recce, boss. It's tomorrow night; you two need to get your story straight."

Paul said, "We really need to make the two guests look legit."

"Fuck me," said Mike. "You lot planned this all along."

"Yep, when I saw your apartment, I canceled my alternate rental and a hotel option I was looking at, and decided I was staying with you in this luxury space." Steph smiled as she spoke.

"Okay." Mike held up his hands, completely disarmed. "What choice do I have?"

Steph laughed. "You've had to put up with me in worse places."

"True." Mike didn't really mind Steph staying; in fact, it would help with the overall plan for the recce of the Red Zone nightclub.

"So, boss, I need to hear it from you. We are *definitely* on?" Paul always wanted the black-or-white answer—no ambiguity, no room for doubt.

Mike pondered this for a minute. Rachel getting gunned down had probably tipped it for him, and he still wasn't sure whether Tommy was at risk.

"Paul, brief the team that they're on notice to move, nothing more," Mike ordered.

"Roger that."

"They'll report tomorrow morning for some training. I need to know they're sharp."

"Roger that, but where?" Paul asked.

Mike handed him a card. "Take them here at 0700. She'll know that I've sent you."

"'She'?" Paul looked at the card: a woman's name, a large Krav Maga logo, and an address.

"Don't be fooled, Paul; she's fucking brutal. She's with the Israeli embassy, so be discreet."

"Roger that."

"We run this as a proper mission. I want total comms silence. The team is to go about their normal lives, aside from the workout. If you need something done, use them one at a time, and make them think they're being watched—they just might be."

"Andy, go gray once you give us the tac comms. You'll only exist while Steph and I do the recce, and then you focus with Paul on The Eagle for a Tuesday zero hour."

"Okay, boss."

"Questions?" None were offered.

"Right. I'll bring my stuff up," said Steph in an almost playful manner.

4

It was Saturday afternoon. Mike and Steph entered the apartment, which was immaculate. Although it got cleaned twice a week by the building staff, Steph, who was self-professed OCD, had also cleaned after them. Andy had gone through the apartment with a fine-tooth comb to ensure that should it be searched, any evidence would be easily explained away. They also had another complication: as Mike was still technically in the army, the Army Special Investigation Branch might search it as well, should he be accused of anything.

The Krav Maga session that morning was as brutal as anything Steph had done before, but she, like the rest of the team, had loved every minute of it. It was not often Steph and Skippy came across another woman who could handle herself against trained men. She was proud of the Skirmishers; they all reported on time, except Andy, who had gone silent, and all of them had put in 100 percent effort. They had also maintained their levels of fitness despite having almost three months off. Only Mark had asked after Andy, and it was an almost half-hearted rhetorical question. A discreet wink from Paul sufficed as an answer; the team didn't need more.

"Right," said Steph. "We're going for a swim, and then I've booked us in for a massage."

"What?" protested Mike, who had just been taken shopping by Steph to make sure he looked the part that evening.

"You've lived in this building for three months, and I bet that the swimming pool and gym are the only places you've visited."

"True," said Mike, and if he was being honest, he had barely seen the pool. "But a massage, Steph?"

"A couples' massage, Mike, or I know you won't go. A perfect way to relax before the recce this evening," she added.

Steph knew Mike well. The reason she was staying with him had everything to do with his well-being. Paul and Steph had talked at length over the last couple of days about the gravity of the decision Mike would need to make. In the army, everything was straightforward: Objective announced, execution plan created, rules of engagement checked, and then mission executed, usually changing the original plan as you went. This was different. Any action they took would put each team member at risk of the law, and that would be eating at Mike's conscience every day. The other issue bothering him was cause and effect. What would their actions do to the overall organized crime picture in London—or more importantly, would there be a chain of events that would put the team firmly on the radar of the so-called kingpins of organized crime?

"Keep an eye on the boss," said Paul.

"I'll stay with him, without him even knowing what I'm up to," said Steph.

They both laughed. He would know straightaway.

Mike's dive into the swimming pool's clear blue waters brought an instant feeling of joy. The water effortlessly supported him, alleviating his muscle soreness. Floating on his back, he felt a profound sense of relaxation. It was as though this brief immersion had cleansed him, washing away the stresses and burdens of the day.

He realized, as he walked into the pool area, that he had never actually been there to swim; he had only looked around briefly.

It was an infinity-style pool with a view of the River Thames and the famous London skyline. Opening his eyes, he scanned the area for Steph. She stood there, clad in the apartment's dressing gowns. She had tried persuading Mike that it was okay to walk around the building in a bathrobe. He didn't understand the need to wear a gown—or realize that nobody else in the building would go to a pool or to a massage in swimming shorts and a T-shirt.

"Everyone just wears the bathrobe provided in their apartments, taking it off at the pool," she protested. It was funny—as soon as he'd entered the pool area, one of the staff gave him a dressing gown!

Steph dropped her phone, untied the belt around the robe, and let it fall. Mike couldn't help but look; he was only human. Steph was wearing a bikini; it wasn't particularly revealing, but her body was that of a goddess—almost flawless. "Fuck," Mike uttered under his breath and then got annoyed with himself for drinking in the view. Worried that Steph might catch him, he glanced away quickly, but it was a little too obvious.

Steph had not noticed Mike staring at her, but she did see him look away like a nervous schoolboy who had been caught doing something naughty. Steph was used to it, though, and wouldn't make a big deal out of it today. The point was to get Mike to take his mind off things, not make him tense. She glanced at him and saw that he was again floating on his back and gently drifting down the pool. She could see the outline of his body and noticed how the lights from the ceiling accentuated his muscles like a well-formed sculpture. Steph now found herself looking away, but she felt a similar sensation to what she'd experienced the other day. Her nipples were hardened and became sensitive, and she noted a not-unpleasant knot in her stomach.

"Snap out of it, Steph," she said to herself.

They had only about fifteen minutes to swim before they had to go through to the massage room. They quickly filled in a pre-massage health questionnaire and were then told to undress to the level they were most comfortable with.

"We won't be wearing wet things, Mike," said Steph, pulling his leg. "Don't worry, we'll be fully draped." She was playing with him; he normally wouldn't care. They had lived on top of each other many times before, but even she realized that these surrounding were very different from the environment they were used to during operations.

Mike's realization dawned late: a couples' massage meant sharing the room. He didn't have to worry, though, as he was first to get onto the massage table and told to look down through the hole.

"Nice butt," Steph called out before the masseuse had a chance to cover him up.

Mike looked up and across just as Steph was lying down, completely naked.

"Not so bad yourself," he said playfully.

"Eyes front, soldier," she shot back with mock sternness, and then in her usual blunt manner, added, "We wouldn't want any... tent formations under those sheets."

Mike laughed; so did both the masseuses.

"You're not a couple, then?" said one of the women.

"Not in the way you might think," said Steph.

"'Couple' . . . you mean *trouble*," added Mike.

Mike had to admit that Steph's idea to spend the afternoon relaxing was spot on.

They got back to the apartment, had a quick chat, and both fell asleep on the balcony. They were programmed in such a way that any microsleep was important, but in the afternoon, they knew to limit it to between twenty and forty-five minutes. They needed to be sharp for the evening's reconnaissance and wanted to avoid the groggy aftermath of a prolonged daytime slumber.

Mike whispered gently in Steph's ear, "Coffee?"

"Oh yes, darling," she replied playfully.

To her surprise, rather than make some, Mike had gone down to the independent coffee shop on the ground floor to get a couple of takeout brews. He claimed they made the best coffee in London. He was right, of course.

"Okay, do we need to go through it again, Steph?"

"No, I'm good," she said.

"We have every contingency covered."

"Yes."

"To confirm, our names will be on the VIP list at the entrance."

"Yes, but we also need these QR codes. I'll send yours to your mobile."

"Your friend is aware that we're going to be there for a short time?"

"Yes, as I said before, he always wanted to catch up with me there. It's been a regular request. I told him that I would be out with my boyfriend, so he invited you along."

"Jon dropped off my suit and your dress, although it doesn't look like much of a dress." Mike smiled.

"Jon said the same when I gave it to him." Steph laughed. "Your microphone is in the neck of the shirt and mine is in the seam of my dress, close to my throat. Jon and Andy said they're state of the art and encryption enabled. No one can listen in, even if they tried. Just the potential for some static radio signatures if we're monitored, so we need to use them sparingly."

"Agreed," said Mike. "If we keep close, there'll be no need to use them. Andy can suppress the broadcast function during normal chat."

It was 21:30 when Mike stepped out of his ensuite bathroom. The clothes Steph had chosen for him earlier were neatly laid out on the bed. All the pieces bore brand names—many of which he hadn't recognized, but he trusted Steph's assurance that he needed to look the part. It wasn't that Mike didn't like fashion, but he probably wouldn't have splurged the way Steph did. The suit was sharp, tailored to perfection, and versatile enough to be worn with or without a tie. It was a pricey Savile Row number, and Steph had to use her connections to have it tailored on the spot, later picked up by Jon. But it was the shoes that truly astounded Mike. They were made by Crockett & Jones and came at a price that he couldn't believe. To be fair, though, he had never seen that level of quality in a shoe. Steph remarked that they were worn by James Bond. Mike liked that, and a smile crossed his face. He thought that if he had bought them, he would not have worn them, as he would always save them for a special occasion. He assessed himself in the mirror; he hoped he looked the part. Playing the role would be easy. He had operated in high-class social settings previously and had always been in his element. That didn't faze him. He just needed to find a way to balance socializing with completing a recce.

"Steph, it's 22:15. We should get going," Mike said.

"Two seconds."

He walked into the lounge and took a final look in the mirror. He heard Steph open the door.

He turned around as she walked out of the room.

"Fuck me." Mike's jaw dropped, and his words were said involuntarily.

Steph was wearing a simple dress that left little to the imagination. Although it was uncomplicated, he could see why she had chosen it. It had a clever—what do you call it?—loop that went around her neck, which was perfect for hiding a microphone. This loop seemed to hold almost no material as the dress plunged toward Steph's waist, leaving the middle of her chest exposed and barely covering her breasts. In fact, he had no idea how she didn't fall out of it. The dress had a slit that showed the lower part of her thigh, but he knew if she sat down, she would expose most of the leg.

"I take it you like it," said Steph, smiling.

"Fuck, Steph, you look stunning," he replied genuinely.

"You don't scrub up so bad yourself, Mike." She laughed. "Can you help me with my jacket?"

"Yes, of course." Mike was slightly embarrassed. For the second time today, he could feel a sensation in his groin.

After assisting Steph with her jacket, he gave her the tiny earpiece that came with the microphone. You would really have to look to see the earpiece, and it was rarely spotted even by the most observant of security teams. If it was noticed, the best excuse was that it was an experimental hearing aid. That explanation worked on most amateur security teams, who were usually too worried about causing a scene with someone who was hard of hearing.

"Sierra Alpha, Sierra 5: comms check."

"Loud and clear." Steph smiled at Mike.

"You also. Out," Mike responded.

They made their way out of the building and to a Mercedes S-Class that was waiting for them out front.

"Evening, folks. Can you confirm where we're going tonight?" Jon Apolosi was driving the car, and from now on, he would play the role of chauffer. He looked the part; you wouldn't know it was Jon.

"To the Red Zone nightclub, please. VIP entrance," said Steph.

"No worries. It will take about fifteen minutes with the traffic tonight," said Jon. "There's champagne in the back if you'd like a glass."

"No, thanks," they both responded.

Jon knew exactly where to go and really did look like a seasoned chauffer as he pulled the car up at the Red Zone VIP entrance. He didn't need to leave the car to open their door, as there were greeters outside. Across the street, paparazzi were lined up, trying to get a shot of an A-list celebrity.

"Mike, get out on my side. It will remove the risk of the paps inadvertently getting a photo." Steph quickly exited the car and Mike followed.

Steph had been in this situation before. Mike was impressed that she gave off an aura of belonging. He needed to act the same.

The VIP entrance to the Red Zone was like an exclusive hotel reception area. The staff there reminded him of an airline cabin crew—certainly not your usual security. There were security protocols in place, though. All bags were passed through a security machine by each hostess—there were lots of them—and they quickly used a wand to check each person. Mike noted that aside from the bags, the checks were almost for show. This worked in their favor, even though he was sure they wouldn't find the comms device.

It was clear that there was no way they wanted A-list celebrities being held up in reception.

The next step was the handing over of his phone to a check-in hostess, who scanned the QR code.

"Oh, you're with Mr. Raj tonight. He's at his usual table, which is number eleven. One of our team will take you up in the lift. What will you be having to drink?"

"Two gin and tonics, Hendrick's with Fever-Tree." Not an overly flash request, but Steph knew that flash was not cool.

"I can take your jacket, ma'am?"

"Oh yes, here you go. And can you please place it at booth two? We'll use the side entrance when we leave."

"Yes, ma'am."

Steph removed her jacket, and no one batted an eyelid. Mike looked around at what the other women were wearing, and Steph was dressed in similar fashion to them.

The club's entry procedure had been practiced by the staff many times; it was all seamless and what the clientele would have expected.

Steph grabbed Mike's hand as they walked to the lift. It was opened for them, and the hostess they were assigned got in with them.

The VIP lounge was just one floor up. *Lazy bastards,* Mike thought.

The doors opened and the sound of music quickly filled their ears. It was loud but not so loud that you couldn't hear people speak. *Clever,* he thought. If the music was slightly quieter in the VIP area, there was more chance of business being conducted. Worst case, though, was that each table was wired, and they were listening in.

Table 11 was situated in a prime spot, Mike noted as he walked to it. It was far enough away from the actual prime table, where the Clover brothers were seated.

"Stephanie," came a genuine welcome from Mr. Raj. "You made it!"

Steph air-kissed him, and then he took a step back. "Wow, you're a sight for tired eyes."

"Thank you," said Steph.

The fact was that Mike hadn't seen so many stunning women in one place, and a few were sitting around Mr. Raj's table. He would swear that Steph's outfit was conservative compared to some of the others.

Mike and Mr. Raj exchanged pleasantries.

"What a polite man you've found, Steph. Please, Mike, call me Simon. Where do you want to sit, darling?" Simon said to Steph.

"You know I'm a people-watcher, Simon. Can we look at the dance floor?"

Steph's decision to orientate towards the dance floor, was a stroke of genius. This design of the table facilitated conversation from any seat and provided a direct view of the Clover table when facing the dance floor.

"Sierra Alpha, Sierra 5, this is Sierra 7: Radio check. Over." Andy had done it. He had gotten the range on the earpieces.

They had three planned responses depending on the situation.

"Do I need to order the drinks, darling?" Mike said to Steph. He whispered so only Steph could hear.

"No, darling, I ordered them on the way in," Steph responded, slightly louder.

"Both loud and clear. Out," said Andy.

As Steph caught up with Simon Raj—they really were old friends—Mike made small talk with the woman immediately to his left. She was quite interesting; her name was Katrina, and she was the daughter of an oil baron in the Middle East, but in her heart was an environmentalist.

Simultaneously, Mike was mentally cataloging every visitor to the Clover table, identifying the security personnel, and zeroing in on the primary target. Positioned between the brothers sat their father, Aaron Clover.

While the brothers' attention was predominantly directed at Aaron, it was the man seated opposite them, guarded by two others, who piqued Mike's interest. Every time he spoke, all the Clover family focused intently on him. Whoever he was, he outranked them all. He was angry about something, and the Clover boys in particular looked worried. Mike checked his watch: fifteen more minutes. He looked at Steph and smiled to acknowledge Simon. He glanced down and noticed that Simon had his hand on Steph's leg. Any higher, and Steph would have broken his fingers. Mike kept the routine going, looking straight ahead and then, after a short while, glancing away to ensure he wouldn't be caught staring at the Clover table. Then he'd continue his conversation with Katrina.

Mike's routine proved beneficial when he nearly locked eyes with Terry Patrick. Mike had seen Terry when he'd first sat down at the table. *This guy is a professional,* Mike thought. Terry was monitoring everyone; in fact, Mike noted that he seemed to be overdoing it. *Is something up? Is Terry worried about something?* He was on his toes, that was for sure, and Mike needed to be careful not to get caught. Steph was busy talking to Simon; however, Mike would be keen to get her feedback on the power play at the table and why Terry looked so worried. Mike then noticed the one Tommy had referred to as the Cockney lad, Nick Clover, stand up.

"Fuck me," said Mike under his breath. Tommy had done a job on him. *One punch, holy shit.*

"What?" said Katrina.

"Sorry," said Mike. "I was just thinking we'll need to go soon."

"Already?" she replied.

"Sierra Alpha, Sierra 5: abort, abort, abort." Their earpieces erupted to life as Andy's voice aired a level of authority.

Steph calmly looked at Simon. "Sorry, we have to go. Remember what I said about Mike meeting my mum first thing?"

"Mothers," said Simon, finally removing his hand from Steph's leg.

Steph called over the hostess. "Could you arrange for my coat to be ready? It's in booth two. My chauffeur will be meeting us at the side entrance."

"Yes, ma'am."

"Simon, thank you so much for the invite," said Mike. "Honey, I'll go with the hostess and get your jacket while you say goodbye."

Mike thanked Katrina, kissed her on the cheek, and walked away.

"Steph, thirty secs," whispered Mike into his mic.

To everyone looking at them, they were just a couple leaving a table and saying goodbye to good friends. They played it out well, but both would have sensed the urgency in Andy's voice.

"Sitrep." Once again, Mike talked in a whisper.

The hostess looked at Mike. "Pardon?"

"Oh, sorry, it's my first time here, and I just wondered whether I collect the jacket from the booth?"

"No, sir. Your partner's jacket will be waiting for us at the exit point."

"Sierra Alpha, Sierra 5: Urgent sitrep. DS Reed and others entering the club. You have two minutes before they try to get to the VIP area."

Of course, thought Mike. Bec Reed had mentioned that there were other ways of putting heat on local firms. Raid them and impact the clientele and revenue on a busy night, such as a Friday or Saturday.

Mike's heart skipped a beat. He heard Steph's voice talking to someone new.

"Going somewhere so soon?" he heard in his earpiece.

"Oh, I have to join my boyfriend. We have a busy day tomorrow," said Steph.

"Pity. You're a very sexy woman. My father would love to meet you one day." Liam Clover was looking straight into Steph's eyes. "He owns this club."

"Wow," said Steph, trying to sound impressed.

"Why don't you join us for a drink?"

"Really, I'm so tempted, but I have to go." Steph sounded genuine.

"Sixty seconds," said Andy.

"My darling, this is my card. Give me a call or join me for a drink. The pub on the card is a shithole, but I'm usually there on Tuesdays and Thursdays. The rest of the time, I'm here."

Steph smiled, thanked him, and walked away.

Liam Clover blew out a whistle as Steph left. He looked at Terry. "Fuck me, the things I want to do with her." They both laughed.

Steph and Mike were reunited by the car and climbed in just as they saw more blue lights coming up the road behind them. It was a full-blown raid. Jon was driving in exactly the way a chauffeur would; he made the easiest turn, which was left, and drove away from the club.

"Sierra 7, Sierra Alpha: Good work. We'll debrief tomorrow." Mike had not realized Andy needed something else.

"Good work, Steph," Mike said.

"Fuck me," said Steph. "What a rush. That, my friends, is contingency plan one playing out: actual contact with one of the Clover family."

They drove for a short while.

"Okay, guys, I need some decoy footage for Andy," Jon said as he pulled the car over.

"Get out here, walk five hundred meters along the river, get seen by the security camera next to the small outdoor music event that is at the one-hundred-fifty-meter point, and then the other camera at the four-hundred-fifty-meter point, stop and chat for about five minutes and then leave the rest to us. I'll pick you up fifty meters up the road from that point." Jon had briefed it exactly as Andy wanted it.

Mike and Steph did as they were told and walked toward the first camera.

"Hold her hand, Sierra Alpha. This is a blossoming relationship," barked Andy.

They held hands as they walked toward the second camera, but Andy stopped them a distance away and got them to pause, talk, and then walk again.

"Stop once again, Sierra 5. Kiss Sierra Alpha." Mike looked at Steph, and they both seemed slightly puzzled by Andy's request. They knew Andy would have seen something from earlier in the evening at this location, possibly that it was very much a couple's event. It was probably what was driving the request.

Mike reached for Steph's other hand and then very gently kissed her on the lips. They both moved away slightly, and then they kissed again, longer.

"Nearly there," said Andy.

Mike and Steph embraced again, this time like the first kiss of two lovers. It was electrically charged and executed with absolute purpose.

"And stop," said Andy.

They both snapped out of it.

"Well done. That last one was on the money; you convinced me," said Andy, watching through the CCTV.

They walked the final fifty meters to the car and got in. They looked at each other and then away like two people determining whether what had happened was real or an act.

Jon turned to them. "Okay, Steph, your replacement dress is here—and, Mike, here's your shirt. We need to get the tac comms you're wearing away from you, but we also need you to go back to the hotel in the same outfits. Get changed now, and I'll you drop you at the apartment before delivering the comms equipment back to Andy."

"Sierra 7, this is Sierra Alpha: Comms black. Good work out."

"Roger. Out." Andy switched off his comms.

Mike took off his jacket and put on the fresh shirt. He looked at Steph as she took off the nipple tape from under her dress and then lifted it off. She was completely naked underneath.

"Avert your eyes, soldier," Steph said to Mike.

Mike tried to avert his eyes, but they seemed to take an age to move away. He once again felt the buzz of excitement hit his body. He couldn't get the image out of his mind.

Steph smiled as she pulled the replacement dress on and then her jacket. *Mike is human, after all,* she thought. Her body betrayed her, though, as it was not reacting in a professional way but gave out a raw charge of energy because of the situation, as it responded in a state of arousal.

"There's a suitcase on the front seat, boss. Could you grab it and put the clothes inside? In the unlikely event these comms are ever tracked, they'll go dead here. We're ten minutes out."

They arrived at the apartment's foyer in good time.

"Night, Jon. Good work." Mike patted him on the shoulder.

Mike and Steph sat down in the lounge room of the apartment, opposite each other. Mike's eyes were hypnotized by Steph as she sat with her legs crossed; her dress had naturally ridden up, and her upper thigh was clearly visible. He looked at the way the dress fell across her breasts, which were now no longer fully hidden. The tape she had used to prevent them from being exposed had been discarded. He needed to get his mind away from the view in front of him.

"Steph, anything to debrief now, while it's still fresh in your mind?"

"Not really, Mike—but fuck, I didn't see that Liam Clover had left the table."

"Me neither, but you handled it well."

"We did rehearse it." She laughed. "Over and over again." She rolled her eyes. "What a fucking rush, though. What about you? Anything on your mind?"

Is that a trick question?

He smiled. "Terry Patrick. Any thoughts?"

"He's a professional. Trained."

"Absolutely," Mike confirmed. "We need to know more about him." He gave a huge sigh. "DS Reed . . . that was too close."

"Yep, we planned for the cops to potentially raid, but not at the same time," Steph said, deep in thought.

"The raid was just for show. She'll call me tomorrow, I guarantee it," Mike said after another sigh.

"Are you okay?" said Steph. Mike looked frustrated as he stared into the distance, thinking.

"Emergency sex." She'd thought it, then said it. The electricity was still flowing through her body.

"What?" asked Mike.

"You know, emergency sex. Maybe it will do us some good." She smiled seductively.

Mike hadn't been thinking about the mission but about Steph, the kiss, the nakedness in the car. He was now staring at her, knowing she had nothing on underneath the dress, and he was aroused. Was she inviting him?

Steph gave him a look that made him go weak and slightly breathless. She traced her finger down the front of her exposed chest and then gently pulled back the little fabric left covering her breast. She traced her finger slowly over her nipple and then stood up. Mike was rooted to the chair like all sense of being had left him. As she stood up, Steph let the dress slip off her body, leaving her totally naked in front of him. She walked over, climbed on top of him, and sat, legs astride. Their lips met tenderly, reminiscent of an artist's delicate brush strokes. Mike's kisses traced a path from her lips to her neck and lower.

Fuck, thought Steph, *this is not emergency sex.* He was going to make love to her. That was not the plan; that would make it complicated. Initially, she thought, *Mistake, move away,* but he was awakening a very guarded part of her inner desires. Her nipples, now sensitive, reacted as his tongue gently brushed over one while his hand expertly, gently rolled the other. She could feel the heat building inside her. She unbuttoned his shirt and began kissing his nipples. *Where on earth is this going?* she thought. She had planned a quick five-minute fuck, that's all.

Mike wasn't sure he was ever going to find himself in this position again. All the years he had known Steph, he—like other men—had marveled at her beauty, but he never felt the way he did about her now. He wanted it to last, fearing it might be fleeting. He was now carefully exploring every inch of her body with his lips and hands, to see how she would respond. She rose, pulling him with her, and he briefly feared it was the end. Instead, she led him to the bedroom.

Steph had given in—no quick fuck, no immediate release of tension. In her aroused state, she thought they might as well move to the bedroom and enjoy it. And enjoying it, she was. She climbed onto Mike's bed, making sure he got her best angle as she carefully laid down in a way that allowed him to drink the moment in. She had seen Mike naked before but never in a sexually charged atmosphere like this one, and now it was her turn to admire his body. She had forgotten just how well formed his upper body was, which was a result of all those years of exercise, carrying packs, chin-ups, and shaping his body for the sole purpose of being ready to fight. She traced her eyes down to his flat stomach, looked at his buttocks in the mirror, and then his muscular upper thighs. Her attention drifted downward, settling on his evident arousal, intensifying her longing.

Mike climbed onto the bed and kissed Steph, moving slowly up her legs. He kissed around her inner thighs, passing gently across her clitoris, and then worked his way back up to her breasts and ultimately to her lips.

"Please, Mike, fuck me," she whispered.

Mike took his penis and eased the tip into her moist opening. Steph let out a gasp as he teased her with just the tip for the first few short strokes.

He then went slightly deeper for the next few strokes and could feel her clamping all her internal muscles around him.

"Please, just fuck me," she begged.

He pushed deep inside her.

Their mouths met, and their kissing deepened. They were, at that moment, one.

They seemed to be made for each other, Steph moving rhythmically to Mike's beat. It was like an orchestra building to a crescendo.

Very soon, she let out a gasp, involuntarily but needed.

"Fuck!" she shouted.

Her pussy contracted, and then, as the orgasm passed over her, she could feel Mike's cock pulsing at the same time. "It's okay, Mike. Let it go."

It was like a pressure relief valve for Mike, all the stress of the last few days suddenly forgotten as each stream of fluid engulfed Steph.

They fell into each other's arms.

"Emergency sex," he said.

"That was not emergency sex," said Steph.

That was trouble, she thought.

5

At 0700 on Sunday morning, the cell phone alarm gently woke Mike and Steph from their sleep. Nestled in Mike's embrace, Steph was wrapped only in a sheet, both naked. *What now?* she thought. Who was going to break the silence? Mike was almost thinking the same, but his own defense system kicked in like he was under some sort of threat.

"Coffee?" he proposed.

Steph smiled. That was one way to break the ice.

"You making it or grabbing one downstairs?" she asked.

"For you, I'm willing to shower, put some clothes on, and go downstairs."

Just as Mike was about to get up, Steph looked at him. "Mike."

He returned the same look. "I know."

"What the fuck do we do now?" said Steph.

"What do you want to do?"

"I honestly don't know. I wasn't expecting that."

"Well, maybe we should just do the life thing."

She smiled. "Live it and see. Just one thing . . ."

"Yes?"

"What happened can't destroy our friendship." Steph offered her hand; Mike shook it and laughed.

Steph watched as he got up, went to the bathroom, grabbed a towel—which he would eventually hang nearer the shower—

and threw it over his shoulder. The door shut, and she leaned back.

"Steph Holgate, what the fuck are you doing?" she uttered under her breath, and then she smiled.

A little while later, there was a knock on the apartment door. Paul and Andrew were standing in the hallway, coffee tray in hand, ready for the debrief.

"Have another." Paul gave out a coffee to Mike and Steph. "I hear you had an interesting evening."

Andy had briefed Paul on the primary points from last night's recce but without the details Mike and Steph could provide.

"Okay, let's go through the main players at the head table using the footage Andy retrieved. Liam was the guy you encountered, Steph?" Paul asked.

It wasn't unusual for Paul to run the debrief. He was here to glean potential insights that might otherwise go unnoticed in a regular debrief.

"Seems like a nice guy on the surface," said Steph, "but you can tell he's used to getting his way. I'm pretty sure he would have made some sort of misogynistic comment when I walked away. He wanted me to meet his father. I felt he was maybe fishing on his behalf."

"'Fishing'?" Paul looked confused.

"Fishing for girls for the old pervert," Steph said in a parodied voice of an old man.

"Okay, what would we expect in a confrontation with Liam?"

"He looks handy—not sure if he's trained or whether it's from the school of hard knocks," said Steph.

"Mike, your thoughts on Liam?"

"Agree with Steph. I think Liam and Karl are both probably handy—they may be receiving some fighting training from their enforcers. Hard to tell, though."

"And Nick Clover?"

Steph laughed. "Tommy fucked him up bad. Did you see him, Mike?"

"His face is a mess, Paul. Tommy made sure he wasn't getting up."

"Dangerous?" Paul asked.

"Really dangerous. He instigated everything, and I believe he was armed," Mike said gravely.

"Agreed." Steph was just as serious. "I think he's the wild card. He can't handle himself, so he probably carries something and will use it as an extension of his penis."

"Okay, next: these guys, the so-called enforcers."

"I saw only two," said Mike. "And I don't know who the other one is who was with Terry."

"Terry Patrick?"

"Yes, he's a pro." Mike was certain.

Andy chimed in, "He certainly is—ex–French Foreign Legion and worked with a couple of security companies in Iraq."

"He was switched on, Paul. Something had him worried," said Mike.

"Agreed," said Steph.

"Could it be the police raid?" Andy asked.

"No, something else," said Mike almost quizzically.

"What are you thinking, Mike? Happy for a hypothesis," said Paul.

"Test this."

Mike stood up with his coffee in hand and began to pace. "Let's go back to Tuesday when Tommy walked into the pub. Suppose Terry had an inkling that Tommy could handle himself. He's being paid to evaluate people and determine whether they pose a threat. Tommy grabs a beer, stares into the distance like he has a lot on his mind, and drinks a pint without thinking. The gobshite Nick stands up and gives Tommy a hard time. Rather than the flight mechanism kicking in like it would with ninety-nine percent of the population, Tommy tries to joke his way out of it and leave. This arouses Terry's suspicions further that Tommy can handle himself. He adjusts his position in the pub to be out of Tommy's field of vision. As Tommy turns and is pushed, Terry is in a booth just out of sight of Tommy. As Tommy turns around and the gobshite attempts to punch him, Terry places himself behind him too late to do anything about Tommy reacting to Nick but quick enough to prevent Tommy from doing anything else. Now, my guess is that if Tommy saw Terry in the mirror, Terry would have clocked it. He sucker-punched Tommy because he knew that a second later, Tommy would prioritize him as a target."

"Fuck, boss, that's more information than Tommy gave us," said Paul.

Andy and Steph were speechless.

In truth, that was one of a couple of theories Mike had about Terry, but he wanted to keep the others to himself.

"So you're saying, boss, that there's a chance Terry is worried about who they attacked and whether trouble will follow?" said Andy.

"Sort of. What I'm saying is that Terry knows that those skills come with some serious training. He wouldn't be sure from where, but he would be concerned there may be repercussions."

"He was really agitated last night—almost nervous," said Steph.

"Thoughts, Paul?" asked Mike.

"We'll use that in planning. Is he problem number one?" said Paul.

"Only number one on the assault, not overall," said Steph.

"Tell me what you saw, Steph," said Mike.

"The father had someone with him. He was the highest-ranking person there."

"A kingpin," said Mike.

"Agreed," said Steph. "The kingpin was pissed, and the family looked scared."

"Confirmed," said Mike.

"Andy?" said Paul.

Andy spoke about the last thirty-six hours operating gray from the team, leading up to last night's recce. He explained how he thought the firm worked, especially the upper echelons beyond the Clover family. They were small-time in the grand scheme of things, but Shoreditch was their lucky card, especially the club. "The kingpin is a guy called John Tort, and he has an interesting background. English and Russian parents, sixty-two years old, and runs about a quarter of London. He's naturally aligned with a Russian kingpin, and together they run half of London."

"What does that actually mean, Andy? He runs half of London?" asked Steph.

"Good question. They feed off—well, run—all the smaller firms. Drugs, extortion, protection, guns, money laundering—you name it, they have a piece of it. The firms are made up of a combination of new and old London crime syndicates: some loyal, some resentful. Tort provides the infrastructure for all the other kingpins. The reason Mike and Steph put John Tort as number one is good. Tort will want to either get behind the Clover family or move someone in quickly. In their world, any gaps will be quickly filled."

"Cause and effect," said Mike.

"The risk of doing the recce was worth it?" said Paul.

"Absolutely. It's clear the club isn't an option; we would be massacred unless we had weapons. The intel it gave us is enough to know the cause and effect," Mike said. "Steph meeting Liam was a bonus, something we could potentially use down the line."

"The police were unexpected. That was nearly a disaster," said Steph.

"Yeah, great work, Andy," Mike said.

"Great work, all of you," said Paul.

"Andy, logistics updates?" Mike asked.

"Comms disposed, clothes gone," Andy replied.

"Bastard." Steph bemoaned the loss of her dress.

"You have another one," Andy said, always to the point.

"CCTV?" said Paul.

"Thirty-nine minutes of the nightclub security tapes are on recycle. It will also look like Mike and Steph spent forty-five minutes at the small music event," Andy confirmed.

"I have no idea how you managed that, Andy, but good work," said Paul. "What about your van?"

"It's clean and parked in a safe place."

"Questions?"

"No questions," said Mike. "I've seen enough. I want you, Tommy, and Mark to work a plan; run it past Andy, Jon, Timi, and Steve. Skippy, Steph, and I will play the cross-examiners. We go to court tomorrow morning. Paul, can you get Jon to find somewhere secure? And, Andy, once you've done the first run-through, go gray again and start surveillance at your discretion."

"Yes, boss."

"Thanks, everyone," Mike said, finishing the meeting.

"One more thing, boss. We need an op name for the guys. Some things need to stay familiar."

Mike was slightly surprised by Paul's request, but it made sense.

"You have one in mind, Paul?"

Paul hesitated. "How would you feel about Op Becker?"

"Naming an op after Tony Becker." Mike almost choked up. "The team would be okay with it? Steph, Andy?"

Steph let out a sigh. Andy rubbed his forehead.

Paul could see they were choked up as well; a tear was in Andy's eye.

"Sorry, guys. Bad call," said Paul.

"No," Andy and Steph replied together.

"It's absolutely fitting, Paul."

Mike kept back his own emotions. "Op Becker, it is."

Paul and Andy got up to leave. Just as he was about to walk out of the apartment, Paul called out to Steph. "Walk with me to the car."

"Sure."

"Andy, you go ahead."

"Okay, Paul," Andy responded.

"Mike, would you like anything while I'm downstairs with Paul?" asked Steph.

"All good."

Steph slipped on some trainers that instantly made the jeans and T-shirt she was wearing look like a carefully arranged ensemble and walked with Paul to the lift, which they took to the foyer.

"How's he doing, Steph?" said Paul.

"He's worried about the team. This cause-and-effect problem is becoming a real issue. We could hit them and just walk away. Mike doesn't want the team to get into trouble with the law, and he's also worried about the gap left after we take out the firm. He's concerned that it will have repercussions for the local community. He fucking cares!"

"That's what makes him stand out from the rest," Paul agreed. "He is okay, though?"

"Yes. I sent him for a massage yesterday." Steph laughed.

"I bet he loved that."

"He was certainly relaxed before the recce," Steph said, still smiling.

"Good," said Paul. "Steph, I'm pleased you're watching out for him, but I really didn't want you to sleep with him."

The words hit Steph like a missile.

"How the fuck did you know that?" she asked.

Paul laughed. "Well, you just confirmed it—but your bed was immaculately made and his was a mess. I could tell the cleaners hadn't been there, and you wouldn't have gone out after the mission last night. You don't need to explain, Steph."

"Shit, Paul. I pulled the emergency sex button."

"But the outcome isn't what you thought?"

"The problem is, it was better than I thought or wanted."

"You're both extremely important to me, Steph; I'm here for you."

She hugged him. He was as sharp as a knife and knew exactly what was going on, and she trusted him like a father.

"Be careful, Steph," he said as he walked away.

"What was that all about?" asked Mike, who had just come out of the lift. "Cleaners turned up early," he explained.

"That's good. It gives us the afternoon to relax after they finish. It's been a tough twenty-four hours."

"Shall we do brunch?" he asked.

"Great idea."

Terry Patrick faced Aaron Clover. It had been a trying week. Aaron had called a meeting with his main enforcer and his three boys: Liam, Karl, and Nick. Liam and Karl were genuinely agitated about the police raid the night before, especially as John Tort had been at the club a minute before the raid.

"That was a fucking shambles, Terry," said Karl.

"You're responsible for ensuring no one gets close," added Liam.

"Even the fucking filth," Nick said, trying to impress his dad.

Aaron had seen it all before. He could also preempt what Terry would say, but he wanted to hear it himself. "Terry, ignore them. What's been bothering you these last few days?"

"John Tort. You know he's losing patience, sir."

Aaron liked that Terry insisted on calling him *sir*.

"I thought he was going to hit us last night and finally snap," said Terry.

Aaron smiled. "These are my problems, Terry. I like that you worry, but your job isn't to run the business—it's to enforce and keep us secure."

Nick snapped, "And you fucking failed at that, Terry." Nick was becoming annoying.

Aaron looked at his sons. "Sit the fuck down, all three of you." They all sat down immediately.

"I can't protect us from the OCD, boss," said Terry.

That got everyone's attention. "The OCD," said Aaron. "That makes sense."

"Confirmed, boss. After we got you out of there, we were faced with—"

"Don't tell me DS Reed," interrupted Aaron. "Why is she interested in us again? We're small fish."

This comment irked the three brothers; their father had always warned them that they were a small cog in a bigger wheel. He had told them about the advantages being a small firm brings, though, especially in terms of operating below the radar of the police and, usually, if they contributed to their kingpin, without the typical territorial battles with other firms. The latter had become problematic, though. Revenue from the club was their main source of income, and it had been doing very well of late, but just about every other area of the business was hemorrhaging money. That was the reason John Tort had suddenly taken an interest. The bastard had offered to buy him out and allow him and the family to retire in peace. *Get weak, and the vulture's pounce,* Aaron thought.

"We should have known the OCD was coming," said Liam, belaboring the point.

Aaron liked Terry, and he was starting to get annoyed with his sons. "Tell me how the fuck Terry was supposed to know the OCD was coming? No firm has a cop on their payroll from that organization. Those officers are fucking monitored more for corruption than the Chinese. Now shut the fuck up; I want to hear from Terry. Tell me, Terry, what the fuck is on your mind." Aaron was clearly pissed.

Terry liked his boss but hated his boys. Spoiled bastards—no code, no honor. Their father was old-school, and even though he was a lifelong gangster, he believed in a code. It was probably why John Tort had made an offer instead of moving in directly.

"I was worried last night that we were primed for an attempted takeover, sir. But once I realized you and Tort were trying to work everything out, I became less edgy," Terry explained.

"So why did the cops raid us last night? The timing was interesting. Hurt our revenue and scare our clientele, and the firm will go under," said Aaron.

The three boys were growing resentful that their father was confiding in Terry.

"I don't think it's Tort," said Terry.

"You have someone else in mind?"

Terry glanced at the boys, sensing a looming betrayal.

"I think OCD raided the club because that was their only way to retaliate for the attack on the kid on Tuesday. And then, of course, that fucking hit on the girl." Terry words conveyed his anger.

"Drop it, Terry, for fuck's sake. You're saying they'd waste all those resources for a fucking nobody? And we keep telling you— we swear it—we had nothing to do with the girl," Liam snapped.

"You're full of bullshit, and you know it," said Nick. "We don't need this cunt around us, Dad."

Terry could feel the hackles rise on the back of his neck but did his best to stay calm.

"What's the fixation with that fucking boy, Terry? He fucking survived, didn't he?" said Nick. "We keep telling you, we did not order a hit on the girl."

It was Aaron's turn to lose his temper. "If Terry doesn't get the chance to tell me what he thinks is going on, I swear I'll cut your fucking tongues out."

The boys immediately sat back. They had never seen their father so livid.

"Terry, tell me, for fuck's sake, what's on your mind?" Aaron looked at his sons. "No interruptions."

"That boy could handle himself," Terry started, looking at each of them in turn.

"He wouldn't be the first guy we met who could handle himself," said Aaron.

"Different," said Terry. "He was trained."

"Go on, take me through it," said Aaron.

"When he first walked into the pub, I thought he was just a normal kid. He seemed preoccupied, probably with meeting the girl, but he acknowledged us on the way in—not unusual but it showed he was confident. I watched him as he drank his first pint. He was just staring into space, almost like he was lost in thought. I've seen that look before. He finished the pint without even realizing it. The barman snapped him out of it, and he ordered another, and once again he went back into a trance. At that point, I was tempted to go talk to him and see if he was okay. That's when Nick decided to start taking the piss."

Nick nearly protested, but his father gave him a look that warned him off.

"Well, when the . . . banter began, most people would have done one of two things: If you're confident, laugh it off and try to defuse the situation, or get up and leave. In the kid's mind, after he tried to defuse it, all seemed okay. But then he did something curious: He got up to leave. I think he knew it could escalate again and it was better to get out of the pub. That's when Nick pushed him."

Aaron knew what had happened at the pub, but this was the first time he had asked for details. "What the fuck did you do that for, Nick?"

Before Nick could answer, Terry cut in. "He wanted to show everyone in the pub he had a big dick."

Aaron smiled. "Not a fucking word." He pointed at all three of his sons again.

Terry went on. "When the lad turned around, I changed seats to get out of his line of sight. I could see Nick was going to follow up. As Nick went to hit the lad, he blocked Nick and dropped him like he wasn't there."

Nick's face went red. His brothers smirked. "Lucky shot," said Nick.

"Look at your fucking face, Nick. There's nothing lucky about that." His dad showed no sympathy.

"You're right, sir. He hit him with an open fist to protect his knuckles—professional. It's what the lad did next, though, that convinced me he was trained. He had to weigh his options quickly, so he checked to see whether he could make the exit. It was only a glance, but had he completely turned, he would have seen me. He realized that Karl and Liam were coming toward him. I'm pretty sure he made the choice to take them out and then run."

"He didn't get the chance, though, because you took him out?" said Aaron.

"Yes, I did. There's something else, and it's this that's been weighing on my mind. In the split second before I hit him, he glanced in the mirror and caught sight of Tibbsy and me. He was about to readjust his target priorities. He was going to take us out."

The room went silent.

Karl was the first to speak. "So what? Maybe he's trained, maybe he's not. He's no longer around, nobody's getting charged, and you're sitting here like some fanboy warning Dad about a kid."

"Terry?" Aaron realized his son was factually correct.

"Did you see the papers, boss, on Wednesday?" said Terry.

"Can't remember them."

"There was nothing in them. Big commotion, lots of people. Nothing—no social media, no nothing."

"And no real witness, thankfully," added Karl.

"So why are you worried, Terry? Humor me," said Nick.

"He dropped you like you weren't there; he was confident he could take out your brothers, and he was prepared to go through Tibbsy and me. I think he's military or something else. I see a lot of me in him. All I'm worried about is if there are a few more like him, where he comes from—if he wants revenge, we're fucked. As each day goes by, I'm getting more relaxed about it, and the raid last night convinced me that the cops were the ones seeking revenge within the law."

"Your problem, Terry, is that you're always worried about something." Nick was flippant, almost cocky.

"Nick, we pay him to be worried, you stupid little boy. You brought the fucking OCD down on us, and if I think you had anything to do with that girl, you better fucking hide." Aaron believed every word Terry had said. "One thing, Terry: You said you were going to talk with the lad before Nick here decided to take him on. Why?"

Terry smiled. "I was going to ask him if he wanted a job."

They all laughed.

"Okay, Tort is off our backs for a while, and the boy has done the right thing and gone quiet. Still, we should keep our ear to the ground on the girl. Really strange if it wasn't us. Make sure her old man has a cushy time inside; he may think we didn't keep our word. The police have also proved their point with the raid. Let's move on from this quickly." Aaron looked concerned despite his words. "Terry, have a drink with me. And, boys, you need to learn from this man."

Liam, Karl, and Nick reluctantly agreed.

"Liam, I need a girl. Tonight. Find me one," said Aaron.

Fuck, what am I doing here? Terry thought. *The money is good, but these guys are fuckwits.*

"He knows," said Steph.

Mike understood right away what she was talking about. "Who?"

"Paul."

"That's why he dragged you downstairs?"

"Yes."

"Are you okay?"

"I am, Mike. I really am. But to be honest, last night wasn't meant to play out like that."

"I didn't think you had planned it that way."

They hadn't really discussed the events of the previous evening—not just the sex but also the fact that they'd spent the night together. It had left them both somewhat confused. Was this an ongoing thing, pressure relief, or something else?

"I thought we were going to do the life thing," said Mike.

"Live it and see—but it could get complicated."

"I know . . ."

It was strange—this was the first real time they'd had with each other since they'd woken up: no kissing, no touching, no awkwardness. They both felt it. Did it mean something or nothing?

"Mind if I join you?"

Mike looked up and then stood. His officer training had taught him some manners. "DS Reed," he said respectfully. "Please do."

Steph was slightly annoyed; this interruption left their conversation unresolved.

"What brings you here, Bec?" Mike asked, getting right to the point.

"We raided the club last night."

"The club?"

"The Clover nightclub." If Bec had been expecting a reaction, she didn't get one.

"Do you want a coffee?"

"Make it two." She gestured to a colleague approaching them. "This is Detective Sean Grimmer."

Sean was clearly in awe of his colleague, slightly on the skinny side, and pale, like he spent too many nights on duty and too many days in bed. He seemed exhausted.

"I better get those coffees, Sean. You look tired," said Mike.

Heading to the counter, Mike left Steph slightly uneasy, seated with the two police officers.

"You two just catching up, Steph?" asked Bec.

"Not exactly. I'm sort of lodging with him, avoiding hotel costs."

A subtle change in Bec's demeanor caught Steph's attention. It was a small signal that she gave off, but she could swear it was jealousy. *Does Bec like Mike?* she wondered.

"How long are you in town?" Bec realized how that might sound. "I mean, in London."

Steph remained guarded. "Oh, I plan to live here full-time, eventually."

"Okay. What have you been up to, then?" Bec was probing.

Steph went straight into disinformation mode. "Nothing, really. We went to a small music event last night near the water."

"Here we go." Mike brought over the coffees. Bec offered to pay, but he refused with a smile.

By now, the café staff was transitioning the space for dinner service, setting up cutlery, candles, and menus. The place turned into a top-notch restaurant in the evening.

"So you said you raided the club?" asked Mike.

"Yes, we wanted to let you know that. They would have lost a lot of money last night and probably some A-list clientele. I know you said you were disappointed the police couldn't do anything to bring to justice the thugs who attacked Tommy, but occasionally there are other ways, such as a well-timed raid."

"Thanks for telling us. Wouldn't it have been easier to call?"

Genius question, thought Steph as she watched Bec's face slightly redden, but she then realized it was not because of her obvious fondness—if that was the right word—for Mike.

Steph noticed that Bec had changed her position in the chair and leaned forward. Detective Grimmer had done the same.

"There was something else going on in the club last night." Bec paused.

"What?" Mike played poker, clearly.

"I thought you could tell us, Mike."

"Pardon?" Mike said, still playing it cool.

"Our comms van picked up static from an encrypted radio last night, on and off for about thirty minutes. It was very active three minutes before the raid."

"How can I help?" Mike was so casual that it seemed to Steph like he was having a conversation with a best friend.

"Well, with your military experience and Special Forces background, what would cause that?"

Sean engaged. "What we're trying to say, Mr. Sharpe, is that only the intelligence services or the military would have that signature."

"Sorry, do you want me to confirm that or make an inquiry to get someone to confirm that? I'm not a comms expert—and, Bec, why on earth do you think I'm Special Forces?" Again, all said without a change in tone, a nervous fidget, or any sort of tell through his expressions.

Bec sat back again. "We tried to look you up, Mike. And your team."

"Why?" Mike remained relaxed.

"No reason but you live in town. Steph is still here." She paused. "As is your former team."

"Sorry, I still don't understand what you're trying to get at."

"When we ask for military records, we get them in about half a day if we can't access them directly. So far it's been three days and nothing." Bec spoke with more authority. "Smacks of SF."

"Or army admin," said Mike. "We've all just left—or are about to leave—the army. Our records are probably being dispatched somewhere for storage."

Steph could tell that Bec was suddenly unsure of herself. It was another clever response from Mike.

Bec changed the subject back to the communications interference. "Well, in your experience, why would state-of-the-art communications be used in a nightclub?"

"I have no idea. Could there have been someone else on the ground? Would you be the only agency interested in the Clover brothers? In my world, these comms are normally used on all missions. I have no idea what you or the security services would use. Could another agency have interest in someone?" Mike made it sound like a throwaway remark for a second time. But effectively, he made sure the seed had been planted.

Bec answered with the same level of authority. "Possibly." She paused. She had received intel that a kingpin may have been present before the raid. "Forty-one minutes of CCTV footage was on a loop. No one knows why, including the club security."

Detective Grimmer looked at his boss. He was confused; that information should not have been given out.

Mike stared blankly. "Look, Bec," he said, leaning forward for the first time and looking her straight in the eye. "Do you think we're involved in something? If so, just say it."

Bec sat back in her chair. *Bastard,* she thought. *He used the eyes on me.* If he had lied, there wasn't even a flinch, nothing— just like when she'd first met him.

"Sorry. I had to ask." Bec tried the soft touch. She wanted to keep Mike as a friend.

"You have to do what you have to do, Bec, but I can certainly help in one area."

Steph didn't look at Mike, but her heart was beating a little faster. Was he about to play with fire?

"How?" Mike's offer had caught Bec off guard.

"I can talk with someone in the army to try to get you our records, if you like."

"That won't be needed—thanks anyway," Bec replied sharply.

Bec and Detective Grimmer got up and left.

"Steph, quick—go to the women's toilet but look out the window at the front of the hotel. Keep it natural, and tell me what you see as they leave."

Steph immediately got up and walked across to the restrooms. She timed it so she was at the huge window that looked out onto the apartment building pickup area and the valet stand. She then carried on into the toilet.

Five minutes later, she returned.

"They met someone out there, didn't they?" said Mike.

"A woman. I didn't see who she was, but she was dressed really casually."

"Contact Andy. Tell him we need a remote sweep of the apartment immediately. Anything that they planted may have activated his security protocol, anyway. We need to get up there and remove or destroy them quickly before they complete a full comms system check."

"DS Reed, we have Mitch Collier on the phone for you from the tech department." Sean Grimmer had just sat down after getting back to the office.

Bec grabbed the phone from him. It was the call she had been waiting for.

"Hello, DS Reed."

"Oh, hi, Bec. It's Mitch Collier. Can you confirm for me again the devices were planted where I briefed?"

"Hold on, I'll put you on speaker. I have your colleague with me."

"Hi, Mitch. It's Petra."

"Er, Petra, can you confirm where you put the two devices?"

"Yep. One is by the TV on the wall-mount bracket, and the other is in the main bedroom, behind a light switch cover."

Bec was concerned. "Mitch, is there a problem?"

"Well, the equipment is working fine," he said.

Bec was relieved.

"The only problem is that I could swear we're recording the reception area."

"Sorry, did you just say 'poor reception'?" asked Petra.

"No, I mean has the building got a reception?"

"Well, yes," said Bec, confused.

"I think that's where the devices are," he replied.

Bec hung up and threw the phone. "Bastard."

"Shit, boss. That tap wasn't sanctioned," said Grimmer.

"Don't worry. Mike Sharpe won't say a word."

The phone rang again.

"DS Reed, it's for you," said Sean.

"Bec Reed."

"Oh, hello, ma'am. This is the front desk at Spear Tower. I'm sorry to bother you, but there's an envelope for you in reception—"

"It's okay," Bec cut in. "I'll send someone to pick it up."

She hung up again, totally humiliated.

6

At 0700 on Monday morning, the team gathered after completing their workout and twenty minutes of Krav Maga. Their training area was an extension on the side of an exclusive gymnasium. To get in, you had to walk through an electronic gate system located at the gym's reception. There was then a code given to get into the studio, which was located at the far end of the gym; in fact, you had to walk down another corridor to get to it. The setup was perfect for training and team briefings.

Mike, Steph, and Skippy rested on benches, water bottles in hand, the team around them. The studio space was used for yoga, Pilates, and dance, as well as martial arts. It was basically an enclosed room that required a code to enter through a nondescript door, but once you walked through it and farther down the corridor, you were met with a glass door and a modern studio. Paul positioned the team so that anyone looking in would think they were talking sport tactics. They were actually briefing Op Becker.

They listened intently to the initial sitrep, which reviewed known details and provided an update on the current situation. Unusually, Mike stopped the briefing at this point just before discussing the mission's execution.

"Okay, we've spoken to you all individually and will do the same now, together. It's important to know that before we brief on the plan for tomorrow, you all have the opportunity to walk away now. What we're going to do might land us on the wrong side of the law, and in the very worst case, we could all be arrested. This will probably be the first real bad decision we'll ever make, but I can't sleep at night knowing what the Clover bothers could have done to one of our own—and that innocent girl. Who knows where Tommy would be today if they had been allowed to carry on. These people have been untouchable until now. That said, there's nothing greater than having the moral fiber to decide to walk away now."

Mike paused for a long time. None of them broke the silence; none of them moved.

Skippy's phone beeped. "Boss, I have a surprise for the team before we get started with the courtroom."

The door opened and in walked Tommy. Mike smiled.

"No fucking way are you leaving me out of this one," said Tommy, grinning but grimacing with pain.

The team spent five minutes with their friend before Paul called them back to court.

"Okay, listen in. Court is in session," Paul said with authority.

"One more minute, please, Paul." Mike hadn't gotten the response he was looking for regarding his previous point.

It was unusual, but Paul relented.

"Tommy, do you want us to do this?" asked Mike.

Tommy hesitated, grappling with the weight of the decision. If he was being honest, Tommy really wasn't sure. On the one hand, the bastards were Teflon-coated and could literally get away with murder. On the other hand, the seriousness of what his mates were about to do weighed on his mind.

"Tell them, Tommy." Mike had read the situation perfectly.

Tommy opened up to the team, emotions raw as he recounted his experiences, described Rachel's ordeal, and explained the immense internal conflict he felt about involving the Skirmishers.

As he finished, he said, "I really can't ask you to do this, but I don't like bullies. They killed an innocent person and are likely to do it again, especially when Nick Clover is involved."

Steve, the most junior member of the team, found his voice. "Boss, it's like you don't want us to do this."

"Honestly, Steve, I'm not sure I can ask you to do this. It must be your choice. This time, I'm not ordering you, but if you want to come along, I'll be prepared to lead you. If we all walk away, I'll still be there for you," Mike said, trying to be as open as possible.

"We can't leave it, boss," said Andy. "We have a mission to complete and payback for Tommy."

"Revenge is the worst kind of motive, Andy. You know that," Mike said sincerely.

"This isn't revenge, boss—this is helping change people's lives for the better. We take them off the streets, and then at least the public can see something can be done."

Mike was surprised by Andy's comment. It was unusual for him to speak up, especially around a cause.

"With all due respect, boss, we need to focus on tomorrow," Andy said, almost challenging Mike.

By using the line *with all due respect*, it meant Andy was calling out Mike's approach here.

Paul stepped in. "You all feel the same way and want to continue?"

Everyone agreed.

Paul moved to the front. "Court is in session. Listen up on the rules. No point raised during this court session is to be immediately shot down; we need to discuss and explore first. Everyone has a voice, but the boss, Steph, and Skippy will determine what's in and what's out. You can use the bullshit card if you disagree with something, but make it constructive.

"Mark, Jon, Steph, and Andy will be your NCOs, just as if we were conducting a normal Skirmishers mission, and are your go-to leaders between now and zero hour. Mark, Steph will likely have an active role due to her bumping into Liam Clover at the club; therefore, you'll be the boss's number two if it goes to shit and will lead half the unit. Jon, you're my number two, as Andy will need to do the intel thing. All understood?"

"Yes, Sarge."

Paul looked at Tommy. "You have an active part to play. Up for it?"

Tommy looked surprised. "Yes, Sarge."

"You'll be well protected, my lad, and there will be no contact on you," Paul said, trying to reassure him.

"Yes, Sarge. Just as well, as I'm not sure my ribs and face could take it."

"Anything else before we start the court, boss?" Paul asked Mike.

"No. Off you go, Paul."

Paul stood up. The team was now to one side of him, and Mike, Steph, and Skippy were on his other side.

"The time is 0815, Skirmishers. Listen in, this is Op Becker."

Two hours later, the team dispersed. Mike, Steph, Andy, and Paul were the last ones left in the studio.

"Sorry, boss, if I overstepped earlier," said Andy.

"It's okay, Andy. I'm glad you spoke up," said Mike—internally, though, he was a little surprised.

"All right. I better be going. See you at the final RV."

"You did lay it on a bit thick about walking away, Mike," Paul said.

"I needed to know."

"I realize it's been weighing on your mind, and I think you've done everything to give the team the opportunity to decline," Paul said, trying to reassure him.

"Oh yeah, and that," said Mike.

"Sorry, you confused me… Why else would you lay it on that thick?" said Paul, genuinely puzzled by the response.

Steph knew but wasn't sure she should say anything. Mike looked at her; he could tell she was onto something. He nodded at her.

"It's Andy," she said but thought better of saying anything else.

"Andy?" Paul looked to Mike.

"I'm not sure yet, but something isn't right. Don't let it get in the way of the mission, though, and don't second-guess Andy or treat him differently. He's been outstanding."

"Okay," said Paul.

"Paul"—Mike looked him straight in the eyes—"that's an order."

"Yes, sir." Paul was smiling inside. Mike knew him well and realized he would set the wheels in motion to find out what they were implying about Andy, and that order had just put a stop to it.

"All right, we meet pre-mission tomorrow morning, time to be confirmed. Mike, are we having our pre-mission catch-up this afternoon?" Paul said, though he wasn't really asking.

"It's a tradition, Paul."

They both laughed.

After taking a shower, Mike and Steph walked back to their car, as they had planned to go straight to brunch. Skippy and Tommy were waiting for them.

"Er, boss, can we have a word?" asked Tommy.

"Of course, what's on your mind? You two must have been waiting awhile!" Mike tried to sound as open as possible.

"I've been trying to think of how to break it to you, and, well. . . let you know that it won't change anything. Everything will be just like normal, but I would understand if you weren't happy. . ." Tommy almost stuttered.

Mike looked bemused by Tommy's tongue-tied words; inside, though, he was smiling.

Steph also had a huge grin on her face.

"Tommy, shut up," said Skippy. "Boss, we're fucking each other—well, we're together, and if you don't like it, tough." She had a way with words.

"Cool. I had guessed that." Mike laughed.

"And another thing. . ." Skippy stopped. "You know?"

Steph completely lost it. Laughing, she grabbed her friend and gave her a huge hug. "I do love you, you crazy Aussie."

Mike looked at Tommy. "Good to see you two together."

"Thanks, boss. And I didn't thank you for everything you've done for me over the last few days—in fact, over the last few years." Tommy reached out and hugged him.

Mike wouldn't admit it, but he was choked up. "Thanks, Tommy. Thanks."

Steph looked at Mike. *Wow,* she thought. With that hug, Tommy may have given Mike the absolute *why* of Op Becker.

"I hope I get a hug, boss," said Skippy, reaching out. They embraced.

Mike and Steph got into the car. They looked at each other and laughed.

"That was hilarious," said Steph.

"Poor Tommy was tongue tied," said Mike.

"So when do I get my hug, Mike?" Steph smiled.

Steph and Mike had spent the previous evening in the apartment going over some aspects of the recce and Op Becker before sitting on the big comfy chairs in the apartment lounge. There had been no mention of the night before, and in fact, the next few hours had been spent learning more about each other. There was no awkwardness until it was time to say good night. It was strange how two highly trained humans suddenly had no idea how to talk about what happened next, and bizarrely, they kissed each other on the cheek and went their separate ways to bed.

They'd each sat up in bed, thinking about the night before and wondering if it was worth visiting the other's room to talk about it. Neither of them did, and until now, there hadn't been even a smidgen of playful banter.

"So am I going to get a hug?" Steph repeated teasingly. She was also hoping to illicit a grown-up response, though, as she had laid in bed wanting to be in his arms the previous night but didn't really know how he felt.

Mike thought about it. "Anytime."

He could see a slight change in the way Steph looked. She was concentrating as she drove, but she seemed slightly disappointed by his reply, he guessed. *Grown-up response,* thought Mike.

"To be honest with you, Steph. . ."

Steph suddenly snapped back from a spiral of potential disappointment.

"I really wanted you in my bed last night." Mike felt a huge amount of pressure lift from his shoulders. He was now letting life do its thing.

Steph's whole being lit up, like a plant that had just been watered for the first time in days.

She smiled at Mike. That was all she'd needed.

Mike and Steph spent about an hour at brunch, most of the time talking about Skippy and Tommy and reminiscing about the army. Afterward, they went for a walk along the river, had a strange discussion about past relationships and then family. They stopped and gazed at each other. "I like this, Mike. You look happy."

"You know, the last hour or two has been good—really good."

Mike looked into her eyes and then took her hand.

They kissed, almost without thought, parted, and then kissed again, longer.

As they made their way back to the apartment, Steph hoped that Mike would drop everything for the next couple of hours and spend it with her, but she knew he would have to go.

"You and Paul need to do the thing?" She knew it meant a lot to them.

"Yes, it's important but also a tradition. A lucky charm."

"I'll be waiting." She kissed him again and whispered in his ear, "Text me when you're five minutes away, if you know what's good for you."

Those words were like an electric bolt through his body, and if he could have gone straight up to the apartment, he would have.

DS Reed sat in front of her inspector, James Miles. His office boasted a glass front, slightly frosted in places to obscure prying eyes from discerning who was currently on the receiving end of a stern reprimand. The inspector's chair was deliberately set high, making his desk with its old-school oak finish appear even more imposing. Conversely, DS Reed's chair was intentionally lower, a tactic to make its occupant feel subordinate. On the opposite side of the office was a lounge, reserved for standard meetings and the delivery of good news.

The inspector was leafing through the Clover file, looking at something that was obviously making him annoyed.

"DS Reed, what the hell is going on?"

Shit, thought Bec. *This is serious. He's using my rank and name.*

"What do you mean, sir?" It was a genuine answer; Bec had no idea what he wanted to discuss.

"You put an unauthorized tap into a serving army officer's apartment."

Shit, thought Bec again. *Mike has reported me. Surely that's not his form—nor Grimmer's or one of the tech team.*

"You're trying to work out who brought this to my attention, aren't you?"

Bec couldn't hide the guilt. Why couldn't she be like Mike Sharpe and treat questioning like it was an everyday conversation?

"I'm sure you're not going to tell me, sir," said Bec.

"DS Reed, do you know the audit trail required for tapping? You should know better than anyone the permissions required to put a device in someone's apartment."

"I did apply, sir." Bec knew it was a hollow comment.

"The same day you placed the device." The inspector was not happy with these games. "You're fortunate the book isn't being thrown at you, Bec, but luckily for you, the devices were not placed and were signed back in by you."

Relief washed over her. *We did collect them and sign them back in,* she realized.

"Had you placed them, I would have had no choice but to suspend you and launch an inquiry. I'm so glad that you had a change of heart and brought them back. Why is a highly decorated army officer of interest, anyway?"

"He's not, sir. I made a mistake." Bec decided that a lot of humility would go a long way.

"So why have you asked the army for personnel files for ten soldiers?"

"One of them was attacked, sir. I was concerned there would be retribution."

"Hmm. . . someone at the army has a sense of humor, Bec."

This sparked her interest. "Why? What have they sent?"

"The man you were interested in, Major Mike Sharpe?"

"Yes?" Bec responded hesitantly.

"This is what we received." The inspector handed Bec some papers.

She looked at one of the pages. It had a photo in the top right-hand corner with a black letter box covering a portion of the face. She couldn't even tell that it was Mike. Then she looked at the elements that would form a personal summary; they all had black lines through them, except name, rank, and blood group. It was totally redacted.

"It's the same for all of them," said the inspector.

"Inspector Miles—James," Bec implored, hoping to connect with him on a personal level. "Can't you see something is off?"

"It's unusual, Bec, but there's nothing we can do unless we arrest him."

"We can't do that. He's done nothing wrong."

"Well, stop, then," Inspector Miles said, raising his voice. He regained his composure. "Bec, stop. I've read the report on the Clover brothers—nothing new, as usual. I'll reassign your team to John Tort. I want him watched."

"We have two more days left on the surveillance operation at The Eagle, sir. We can stand them down tomorrow." Bec was almost pleading now.

"Today, Bec. Please do me a favor and leave the pub and concentrate on Tort."

"Yes, sir," she replied reluctantly.

Bec walked out of the office, fuming. All she wanted was a weeklong surveillance on the pub so she could swoop in if there was any further trouble. She quickly composed herself, though, as she realized that what the inspector had actually done was finally give her one of the big jobs within the division. She was about to go after a kingpin—a gangster godfather.

Mike found Paul at the Temple Church, located near the River Thames and Fleet Street. The beautiful building had been constructed by the Knights Templar, a subject that always fascinated Paul. What set this church apart from others was its unique round architecture, giving it an appearance similar to a fortified castle. Despite its rich history, the church attracted only a few tourists, as it wasn't typically on most people's must-see lists.

"Ready," said Paul.

"Ready," replied Mike.

Neither Mike nor Paul was particularly religious. However, after their initial missions with the Skirmishers, they began to wonder if fate played a role in their lives. They had witnessed people die in the strangest of circumstances, as though no matter what they did, their time was up. They had heard similar stories from other units and security forces. "Some days, an IED would go off in front of us, sometimes behind us, but it never hit us," he recalled a former SF operator, who was now working for a security firm, telling him. On one occasion, the Skirmishers went out on a coalition mission near Kabul, supporting a US SEAL team mission. They had been asked to create a distraction in a part of a town called Etefaq. On paper, it had been relatively straightforward: create a distraction, return fire if necessary, and then retreat, making sure to lure the enemy.

Prior to the mission, Paul and Mike had been seeking a padre to say a few words to the team. This practice began early in the Skirmishers' history. Their initial missions were plagued with unforeseen issues, like malfunctioning vehicles or helicopters rendered unservicable before extraction. However, just before one mission, Mike encountered an RAF padre and half-jokingly asked for a prayer for the Skirmishers' safety and good fortune.

The mission proceeded perfectly, and a tradition was born.

Just before the mission in Etefaq, Paul had told Mike that the priest had been called to an injured soldier to issue the last rites.

Paul had laughed. "Well, the helicopter will probably break down."

Two hours later, the mission was going far worse than a broken helicopter—the Skirmishers were having to fight their way out of the town and were in danger of being overrun. Meanwhile, the SEAL team confirmed they had their target and had gotten them out easily.

Mike remembered radioing the task force HQ, expressing their predicament. "We've drawn all the fire and might be overrun."

"Don't worry, we have a bird and fire support two minutes away." He had never been so grateful upon hearing an American operator's voice. Two Black Hawk helicopters touched down, successfully extracting the team.

Mike recalled climbing aboard, the helicopter under fire, and being relieved to see his team all there. The pilot let him know that all of Paul's team was also accounted for.

Once it was safe to do so, Mike checked on his team—all were okay. He remembered seeing how quickly the stress was relieved from each of their blackened faces.

"Five minutes to landing," the pilot announced.

There was a whistle and a small pressure wave.

"Incoming," said the gunner, who was now returning fire, probably to someone on the ground who had heard a helicopter and taken potshots.

In military life, there are two words that a commander never wants to hear, and these words were spoken loudly but calmly by Mark Jackson.

"Man down, man down."

Mike turned around immediately to see Skippy busily trying to get Private Tony Becker out of the chair and onto the helicopter floor.

Mike got on the internal comms system. "Man down, man down," he told the pilot.

He could hear the pilots asking for a medical team to meet them on landing.

Mike, Mark, and Skippy were busy trying to plug the wound. The bullet had found a gap in the body armor and had entered Tony's side. They couldn't find the exit wound.

"It's higher up!" shouted Mark.

Mike took a field dressing and tried to maneuver it between Tony's back and the body armor. The exit wound was big.

"Landing," said the pilot.

Mike could see the headlights of the ambulance. Jon Apolosi had run across from the other helicopter and helped Mike lift Tony out.

They put Tony onto the stretcher. A medic shouted, "Let him go, we have it from here!"

The helicopters shut down, and the area was suddenly eerily quiet.

Paul waited while Mike got on UKSF secure comms.

"Alpha Zulu, Sierra Alpha: contact report."

"Sierra Alpha, Alpha Zulu: We have the information already. Get to a landline and ring Blue Line figures 75117. Repeat."

"Alpha Zulu, Sierra Alpha: Blue Line figures 75117." Mike's brain was fried, but training had taken over as he repeated the message.

"Roger. Out."

Tony had died that night. It hit the Skirmishers hard. The only member of the team to have been killed in action. After that, the tradition of seeing a priest or receiving a religious blessing for each mission had been cemented.

Losing Tony had changed Mike forever.

"Padre, thanks for taking the time to see us," said Paul. "We need a small blessing for our team. It's tradition before a mission."

The priest had little idea of what Paul was talking about but offered a blessing nonetheless. Much to his surprise, Paul pulled out a hip flask and three small glasses. "Join us for a toast, Padre, would you?"

"Would never say no to a small nip," he replied.

"To Tony Becker. May he be watching over us."

The three clinked glasses.

"To Tony."

Paul and Mike left the Temple Church and began walking toward the River Thames. They were going to catch the underground train at Temple station but decided to walk for a while along the river.

Mike's phone buzzed with a text message: Going to the spa. It was from Steph.

He responded, Okay, will be back in an hour or so x.

"Is that Steph?" said Paul.

"Yep, doing her routine."

"The only woman I've ever met who believes feeling your best also applies to a battlefield."

Mike laughed. "She always looks her best."

"We all have our funny little traditions," said Paul. "Look at us—we've always gotten together for our ritual since we lost Tony."

"Besides, Mark started joining her for beauty treatments," said Mike.

"That's right, and not one of the team batted an eye."

"Timi and Jon would be eating with their families. It's just another day for them, but on ops, they always have a big meal the night before a mission. Young Stevie will be watching war movies or playing shoot-'em-up video games," Paul added.

"Do we even want to know what Skippy and Tommy are doing?" Paul laughed.

"Probably not, although Skippy always writes the night before. No idea what about, though," said Mike.

"What about Andy?"

"Andy is an odd one. As he got more involved in intel, he became more withdrawn," said Mike.

"No, I mean, why are you concerned about Andy?"

"I guess it's a fair question, but I really mean it when I say I don't want you to do anything about it or treat Andy differently." Mike looked at Paul with his laser-blue eyes.

Paul was concerned. "Okay, I get that part loud and clear. But Andy is a good lad. Why are you worried?"

Mike thought before he spoke. "How would you describe Andy before a mission?"

"Like you said: withdrawn and focused, I guess."

"How would you describe him yesterday during the briefing?"

"You mean, when he challenged you?" Paul thought and quickly realized that wasn't what Mike wanted. "He was punchier than normal—in fact, really punchy."

"Yes, it's like something is driving him. He wants us to act. That's just not the Andy we know."

"I have to admit, he has worked some bloody wonders, though, with what he's achieved," said Paul.

"He always does, but this time his performance—bearing in mind we're acting outside the military—is above anything else I've seen him do," said Mike. "It's bothering me."

"Care to share your theory with me?"

"No, I can't because I'm really not sure, and I have to give Andy the respect he deserves for all he's done for us. But when the time is right, I promise I'll tell you."

"Okay," said Paul. "Can I speak freely?"

Here it comes, thought Mike. "Of course."

"If we were in the army, and let's just say I was your sergeant or WO1, I would be kicking your arse all over the barracks."

"Steph?"

"Steph," said Paul. "We're not in the army—well, actually, you still technically are—but are you sure you're not compromising the team?"

"I don't know," said Mike. "It just happened, Paul, but it hasn't happened again. The time we're spending together has been awesome—but in the last twenty-four hours it's been more spiritual than, you know, the other thing."

"That might be worse, Mike. It sounds to me that this could be developing into something else."

"Worse?"

"I mean, you're starting to care for her."

"I always did, like the rest of the team," Mike retorted.

"I don't mean like the rest of the team. I'll only ask you this once: Is there any danger the mission will be compromised?"

"None." Mike was firm in his response.

"What about Tommy and Skippy?"

"I actually think that might work to our benefit; anyone gets near Tommy, and Skippy might kill them." Mike was deadly serious.

They both laughed.

The two friends departed, and Mike sent a text message to Steph: Fifteen minutes x.

Mike had gotten back to the apartment block before Steph responded to the text: Will be another ten minutes, make me a drink!

Mike took a shower to freshen up, poured a couple of drinks, and sat on the big sofa in the lounge. He completed another active sweep for devices; there were none. He heard the door lock turn and in walked Steph in the spa dressing gown. She discarded the slippers and approached him.

"Hey, how was your spa?" said Mike.

"Perfect, and how is Paul?"

"He's good. It was really great to catch up with him. So what did you do in the spa?"

"Well, I had a swim, a massage, and then a facial." She took a sip of her drink. "I then had a little tan applied." She smiled.

Mike could tell that her skin seemed to be radiating from a couple of hours of spa treatment.

"You look really, really good, Steph."

"I feel good," she said, "and when I feel good, I get really, really horny." She was almost purring.

Mike could feel himself stirring. Steph slowly undid the cord to the bathrobe.

"You see, Mike, I've just walked back to the apartment, wearing nothing but this gown."

Steph dropped the robe. The last two hours of treatment had seemed to make her entire body glow. The tingling between her legs was almost too much.

Mike stood up and quickly discarded the shorts and T-shirt he'd put on after his shower.

In almost no time at all, they were making love on the sofa. For the rest of the day, Mike and Steph were in each other's arms, surfacing only for something to eat and drink.

7

It was 0700 on Tuesday morning when Mike awoke. He gently moved his arm out from under Steph and checked his phone. There was an encrypted message from yesterday evening from Andy: Intel good, D will be 1210 hours, meet sixty minutes prior at K1 warehouse.

Mike watched Steph as she slept. He couldn't believe how peaceful she looked, how beautiful she looked, and—as he glanced at her half-covered body—how sexy she looked. He then thought about how violent she could be, how many firefights she had been in, and how close to death she, like the rest of the team, had been.

Steph stirred. "Morning," she said, half-asleep. "Can we stay in bed?" Then suddenly: "I need the bathroom." She jumped up and skipped to the bathroom. When she got back, Mike noticed she had straightened her hair. He grabbed her just as she was about to jump over him and back into bed.

"You dare to come past me with that cheeky grin and sexy arse?" He pulled her to him.

"Not forgetting the hot body, great tits, and very, very tight. . . abs." She was posing.

They both laughed.

"We have time, you know," said Steph with a smile.

"You might take all my strength away." Mike was also smiling.

Steph lowered herself onto him. "It's okay, I'll protect you." She sighed with pleasure. *"Always."*

Zero minus one hour. Location: K1 warehouse Shoreditch.

K1 was an old abandoned warehouse near the railway, which probably served as a place for bored teenagers to take refuge after dark with their mates and use recreational drugs. It was a perfect location for the team, as it really was a dump, and it was unlikely that anyone would enter it during the day—certainly not the hour they would be there.

Steph and Mike were last to arrive at the warehouse, twice changing their route in order to spot anyone following them. "Everyone ready, Paul?"

"Yes, we've rehearsed many times, Mike."

"Okay, everybody gather round."

Paul briefed the plan and objectives once again. It wasn't really necessary, but they always did it. Mike then briefed an abridged version of the SMEAC format of briefing troops—Situation, Mission, Execution Admin, and Check for understanding. Then he would ask questions of the team to check understanding. Not everyone used the briefing format anymore, but Mike had tailored it over the years to ensure everyone knew what their individual objectives were as well as those of the others. Paul had already briefed the plan and objectives, so to an outsider, it was a rehash.

After briefing again, Mike took command. "Okay, overall exec control of the mission is me; I go down, it's Paul, and Paul goes down, it'll be Steph. Mark, Jon, as briefed, you'll be section commanders and take exec control if it's been a total cluster. Any questions?" Silence. "Okay, Mark, Skippy, it's time for you to go to the pub. Good luck, everyone."

Zero minus thirty minutes.

Terry Patrick was sitting at his usual place in The Eagle next to Kurt Tibbs. He enjoyed people-watching but was also looking around the pub, thinking how shit his Tuesdays had become. He was monitoring everyone coming through the door and drinking there. The pub was a shithole as far as he was concerned. He could not understand why anyone would want to be there. Most Tuesdays were quiet, with only a few local punters present. Today had been a little different, as a bunch of students had been in the pub following some shit demo, all trying to save the world. They would stay for one and then move on. His job obviously was to ensure the Clover firm could eat, drink, and play without fear of a rival gang or some afternoon drunk getting out of hand. Last week had been different, and as he sat there, he thought about Nick Clover and the trouble he had created.

He looked at a couple of the students and wondered whether they had any idea the potential danger they could be in should Nick have one of his dick-measuring moments. Nick was desperate for his brothers to take him seriously, but they largely brushed him off. Over the weeks he had been working with them, Terry had thought several times about leaving, but the money was great, and he really didn't want to go back to a war zone and work for one of the many private security companies.

A few more students rolled into The Eagle, clearly on a bit of a pub crawl. Tibbsy glanced at Terry with a look of *Fuck me, she's hot.*

"These girls look so young, Tibbsy," Terry said.

"I know—fuck, if you didn't know they're uni students, you'd think they were jailbait. Thank fuck it's busy today," said Tibbsy. "At least we have something to do."

The door opened again. In walked two older-looking kids who went straight to the bar. The girl was cute, innocent-looking but very pretty. He heard her order a drink. *Australian,* he thought.

Holiday? Could be studying as a mature student. The guy next to her, immaculate—must be the gay friend.

Skippy and Mark took a seat at the bar at the far end nearest the entrance, with their backs to Terry and Tibbsy. They could see the two men through the long mirror that ran the length of the optics area behind the bar.

Terry had fun allocating a risk between one and five for anyone walking into the bar. Students would always be a zero, even the ones who were gym monkeys. He looked at Skippy; she seemed fairly fit. *I'll give her a one for risk and a five for looks.* He made himself smile. He looked at Mark. *He would probably slap me,* he thought. *Another one.* He couldn't believe this generation coming through and their fixation with mobile phones. *The students and these two, they're hardly talking to each other.*

Skippy sent a text: Alpha 2 and 6 in position, door watched as usual, all targets present.

Zero minus fifteen minutes.

Steve Kenny watched from across the road as his boss, Mike Sharpe, made his way into the pub. Mike was holding the *Sporting Life* newspaper and really did look like a local. He was wearing a Tom Ford jacket, which helped disguise his shape, and had on a pair of glasses with clear lenses. It was just enough to ensure Terry didn't recognize him from the Red Zone but also enough to soften him a little so that he wasn't immediately marked as a threat. At this stage, it didn't really matter, anyway, unless Terry was absolutely on edge. Mike walked straight to the bar, put the paper down, and ordered a pint. The barman noticed the paper and asked Mike for a tip. Mike had already noted in the paper several horses to watch. He had gotten some inside knowledge through a mate of his.

"I hate giving tips, mate, as I'm always worried about how much money people might bet." Mike was very casual and acted like a seasoned punter.

The barman was persistent. "Don't worry, mate—I always lose, anyway. Let me have a tip. It might change my luck."

Mike couldn't believe his own luck. The barman had just solidified why Mike was in the pub.

"Try Strawberry Blonde in the two o'clock at Fakenham," Mike said with authority.

"I appreciate that, governor," said the barman.

Mike took his pint and seated himself at a table with his back to the wall, where he had full view of the pub. He would have been sitting opposite where Tommy had sat at the bar last week and close to where the Clover firm was sitting. Mike started to look at the tips and place bets on his cell.

Alpha in position. He sent the text message.

Terry watched Mike come in and observed the interaction with the barman. He then made a mental note of the horse racing tip before watching Mike sit down. *Punter, mugs game,* he thought. *Looks a bit handy, though, might score him a two.* He looked at Mike a little more carefully, not for any reason other than where he sat. He referred to it as the king chair. It was the chair he would choose if he couldn't sit near the entrance. *Just for that, he goes up to a three*, he thought, more for his own amusement.

One of the students departed the pub; three others remained. Terry was really hoping no one left. It meant he could people-watch rather than die of boredom.

Zero minus five minutes.

Terry's jaw dropped. In walked a stunner: baseball cap, denim jacket, T-shirt, no bra, and jeans that were painted on her body. *Fuck,* he thought. *Trouble right there.* The boys would have their dicks hanging out in no time at all. Steph ordered a gin and tonic and then sat at the bar where Tommy had been sitting. Terry immediately thought, *Risk four because the boys would be all over her; a fucking ten for looks.*

Zero minus three minutes.

"You all right, darling?" called Karl Clover from the table. "You want to sit with us?" Although the baseball cap covered her face a little, Steph wanted to try to initially avoid actual contact with Liam if she could, just in case by some miracle he recognized her. Steph was lucky in that Liam sat opposite Karl and would struggle to see her, although they were all trying to get a look.

"Wow," said Nick. "She's mine. Hands off." He didn't get up, though. He had a very good poker hand. "You waiting for someone, darling?" said Nick.

"Yes, a guy I was meant to meet the other day, but we missed each other," Steph replied.

"He must have been some sort of arsehole to not meet you. Don't worry. When he gets here, I'll show him what a real man looks like," said Nick.

Zero minus one minute.

"Really, what happened to your face, love?" said Steph, hamming up the East London accent.

"Yeah, Nick, what happened to your face?" The brothers laughed.

"Cage fighting," said Nick. The brothers and the rest of the firm laughed together.

"Wow," said Steph, "The other guy must have been enormous!"

Nick looked red-faced.

Zero hour.

Steve moved to the door. He was prepared to stop anyone trying to enter the pub and only let non-targets out.

Andy sent a burst on the net: *"Zero hour, standby—go, go, go."*

Tommy walked into the pub, followed by Paul. They went to opposite ends of the bar, with Tommy heading straight to Steph.

Terry and Tibbsy had been watching the banter between Steph and the Clover brothers when the door opened. Terry was momentarily distracted, allowing Paul and Tommy to enter. As Tommy moved toward Steph, Terry felt his adrenaline surge and his pulse rise rapidly. He quickly surveyed the pub. *The fucking kid from last week is with that girl, the guy who just walked in, short, stocky. Fuck, he's a five.* He looked to his right. *The barman was missing, and where the fuck did those two Black guys come from?* He looked at Mike, who had removed his glasses. *Fuck, another five.* His risks levels were all going up rapidly.

He noticed the Aussie and the guy next to her. "Oh shit," Terry said, just loud enough for Tibbsy to hear.

Tibbsy, still stunned by the return of the kid from last week, remained seated at Terry's insistence. Jon and Timi gestured to stay quiet and remain seated.

"Do not fucking move, Tibbsy." Terry looked directly at Jon and Timi.

They both gestured to say nothing and sit.

The Clover firm at the table hadn't even noticed Tommy until he greeted Steph and gave her a hug.

"Hello, darling," she said.

It was Nick Clover and one of the bigger guys who saw Tommy first. "What the fuck are you doing here?" said Nick.

"Meeting my girl." The Scottish accent made them all look up.

"What the fuck?" said Karl, and he stood up. "Have you got a fucking death wish?"

"Leave it, Karl," said Nick. "He's mine."

At this point, it was a classic distraction. All eyes were on Tommy and Steph, but in the time it took Karl and Nick to engage with Tommy, Paul, Mark, and Skippy were now at a stand-up table in easy reach of Tommy and Steph. Mike had gotten up like he was about to leave.

"Stay back, you, and sit back down," Nick said to Mike.

"Sorry, mate, just wanted to leave." Mike chose a chair that was one step away from Nick and anyone else who decided to stand up.

Terry was watching it all unfold. *Trained unit,* he thought. *Those fucking amateurs won't know what hit them. The fucking lad came back; he actually came back. I knew he had balls.*

Nick was now within punching distance of Tommy. Steph was poised, but that had gone completely unnoticed.

"You got a lucky fucking shot last week, you jock cunt," Nick said, almost spitting with rage. "After I take you down, I'm going to have my way with her."

"That's no way to talk to a lady," said Steph.

"I agree, love," said Skippy.

Nick looked at Skippy. "Shut the fuck up, or it will be you next."

Everything seemed to happen in slow motion. Terry noted that no one else had moved from the Clover table even though they were standing up. They couldn't see the threat beyond Tommy and clearly thought if there was one that Terry and Tibbsy would be over.

"You've got an anger problem," said Steph to Nick.

Nick reached out to grab Steph. Just as he was about to make contact with her T-shirt, she seized his hand. She twisted until it bent back on itself and then broke a finger. Nick screamed as the pain went through him. He was also in shock because he suddenly sensed something was very wrong, as did the entire Clover table.

As Nick looked up, Steph delivered a blow to his neck, temporarily cutting off the blood supply to his brain. He passed out immediately.

Finally, one of the men nearby reacted, launching towards Steph and Tommy. He didn't see Mike move, but he felt like his momentum was being used against him as he was guided toward Skippy like a rag doll. Skippy jabbed two fingers into his throat. He gasped for air, and Mark delivered the blow that took him out.

"Two down," Jon called into his microphone.

All the men at the table were now scrambling over themselves to get up. The students and the locals quickly tried to exit the pub. Steve processed them rapidly.

"The authorities are on the way," he said. "If you're asked, you saw nothing. It's just a gang fight, and they all hate witnesses." Steve was making it up; he just wanted to scare them off.

"All nontargets out," Timi informed the network.

"You're clear, Sierra 10."

Steve opened the door to the pub, walked through, and locked it.

He would begin putting plastic cuffs on each of the fallen targets and getting them out the back.

The third man from the table launched at Mike, missed with the first punch, and then somehow found himself in front of Paul, who put him down with a single punch and then threw him toward Steve. It was happening so quickly that Timi had started to help Steve process them.

Terry looked up and noted that there was now just one guy guarding them. This could be an opportunity. Jon had already anticipated this. "You're not thinking about doing anything, are you?" he asked with a smile.

Terry was conflicted. *Why hadn't they taken Tibbsy or me out?* They were the most dangerous threat to them. *Are they saving us for last or something else?* He decided to wait. He looked at Tibbsy and shook his head.

The Skirmishers worked with such efficiency that they were quickly left with just the two remaining brothers. Each of the Clover gang had been taken out proficiently and with minimal force. Now the Skirmishers had a numbers advantage, and they could process the targets easily. All would be taken to the back of the pub.

Zero hour + four minutes.

"Sierra 7, Sierra Alpha: last two prime targets," Mike informed Andy.

Andy responded, "Net is good, no incoming."

"Karl and Liam Clover, you have a problem keeping your little brother under control," said Mike.

There was no doubt that Karl and Liam were scared. They had never been in a situation like this before.

Karl responded, "Do you know who you're fucking with?"

"You're Karl Clover; you were responsible for breaking this kid's ribs, and you kicked him when he was on the floor."

"So fucking what? He shouldn't have hit my brother." Karl knew the response was lame.

"Like I said, you need to keep your family under control," said Mike.

"You have no fucking idea what's going to happen to you," said Karl.

"Broken ribs, kicked him in the face, and then beat him when he was down. Eight of you on one person. Is that what we're dealing with?"

Karl looked at Mike. "I'm going to fucking cut you up."

"You can't," said Mike.

"Why not?" Karl looked confused.

"Because your ribs are broken, and your nose will require resetting in hospital. From there, you'll be in jail," Mike said matter-of-factly.

"Ribs and nose broken? What are you talking about—"

Before he could finish, Mike had broken Karl's nose and pushed him toward Paul, who hit him in the ribs. Karl collapsed.

Liam launched at Mike. It was a clever move, as Mike was still readjusting from the attack on Karl.

Steph was quicker, though, and jabbed Liam in one of his eyes. She grabbed him by his hair and brought his face down on the bar. She lifted it up and slammed it down again.

"Fucking finding girls for your perverted father?" She was about to smash his face a third time when Tommy stopped her. She looked at Tommy and then immediately reverted to being Steph. "Don't worry. I'm in control."

Zero hour + five minutes.

"Sierra 7, Sierra Alpha: plan A3 in play," said Mike.

"Sierra Alpha, Sierra 7: repeat, you have two more targets." Andy was concerned.

"Negative, Sierra 7: they're not targets."

"Sierra Alpha, Sierra 7: we're off mission." Andy was now a little too on edge.

"Sierra 7 and all call signs this is Sierra Alpha: This is an exec order. Plan A3 out." Mike was in total command of the situation.

Andy was left stunned by the radio call.

The team in the pub looked at Mike, confused. "Bring those two to the table." He pointed at Terry and Tibbsy.

"Sit down, Terry. I trust there'll be no trouble," said Mike.

Terry was confused. *What is going on?* He was sure he would be beaten to a pulp.

Paul was also slightly confused. He looked at Mike. "Everything okay?"

"Get them all out back, Paul, and then get back here," said Mike.

"Are we taking these two out?" Paul was still confused.

"No, we're not touching them," Mike said with force.

"Boss, what?" Paul was really confused.

Steph was also looking perplexed.

"I'll explain, but there's no time now." Mike looked at Tommy. "Trust me, we have a couple of minutes."

Steph, Tommy, and Mike sat down in such a way that Tibbsy and Terry couldn't run. In a matter of moments, Paul was back, still slightly bewildered by where Mike was suddenly about to take this and why the plan had changed. He had no problems with Mike changing a plan; it always happened, because rarely does a plan survive first contact, but this was not even a contingency or an alternate. It was almost like Mike had a plan of his own.

Steve and Mark arrived at the table as well. "Plan A3 complete, sir."

"Good work."

"Sierra 7 and all callsigns, Sierra Alpha: move to plan A4." Mike's message was for the entire team.

"Sierra Alpha, Sierra 7: but the plan . . ." Andy paused. "Roger. Out."

Mark dispersed the team.

"Steve, get people from the street into the pub, now. As many students as you can," said Mike.

Steve smiled. "Free booze it is, then."

Mike called the end of the operation. "All callsigns, Sierra Alpha: endex."

Mike, Paul, Tommy, and Steph removed their comms equipment and gave it to Mark.

"Don't worry." Mike saw the look in Mark's eyes. "We're okay."

"What do you want us to do with the books we found?" said Mark.

"Copy them quickly; send them to Paul and me encrypted. After you've copied them all, plant the originals with the Clover brothers for the police," Mike said.

"Take the names out of the last pages, though," said Terry.

Mike looked at Terry. "Do as he says, Mark."

Mark had total trust in his boss. He nodded and walked away.

In almost no time the pub was starting to fill with students thirsty for a free pint, with no trace of anything that had gone on before. Steve had done an amazing job getting them in so quickly.

Terry decided to speak. "I'm confused. I thought Tibbsy and I would be your main targets."

Skippy joined them. "So did I, you cunt," she said.

"You need to get out of here, Skippy," said Paul.

"No, my job is to protect him." She looked at Tommy.

"To be honest, boss, I can't believe these two are standing. What the fuck?" Tommy looked dejected.

"Terry, you're a professional, and we can sit here all day and bullshit each other, but tell them what you did for Tommy," said Mike.

"For Tommy?" Steph asked. "Mike?"

Terry looked at Tibbsy and then back at Mike. He knew exactly what needed to be done.

"Tibbsy, leave. I'll be okay."

Tibbsy tried to protest.

Terry wouldn't take no for an answer. "Leave."

Tibbsy looked at Mike. "Touch him, and you're dead." He got up and walked out through the crowd.

Terry looked at Paul and Mike, then directly at Tommy. "I'm sorry, lad, but this is going to sound a little far-fetched, although it's true."

"Go on," said Tommy.

"I knew you were trained when you hit Nick in fact, a little earlier on, I had guessed you were ex-military. I saw the girl outside watching, and it was clear she was about to call the police. Right before I hit you when you saw me in the mirror, it confirmed to me you knew what you were doing. I had to get you down, to get you out."

"I got thrown through a fucking window." Tommy was pissed.

"Luckily that window has been put through so many times that they use a safety compound that doesn't form shards. You can still get cut, but it won't kill you." Terry was calm externally, but internally his stomach was churning.

Tommy was unconvinced. "You believe this shit, boss?"

"Yes," said Mike. "He's ex–Foreign Legion and has worked security in Iraq and Afghanistan."

Mike looked at Tommy and Skippy; he could see Skippy was ready to explode. Paul appeared confused but was also clearly annoyed, and Steph was wondering why the person she had spent almost the whole of yesterday making love to had another agenda for this mission.

It was Tommy who calmed them down. "Boss, I've trusted you with my life on countless occasions. In fact, your decisions have kept me alive. If you think this is true, then I'll accept that."

Mike couldn't have been prouder of Tommy at that moment; he'd displayed the type of maturity that would have led to a promotion in the army. Mike was still holding something back from them all, as he thought Terry might be doing as well.

"Tommy, thank you. This might also be difficult to believe, but Terry could have taken you out from behind and he chose not to."

Skippy looked confused. "But he did, boss."

"No, I mean killed you." Mike's eyes were like lasers.

Terry looked at Mike. Mike glanced at Terry's jacket.

"Carefully take them out and give them to Skippy," Mike ordered calmly.

Terry pulled out a knife and then a pistol.

"That would have been a bit excessive, though," said Skippy.

"In my game, it's expected of me," said Terry. "I hit him hard enough to take him down. I made sure he had enough about him to curl into a ball, and as soon as I heard the sirens, I told Tibbsy to make sure we got him outside quickly. We work for real dickheads."

"Skippy, Tommy—take the weapons to K1, hide them, and give me the details. I'll pass it on to Terry after the cops have raided this place." Mike looked at Skippy and Tommy reassuringly.

"Okay, boss."

There was so much more that Tommy wanted to say, but he knew they would need to leave to avoid the inevitable police presence once they located the Clover firm.

Steph, Paul, and Mike were now left with Terry.

"So we're waiting this out until the police arrive?" Terry was resigned to it.

"Maybe, or maybe just you and me, Terry," said Mike. "I have one last question so these guys can hear it from you."

"I guess I owe you that."

"Who do you two really work for?"

"What do you mean?"

"You're not working for the Clover brothers."

Steph and Paul looked at Mike, both thinking, *How does he know this shit?*

"I don't know how you know that," said Terry, who wasn't too sure how far Mike was going to take this.

"We were at the Red Zone on Saturday in the VIP area," Mike said.

Terry leaned back and smiled. "You're a people-watcher, like me. I dropped my guard," he said.

"You were nervous," said Mike.

"I told Aaron Clover I had been worried about your boy and, more importantly, John Tort deciding to extinguish the Clover firm and moving someone else in," said Terry.

"All the time you were standing there worried about John Tort, and you're actually protecting him?" said Mike.

"Yes, I work for him. So does Tibbsy. You knowing that could get us killed."

"I'm counting on it," said Mike. "Steph, Paul—you need to go. I'll brief you later." They could all hear the sirens.

"I still have little idea what's going on, boss, but you seem to be on it, as usual," said Paul.

"Terry, just give me two secs," said Mike as he walked over to Paul.

"Paul, I trust you with my life. If anything happens to me or I go missing, open this. Do not open it beforehand. Make sure you keep it well hidden," Mike whispered, handing Paul a USB.

Steph gently brushed Mike's hand as they passed each other. She was worried for him.

"Just you and me," said Terry.

"It's Mike."

"I timed that at around five or six minutes, and had you not changed the plan, it would have been quicker. Who are you guys?" Terry was genuinely impressed.

"Sorry, Terry, I can't tell you that, but we're the people the army didn't want. Can you get me a meeting with John Tort?" said Mike.

"That's a guarantee," said Terry. "He'll come looking for you." Terry leaned forward. "To be honest, you've done him a favor. The only shit bit is that you're giving the books to the police."

"Would it come back on Tort?"

"No way. He's the most Teflon of them all. Besides, if your boys took the names out of the back pages, Tort will be pleased."

"If I see him, am I in danger? I mean, are there any trigger-happy people around him?"

"No, not at that level. If they wanted you out of the way, it would happen elsewhere." Terry was sincere.

"Punishment is the only thing that may be dealt out. I can smooth it over, but you have huge balls wanting to see him after this. I can make the meeting for you, Mike, but it'll have to be soon. The problem you give him is that he needs to move someone into this area quickly. Others will be swarming once this gets out, plus the locals will be grumbling very soon."

"Why?" said Mike.

"They pay for protection, and they expect it. It's a pretty good revenue stream."

Mike and Terry heard a slight commotion outside, which probably signaled the arrival of the police. They had about two minutes before the cops would get to them.

"Why do you want the cops to see us and record that we're here?" said Terry.

"Insurance."

Terry was confused. "Humor me."

"You're the enforcer for the Clover brothers, and I'm a guy who may have a motive for what happened out back. If we're seen together having a quiet drink, it produces many, many alibis." Mike smiled.

Terry wasn't sure the alibis necessarily worked in his favor.

Mike began to weave a cover story. "We're old friends, Terry. We met in Kabul when you worked for the Armed Response Group."

"You know a lot about me."

Mike smiled. "That's why you're sitting here talking to me and not waking up in hospital."

DS Bec Reed was in her office, typing up a report.

"Ma'am, you've got to see this." The ops officer tried to hide his obvious excitement.

Bec got up quickly and moved into the main operations office. Inspector Miles had also entered the ops room.

"I'm just getting Fred Birkinshaw on the comms link," one of the ops team called out.

"Fred, what's going on? It's Inspector Miles at OCD."

"Sir, it's unbelievable—we have them all with evidence."

"Sorry, it's Bec Reed. Who do you have?"

"Ma'am, I think you'll be pleased. It's the entire Clover firm."

"What? I don't understand." Bec's heart started racing.

"Ma'am, around thirty minutes ago we got a call to The Eagle in Shoreditch. I'm sending through the pictures now."

As the images appeared on the big screen in front of them, they saw seven bodies lined up in a sitting position but looking like they were asleep. In front of three of them were three books.

"Ma'am, I'm not sure if you can see it, but those books are resting on the legs of the three Clover brothers. It's their entire operation."

"They look asleep," said Bec.

"I think one or two may have taken a beating, but they've also been drugged, I believe."

Bec was happy but also pissed. She had removed the surveillance the day before. She looked at the inspector, who stared at her with a slightly ashen face.

"Fred, is that a sign around one of the brothers' necks?"

"Oh yes, ma'am." He laughed. "It says, 'To the good guys, here are some bad guys. Love, the good guys.'"

"Any witnesses?" Bec already knew the answer.

"Oh no, nothing. The pub was the busiest I've ever seen it—not sure any of the punters knew what was happening around back. We've taken the seven to hospital and arrested them all. With this evidence, we can take down the entire firm," Fred said.

"I'll come down and see you, Fred." Bec's adrenaline was pumping.

She looked at the inspector and turned away.

"Good results all round, Bec," he called after her. "Do you think it's the takeover you talked about?" he added almost sheepishly.

Not exactly, she thought.

Mike fucking Sharpe!

8

It was late afternoon when Mike arrived back at the apartment building. He had gone to see Paul first to debrief the mission and do a final check on how the team was doing. Mike was now putting into place deception plans wherever he moved to throw off anyone tailing him. He had learned from Paul that the team was obviously surprised by the change of mission plan and the moving up of the order of schedule to achieve an outcome. Paul had also advised that Andy had gone gray and would clearly remain gray for a few days as he tried to mop up intel. The team was okay; Tommy and Skippy were able to give their thoughts on Terry Patrick, and they had surprisingly remained positive about the situation. They trusted Mike.

"What's that USB about, Mike?" Paul inquired. "And why have we decided not to give Andy the copies of the Clover books?"

"I have a hunch, but I can't share it. If I'm wrong, it will put you at risk. If I'm right, it might put you at risk only if you're aware of the hunch. Again, I don't want you to second-guess anyone, including Andy. I need you take them at face value. If I disappear, it might not be for long, but so you're aware, I'll now contact you every four hours during the day, between seven a.m. and nine p.m.—normal mobile text, not encrypted. They won't take me while I'm in the apartment—too much heat."

"You mean the police or the bad guys?"

Mike laughed. "I've contacted the bad guys already, and the police are a no-brainer; I'll be questioned by them. The problem is, I'm not sure whether I'm talking to the right bad guy."

"Fuck, you have a way of complicating things," replied Paul, confused.

"Remember, only open the USB after I miss a check-in and only if it's not the police or John Tort."

"You're meeting Tort?"

"Maybe. It was always necessary, Paul."

"I see. Cause and effect." Paul was piecing a few things together.

Mike raised his eyebrows. "Spot on—cause and effect."

"You can brief Steph in if this shit actually goes down. I don't want her suddenly turning into my bodyguard," Mike said and meant it.

"Roger that."

"Steph, I'm home." Mike walked into the apartment.

Steph launched off the sofa and gave Mike a hug.

"All okay?" she said.

"I think so. Some loose ends, but all okay. Have you swept the apartment?"

"Yes, of course—like a good little housewife." She laughed. "All clear."

Mike was keen to freshen up. "I'm going to take a shower."

"Okay. I'll fix you a drink."

On the sofa, Mike and Steph sat almost entwined with each other. Mike was against one of the ends, and Steph sat between his legs, lying back in his arms.

"Andy?" Steph asked.

Fuck, she is observant, thought Mike.

"What's going on, Mike?"

Mike hadn't wanted to tell Paul his insane hunch; he also didn't want to share it with Steph.

"I haven't put my finger on it yet, Steph," he lied.

"You don't have to tell me, but I want to know he's okay." She was concerned about her friend.

"I think he's fine. He may have just got himself involved in something a little over his head. Steph, if I go missing for a while and it's not the cops or a bad guy, then call Paul."

"You're worrying me. A bad guy?"

"I need to meet John Tort," Mike said, getting right to the point.

"Why?" She looked concerned.

"Remember how I told you about cause and effect? The effect bit—the what happens next."

"I'll go with you."

"No, you won't. In fact, if my hunch is correct, I'll be safer on my own."

"So if it's not the cop or Tort, who else will take you?" Steph now looked as confused as Paul had earlier.

"Maybe someone I haven't yet thought about." Mike was concealing his true feelings. "I'm only telling you this because you've made some observations about Andy—and to be honest, Paul has access to the theory and will be in touch if there's an issue. I don't want to worry you."

"I still think you need me as a bodyguard." Steph smiled.

"You might end up breaking too many fingers and skulls."

"If you don't stop being mysterious, I might just break yours." She turned around and playfully bit Mike on the lip.

She pinned his arms down and looked at his bare chest. She appreciated the way his biceps seemed to pump in resistance as she applied a little pressure to his arms.

"Be careful," she said. "Without me, you're weak." She teasingly applied more pressure.

Mike laughed. "I keep forgetting you're the one who provides the personal protection in this relationship."

"Don't forget it, Mike Sharpe. Rather than personal protection, maybe I'm your personal motivation."

"'Motivation'?"

"Motivation," said Steph, and she lifted the long T-shirt she was wearing over her head. "This is what you'll be missing if you don't come home." She removed his shorts and gently kissed her way down his body.

Mike's phone burst into life as a text came in. He reached over and looked at it: 6pm, meet me outside St Clements Dane, Church TP.

Fuck, that was quick, thought Mike. An hour and fifteen minutes' time.

"Who was that?" asked Steph.

"Just some bad guys."

Steph slapped his penis, which she had in her hand.

"Fuck, Steph!" he shouted.

"Start taking things seriously."

"That actually hurt."

"Oh, poor baby. Let me kiss it and make it better." She gave him a mischievous wink.

Mike had convinced Steph all was going to be okay. He was confident that the meeting with John Tort would be fine. His only fear was whether he was trusting Terry Patrick too soon.

He arrived at the church of the Royal Air Force five minutes early. There was a no-parking zone, but just in front of it, parked there five minutes early, was a Mercedes. He walked over and the door was opened from the inside. He got in the back seat, next to Tibbsy. They nodded and the car pulled away. In the front next to the driver was a hired hand, but to be fair, it was all low-key and professional.

Tibbsy looked at him. "It's not far, maybe ten minutes. Any chance you were followed?"

"No," said Mike.

"And your team?"

"A couple know I have a meeting, nothing else."

"Good," said Tibbsy. "Just play it straight and you'll be fine."

The car pulled up at the back entrance of a gentlemen's club.

"When we get out, you'll follow me up two flights of stairs and into a waiting area. You'll be searched there and then led through to see the boss."

"Okay, thanks." Mike felt reassured.

Tibbsy was a professional, explaining everything so there were no surprises and nothing to make Mike react and start anything.

As Mike walked up the stairs, he felt a few butterflies in his stomach, but he was more at ease by the way Tibbsy walked ahead of him and the other guy stayed a distance behind him. Once again, it demonstrated professional courtesy.

It was all fairly informal as he arrived in the waiting area. He smiled at the number of men outside. *Shit,* he thought. *A kingpin needs a lot of protection.*

"Legs apart, please, sir, and arms out like this," said one of the guys who was standing in front of the door. Again, by showing him what to do, it allowed Mike to comply without additional manhandling. The guy professionally searched Mike, who had only a credit card on him and his burner phone. "You travel light, brother," he said.

"Makes your job easier." Mike smiled.

The guy nodded in approval. "I'm just going to do a final electronics check."

Really thorough, thought Mike as the wand was passed next to his ears and around the top of his shirt. "All clear." He then nodded at another guy, who picked up the phone.

"You may go in, sir."

Terry Patrick opened the door and motioned for Mike to enter. It was probably the largest office Mike had ever been in. He was immediately drawn to a huge series of what were likely one-way glass panels that looked out onto the gentlemen's club. It was like a VIP area at a concert venue, only the talent onstage was naked. He looked across to the far side of the room, stacked full of boxing memorabilia; on the opposite side, some distance away from the opulent desk, was a collection of more general sporting memorabilia. What set the office apart from any other was the desk—clearly oversized and handcrafted to fit John Tort.

As he inspected the decor, Mike simultaneously checked out the five men in the room. John Tort sat at the desk in a chair that had also been custom-made to fit him. Mike imagined Tort spent a lot of time in this room.

Tort was around five eight, maybe a little taller, but Mike could see the commanding presence he brought to the room. Over the years, Mike had noticed how some people could elevate a room simply by walking into it, and he knew John was likely one of those guys. It could be the power he held, but he definitely had something about him. He had once been told by a friend that he had the same effect, but Mike could never see it in himself.

John was probably in his early sixties but looked younger. He obviously kept himself fit and hadn't succumbed to the trappings of success. In fact, he wasn't a bad-looking guy—black hair, probably dyed but not out of place, green eyes with a tinge of brown, and a few wrinkles, each likely holding a story about his life.

"Michael Sharpe, isn't it?" said John Tort as he gestured for him to take a seat.

Mike thought about how to address John. *Should it be sir or Mr. Tort?* What would work for the position he was in right now?

Go with polite, he thought. *But don't relinquish too much power.*

"Yes, it's Mike." He quickly added, "Thank you for inviting me, Mr. Tort."

John laughed. "Invite? You requested the meeting. I've been doing this since I was a kid, Michael, and in all that time, no one has ever taken out one of my firms and then sought an invitation to see me. It's usually the other way around."

Mike sat back a bit farther in his seat but kept his core a little tense. He wanted to move fast if anyone tried anything. John had said *Michael* instead of *Mike*—only his parents would use *Michael*. Therefore, John was going to use a parent–child relationship here. That wouldn't be an issue unless John decided the child needed punishing.

"So I'm intrigued, Michael—not only do you take out my firm in Shoreditch, but also you have the balls to ask for a meeting and don't even propose neutral ground. You're either very, very stupid, have a death wish, or something else. The only reason you're here is that Terry said you're a professional and a soldier. You're lucky, Michael. I have a soft spot for our military, but don't take the piss, or I won't hesitate to teach you a lesson."

Mike could tell John wasn't joking. He chose his words carefully. "I'm actually here for some advice."

"'Advice'?" Even John hadn't been expecting that. "You've come to see me for advice?" John paused. He looked at his men, and they gave out a bit of a laugh. "You're coming to me for advice." John had to say it again; he didn't quite believe it.

"But not with these people in the room—except Terry," said Mike.

Mike knew this was a power move, and a very dangerous one at that, but he was hoping that John's competitive nature would be intrigued enough to allow it to happen. He was also hoping that Terry had told him enough for John to think of Mike as a bit of a maverick.

"You want me to clear the room of my people? I don't do that for anyone." John was slightly agitated.

"There's no point in them being here," said Mike. "Too many ears—and right now, none of them except maybe Terry could stop me, anyway." This was Mike's huge power play.

John stared hard at Mike. He could see it, the fire that was raging in those deep-blue eyes. He recognized it before in soldiers who had seen battle.

John sat back. "When I first took Terry on, he profiled everyone in this room." He looked around. "Tell me what you think about each of them, and I'll consider it."

Terry looked at Mike and John. "If I may, sir," he said to John. John nodded.

"Mike, do a risk profile on each, as if you had just walked into a bar, just like I guess you would have done on the Clover brothers." Terry was professional enough to know Mike had already done one.

Mike turned to John. "I don't need to look around. I already made an assessment when I walked in."

Terry smiled. John knew Mike had done this, and it pleased him.

"Well, go ahead," said John.

"I'll start with the guy closest to you on my right, your left. Gym junkie, probably on the 'roids, would have a short fuse." The guy actually flinched when Mike said this, which confirmed it. "This is his weakness. Aside from that making him slow, he would have a shit center of balance; that said, he conveys a presence that would put most people off, which is clearly a good thing, and if he connected with a punch, you'd be out cold." Mike was using the bathtub effect; he didn't want to go pissing off the people closest to John.

"The next guy over there is an SAS wannabe. He has all the gear, like the Danner boots and the tac pants—he probably has a multi-tool on him somewhere. I'm guessing he may have been a bouncer at a club and got promoted into this team. Would be handy, though; street fighting is a hell of a place to learn.

"The guy behind me to my right is small, fast, and agile. He'd struggle with a direct hit from a bigger guy, assuming the bigger guy could hit him. He's trained in martial arts and is probably a bit of a weapon.

"Left shoulder, not trained—possibly a lawyer or something. No threat at all.

"The guy to my left is possibly a career criminal. Maybe an enforcer; he's dangerous in every scenario. He would probably shoot you before the argument even began."

Terry was smiling inside, as he had assessed the team roughly the same, although he had missed the enforcer in the room. He hadn't been sure who he was, as even he hadn't met him before.

"So, Mike, who would you take out first?"

John had called him *Mike* instead of *Michael*. He had passed the test.

Mike smiled. "The lawyer!"

John laughed, as did one or two members of his team.

"Good choice, good choice," he said. "The most dangerous of them all. You lot—out."

After they left, John looked at Mike. "Advice?"

Mike already learned from Terry how much John knew about the events of the last week, including the conversation about John's own view of the Clover brothers, so it was fairly easy to lead with the question Mike wanted answered. He went over some detail but got to the point as quickly as possible.

"Mr. Tort, I don't fully understand cause and effect."

"Call me John. Cause and effect. . . you're a smart guy, Mike. From my perspective, your actions were timely, but according to the code, I should have sanctioned them, and I was close to doing that with my own people. The problem for Aaron Clover was that his sons wanted more—first Liam and Karl, and then of course he had his younger son to contend with. I noticed early on that Nick Clover would be a problem, always needing to prove something and then constantly breaking the code."

"I'm sorry, John, you keep referring to a code. I don't understand what you mean," said Mike.

"Good point, and it would seem most of the youth of today don't get it either. Take the incident with your boy—that would rarely happen a few years ago unless a punter was drunk or had done the wrong thing with a girl or started a fight, of course. No member of a firm would ever confront someone outside of the criminal world. You see, you can't ask someone to pay you protection insurance and then start knocking their punters around; it doesn't make sense."

"Isn't extortion the same thing, though? You know, don't pay and we'll do something?" said Mike.

John smiled. "Yes, but no, Mike. We apply pressure, but only when we know a business can afford to pay. Our methods might not always be logical, but the disorder we're witnessing now is far more chaotic."

"What do you mean?"

"Well, when a crime organization runs an area, most criminal elements adhere to a code. Yes, there are killings, burglaries, drugs, but the majority of the general public go about their lives unaffected. Nowadays, you have young working-class kids—white, Black, Asian, it doesn't discriminate—who have been forgotten about, who want it all now, at once. No code—they're fighting each night on the streets, driven by drug money and success. Have you seen how many young kids are dying here in London? Would never happen under a code." Tort was adamant.

"You see, that's the problem for law enforcement; three or four large crime organizations were easier to police than the hundreds of kids who think they're some sort of gangster and end up being killed before they hit twenty. You know, Mike, in places like Liverpool, kids as young as eleven and twelve are acting as drug mules. No code.

So that brings me back to cause and effect. Taking out the Clover brothers leaves a vacuum—and a pretty big one with that nightclub. I'm stretched thin, to be honest, and there's always a risk that one of the other syndicates outside of the code will make a play. The worst outcome for Shoreditch is these smaller gangs moving in." Tort stared off into the distance.

"We have a little bit of time, though; word has got around that I removed the Clover brothers and that they've been replaced. The problem will come from the businesses that we're giving insurance to. If they're hit by a local gang or a tourist gang, we'll look like mugs. The problem is, Mike, you gave the cops the books that the fucking idiots kept rather than using an encrypted computer. Aaron was old-school, and now we're unsure who paid into the insurance fund. Above all else, that's where you've pissed me off the most." Tort looked Mike directly in the eyes.

"I have copies of those books," said Mike.

"Copies? Why do I feel like you're going to ask me for something else?"

"Yes, but hopefully it's simple," said Mike. "If you guarantee me that no one will pursue my team after what happened this week, I'll give you the books."

Easy enough, thought Mike.

"That's all you're asking for?"

"I would have thought that their *freedom* was enough," Mike said, emphasizing his point.

"Maybe my advice will be slightly different," said John. "Those books are important, Mike. They make a big, big problem go away. Of course, I could just extract them from you and kill everyone involved."

There was silence, and then John broke into a smile.

"So I have an idea that I was mulling over before meeting you. It has to do with the effect, Mike," Tort added. "Terry told me your team has just left the army and are looking for work."

"Yes," said Mike.

"What if I give each of them a job at the nightclub, from management downward, and put you in as a shareholder and director?"

Mike was stunned and a little on the back foot.

"I'm sorry, John. I can't ask the team to cross the line, and I'm already worried we did that earlier today."

John laughed. "You fear the worst, Mike. The nightclub is completely legit. The board members are all businessmen, and the nonexecutive directors are selected from former FTSE top one hundred companies. The Clover brothers' involvement was actually harming the club—that's why I made them do business at the pub. Yes, the security was tight at the club, but it wasn't to protect the Clover brothers. It was to stop anyone from getting a stupid idea about muscling in. Your team spotted the main weakness in their organization: the Clover brothers would conduct business at The Eagle. Even if they had done their business at the club—I mean, even with the books—and it got raided, it would have made little difference there." John appeared thoughtful as he spoke.

"I'm sorry, John, but that doesn't make sense. I thought Aaron Clover owned the club?"

"No, he sold it to me a while ago. We had a gentlemen's agreement about the final payment, which was linked to how the club was performing at the point he finally moved on. He moved on yesterday."

"Is there any risk to the team from the Clover brothers?" Mike asked.

"Yes, when they get out of jail, which will be a long time in the future. It obviously depends on where your team members are in ten to fifteen years' time. The brothers will get thirty, guaranteed."

"And Aaron?" said Mike.

"Slipped the country and never looked back. He's pissed, but I told him part of the payment is not to pursue you and that I would deal with it. So, Mike, thoughts?"

"The effect of what we did today has been weighing on my mind. I'd like to put it to the team and give them the chance to walk away. Aside from their perception of what is being offered, London is an expensive place." Mike wasn't sure whether he had just entered a negotiation.

"Tell them the job comes with an apartment. I have many." John laughed.

"Aside from giving you the books with the names, there are no strings attached?"

"One: security. I want the club to be London's crown jewel and to have the best record in regard to how our clientele are treated and how safe they feel. That's what I'll measure you against, Mike." John was back to being a businessman.

"When do you need to know?" Mike was also now deep in thought.

"One week from today or sooner. Starting you on Friday night would be good, but if not, the following Friday." Tort smiled.

"Okay, I'll try. I'm expecting DS Reed to take me in for questioning soon."

"DS Reed." John laughed. "Yes, well, I'm sure she has no evidence, so it should be straightforward. If you need a lawyer, let me know."

"Thanks, John, and thanks for meeting me." Mike shuffled in the chair, ready to stand up.

"My pleasure, and when you come back here, I'll show you the sports memorabilia. I noted you were impressed when you walked in."

Mike smiled. "That would be great. It is truly impressive."

"I'll get my lawyer to send you all the details. I promise you your team will be well compensated."

As Mike walked out, John looked at Terry. "I can see why you encouraged me to meet him, Terry."

"Yes, sir. I wasn't expecting it to end with a job offer, though." Terry smiled.

"Terry, a lot of people look at kingpins as gangsters, but I genuinely have a soft spot for military people. This whole fucking world seems to be losing direction and respect, but you lot still get it." John nodded at him.

"Mike might not join the firm, but we have many legit businesses, and judging by what he's done to date, he could make it a success. He lives a code whether he realizes it or not," said John.

There was a knock on the door. "Come in."

It was the lawyer. "Mike transferred the books to us electronically."

"See," said John. "He accepted my word, and I'll honor it, and that's before he's talked to his team about the job offer."

"Just one more thing, sir," said the lawyer. "All of our comms have been offline, including the cameras. They're now back up."

"Thank you," said John.

"Clever bastard. He was never here," said Terry.

"I like him. I like him a lot," said John.

Mike was returned to the Saint Clement Dane church and immediately texted Paul and Steph. It took him an hour to get back to the apartment after ensuring he wasn't being followed. Steph was asleep in his bed, evidently worn from the day's excursions. Adrenaline was a funny thing—once gone, it could leave you overwhelmed by sudden fatigue.

He took a quick shower, freshened up, and then cautiously climbed into bed next to Steph. It was only 2230, so he wasn't sure how long she had been asleep. She looked serene and beautiful. Although they had been together only a few days, he loved watching her sleep. He found the contrast between her violent capabilities and her current peaceful state fascinating. He loved everything about the way he felt right now about her and the way it made him feel. "Shit," he muttered. "I'm falling in love with her."

Steph's eyes fluttered open, locking onto Mike's. She smiled as though she had been feigning sleep. "The feeling is mutual," she said.

Mike decided to explain to Steph the conversation he'd had with John Tort and told her he would brief Paul in the morning.

"Run their whole fucking nightclub, with you as director?" said Steph. "Wow. And it's legit, not illegal?"

"Seems that way. I'll get some checks done to ensure that's the case. But it could be a huge opportunity for the team." Mike sounded enthusiastic.

"Maybe," said Steph. "What do we know about running a nightclub, though?"

"Not a lot, but we can learn. They have staff there already, and the security issue seems to be their biggest problem. I'll just make Paul head of security."

"Fuck, Mike, you're seriously thinking about doing this?"

"Maybe. It would help satisfy the problem I've been mulling over for a week."

"This effect thing?"

"Yes, the gap we just created today. From my understanding, things could go south very quickly if the wrong firm takes over." Mike was convincing himself as he spoke.

"So how does us running a nightclub change that?" It was a good question.

"It's the crown jewel in that area. It's the only reason for a firm to really move in."

"If that's the case, though, the club will be targeted whether it's legit or not," said Steph.

"Yes, and it was already at risk with the Clover brothers, hence John's visit there the other night. The difference is that if anyone tried anything, they'd be in for a shock with the way we'd do security."

"It sounds like a slippery slope to me."

"Maybe." Mike knew Steph could be right. "I'll make you manager; you have a sound business background through your father."

"I don't know, Mike. This wasn't how I envisioned my future outside the military. I want to travel, have fun, get away from the violence." Steph looked forlorn.

"You mean, if I accept the offer, you might not be in?" Mike was concerned.

"Maybe not. I need a break, just to get away from it all. I have to find peace again. This morning, the adrenaline rush was intoxicating, and the fire coming on inside me was overpowering. When I was hitting Liam's head against the bar, I was enjoying it a little bit too much—and then, afterward, the guilt. I want to get away, and I want you to come with me."

"It's not just about me, Steph; it's about the team. I need to talk to them tomorrow." Mike wasn't sure of the words to use. "I have a week to respond."

Steph hugged Mike as she laid in his arms. She realized that this alone could be the biggest hurdle in their short relationship and one for her that may be insurmountable.

9

It had taken Mike a long time to fall asleep, given his contemplation of Steph's words. Rising early, he went for a run to clear his head before heading straight for a shower. Steph was already in the bathroom, wrapping up, as Mike began brushing his teeth.

Knock, knock, knock!

"Hold on, just coming!" shouted Steph. "Who the fuck's that?" Steph looked at Mike.

"A knock like that's got to be Bec Reed."

"The police, Mike! Shit!"

"Go answer it. They've come for me, not you." Mike had been expecting it.

Steph scowled. "In just a fucking towel, thanks."

The knock came again.

"I'm coming," said Steph.

She checked the VIDCON system and saw Bec Reed and Detective Grimmer.

She opened the door. "Hi, Bec, how can I help?"

"Is Mike here?"

"He just got out of the shower."

Bec glanced at Steph, clad in a towel, and felt a surge of jealousy. "Can we come in?"

"Um, yes, sure."

Steph led Bec into the apartment and called out to Mike, "It's Bec."

"Two minutes," said Mike. "Hope you brought coffee."

Steph noticed that due to the positioning of the mirror and because the door to the ensuite was open, Bec could see Mike getting dressed. His back was visible, but she might have seen him naked.

Mike put on a T-shirt and jeans, socks, and trail shoes. He walked out of the bedroom and greeted Bec the same way as normal. Bec found this slightly off-putting, as she was there on business.

"Mike, we'd like you to accompany us to the station to help us with ongoing inquiries."

"What? Am I under arrest or something?" Mike feigned surprise.

"No, sir," said Detective Grimmer. "But we'd like you to come voluntarily, or we may have to consider arrest."

Bizarre, thought Mike. It confirmed they had nothing.

"Okay, no worries. But can I ask what it relates to?"

"We'd prefer to talk about that at the station," said Bec, looking at Steph like she didn't want her to know what was going on.

"Okay, then. I guess we should go."

Mike winked at Steph, who put her arms out and wrapped them around him. Mike gave her a kiss. They moved in close. "Don't worry, I'll be back soon. I have no idea why they want me."

Although it was an act, it was pretty convincing. Suddenly Steph's towel fell to the floor. Detective Grimmer's eyes almost popped out of his head as Steph used Mike to cover most of her modesty, and Mike lifted the towel back up. It was a classic deception move that enabled Mike to say, "Inform Paul." Steph also knew that Grimmer would be thinking about that moment all day.

Mike found himself in a small office inside a police station not too far from where he lived. He guessed that this was not the OCD headquarters but rather somewhere convenient that DS Reed could use to work out whether she could get anything useful from him. The journey into the station had been very quiet, and Mike was careful not to say too much except the usual small talk niceties.

Mike sat in the modest room, scanning his surroundings; it was a typical setup used to intimidate those being interviewed: a table and two cheap chairs, similar to what you'd see at a budget café, designed to be uncomfortable over time. Mike had been given a form that explained he was not under arrest but reminded him that he was helping police with their inquiries and that he had certain rights. He could also leave at any time, which he guessed in his case would lead to an arrest at some point. Mike had already decided to cooperate as much as possible and hopefully avoid arrest.

In walked DS Reed and Detective Grimmer. They started their own preliminaries and then reread Mike his rights.

"Okay, Mike—do you mind if we call you Mike?" said Detective Grimmer.

Playing the good cop, thought Mike. *Is this really going to be a textbook interview?* He knew the first question would be the primary one, and the way he answered would determine how long they kept him.

Bec got right to the point, as expected. "Where were you at twelve thirty p.m. on Tuesday, October 23?"

"I was at The Eagle, meeting a former acquaintance," Mike answered directly.

Mike saw the unintentional sign in Bec straightaway; she hadn't been expecting that response and was almost already resigned to the fact that the interview was over before it began. She changed her posture during the answer, stopped looking him in the eye, and glanced down at the file in front of her.

"Who were you meeting?" she asked.

"A guy called Terry Patrick. He's ex–Foreign Legion, but I met him briefly in Afghanistan. He was working for one of the security companies over there, and our paths crossed briefly in Kabul."

"Why were you meeting him, Mike?" It was Detective Grimmer's turn.

"Mainly inquiring about work; I'm on the market," Mike replied.

"No, I mean, why did you contact Terry? And why The Eagle, the very pub where Tommy Stewart was attacked?"

"Terry has been involved in security at some nightclubs around London. I thought that not only could he give me some ideas on potential security work—not just for me but for the team—but also, I wanted him to give me a layman's overview of organized crime in London and gangs like the Clover brothers."

"You know that you met him at around the same time that the Clover firm members were found beaten and drugged at the back of that very same pub?"

"No, we didn't know about that until the police came in and took our names, along with the names of the pub's other patrons. The police let us know there had been an incident, though." Mike hadn't strayed far from the truth, which made it all the more convincing.

DS Reed was direct and to the point. "Terry Patrick is the enforcer for the Clover brothers. Your own man told you that." She was annoyed.

"He was with me during this incident, so I guess you're telling me he's not very good at his job?"

"Mr. Sharpe, you're saying that Terry Patrick is your alibi?" Detective Grimmer was also being direct.

"Sorry, alibi for what, exactly?" Again, Mike was so cool that it could have been a friendly conversation.

"Come on, Mike, there isn't one firm out there that could take out the Clover brothers with that level of efficiency," Bec pushed.

"I'm sorry, DS Reed, but I have no idea what you're talking about. I was in the pub, having a pint with Terry." Mike played the same card, in the same tone.

"So you met with the guy who you already knew was an enforcer for the Clover brothers?"

"Like I said, if he was and something happened to them, he's rubbish at his job." Mike kept to this line of response, as it also protected Terry.

"Did you get any work?"

Mike noted the change of tact. Worth answering truthfully.

"Maybe. The nightclub in Shoreditch."

"The Red Zone?" said Bec.

"Yes, to take over the security."

"That was the Clover nightclub," said Detective Grimmer.

"I was told that it's owned by investors. I've already checked it out." Mike's answers all offered information, like he was trying to be open and cooperative. It had completely disarmed the situation, even though he knew the Skirmishers would remain prime suspects. Without evidence, though—and there was less evidence here than when Tommy was attacked—the police had nothing.

"It still has links to a kingpin, John Tort," said Bec.

"I don't know about that. The money offered is very good, and the club is one of the best in London. Besides, all the directors have run multinationals."

Bec looked at Mike carefully—not even a sign of duress or a flinch at any question, even though she knew something was off. She wasn't going to get anywhere with this approach.

"I trust you would have no issue with us searching your apartment?" This was Bec's last change of direction to try to salvage anything from this interview.

"No issue, but I trust it would be done with the correct paperwork. I mean, we wouldn't want to make the mistake of getting protocol wrong." This was the first and only time Mike would push back.

"Interview suspended," said Bec. *Bastard,* she thought.

Bec had to stop the interview; she couldn't afford to have anything recorded that referred to the tapping of Mike's apartment. She decided to alter her line of questioning and intended to ask Mike on the way home. She was willing to risk talking to him alone to try to get more information.

"What happens now?" said Mike.

"You can go home." Bec almost knew what Mike's next question would be and the subsequent response to her answer.

"You brought me here for that?" he said, keeping up appearances.

"It's protocol, Mike. We have to rule people out of our investigation."

Mike immediately saw what Bec was trying to do: disarm him and try to catch him off guard. Mike knew a lot about interrogation techniques due to the training he had received as part of the Skirmishers. They were trained to interrogate and to endure interrogation, preparing them for the risks they might face in their operations.

Mike was surprised by how quickly Bec had changed the situation from the interview room to a more relaxed car journey home.

"Sorry about that, Mike, but you can see how it looks from our perspective." Bec was almost too friendly.

"I understand, I guess. But as I said, if I had anything to hide, I surely wouldn't have been anywhere near the pub." Mike knew his words would fall on slightly deaf ears.

"Perfect alibi." Bec said it out loud so Mike knew she could see through it as well.

"So what happened to the Clover brothers?"

"I'm not sure I'm going to humor you with a response. The Red Zone is on our watch list."

"Why?"

"For organized crime—but you know that—no matter how legit it appears on paper."

"Why would I know that?"

"You've been there," said Bec, fishing.

"Pardon?"

"Come on, Mike, we spoke about this. The raid we conducted a few nights ago and the fact we found that there was someone else conducting an operation at the same time."

"Like I said, another department or intelligence services?"

"Like you said," replied Bec sarcastically. "You know, good looks and personality won't get you out of every situation."

That statement caught Mike out. "Is that some sort of compliment, Bec?"

Bec lowered her guard and smiled. "No . . . well, maybe a backhanded one. You're sleeping with Steph, then?"

Now that *did* catch Mike out.

"Sorry, you don't need to answer that. Just being a cop."

Mike decided to stay silent.

"Mike, I don't know what's going on, but you're treading in dangerous waters. John Tort is one of the last of his kind, and he's a scumbag, but those moving in make him look like a puppy. You work at that nightclub, whether it's legit or not, and you leave yourself and your team open to that threat every time you step foot in there—and with some of the gangs, every time you step foot anywhere. Don't cross the line between normal security work and wider requests that are outside the law."

"I wasn't planning on that, Bec."

"Do you want to live with that danger every day?"

Mike looked at her with those laser eyes. "I've spent most of my life doing exactly that."

As Mike entered the apartment and walked through to the lounge, he found Paul and Steph having coffee together.

"That was quick," said Steph. "I just about had time to get Paul up to speed."

Mike laughed. "It was a straightforward interview. What do you think, Paul?"

"The nightclub?"

"Yes."

"Seriously, can we trust John Tort? He's a gangster, a thug— do we really want to be associated with that?"

Mike knew that Steph would have given a thorough debrief to Paul, including her own fears of taking on a nightclub.

"He is a gangster and a thug, but he's also the last of his kind; there aren't many like him out there anymore. The club is legit. I've just about heard that from the police. We always wondered what the team might do after our army service, and this could be the answer: working together on a legit project. The money is very good." Even as Mike said it, he understood how it sounded.

"The fact is, Mike, it's an integrity issue. We know that the club has links to organized crime, even if it is legit." Paul was spot on.

Mike sighed. "How many times have we been worried that the team might spiral and end up on the wrong side of the law? This opportunity means we'll be working together on our terms and watching what the team does and how they behave."

Paul was his usual calm self, but he was worried about Mike. "You believe that? So we go in and do the security, run the business, and effectively have a part share in the club—sounds great, doesn't it? Until another firm decides they want to have a go, then we're in the middle of it all—or Tort decides he has a little job for us to do and we're expected to take someone out. Are you so naive that you can't see this?"

Paul's words felt like a bullet to Mike. He had so much respect for Paul that it hurt all the more to hear him say *naive*.

"Maybe I am being blinded by the situation, but I can see the opportunity here—for the team and their future. That said, I won't agree to anything without you, and I'm already reluctant because Steph wants out."

Steph looked at them both. "It's not for that reason, Mike. It's the other stuff that goes with doing a job like that. I want out from the violence—or at least a break from it so I can see what peace looks like."

"So the one person who actually knows something about business won't be there," said Paul.

"I'll do the first two weeks, and then I'm gone." Steph looked at Mike.

He was at a loss for words. "What, you are saying you support it?"

Paul was equally bewildered, especially after the discussion he'd had for the last ninety minutes with Steph. "Why the change, Steph? And why two weeks?"

"Mike has given up everything for us over the years, Paul, and now he's prepared to give up our relationship to support this."

She looked at Mike to see his reaction, and she wasn't disappointed—he really did love her. "If this is so important to you, then we should take it to the team."

Paul looked at Mike. "Do you really know what you're doing? And potentially what you may lose?"

"Unfortunately, yes." He looked at Steph, his eyes slightly glazed but showing no emotion.

"Okay, we take it to the team," said Paul. "I'll do it. Give me the details."

As Mike explained the opportunity, Paul began to realize why Mike was interested in getting the team involved in such a venture, but he had to keep reminding himself of the links to organized crime. Mike systematically broke the roles down for each of the team, including what his own role would be. The only humor came when Mike relayed to Paul that Terry had told him how much a head of security could earn.

"Fuck me, if you'd mentioned that first, I wouldn't have given you such a hard time!" Paul laughed. "I'll brief the team tomorrow and let you know by tomorrow evening. Time I was off, though."

"Thanks, Paul."

"You're not off the hook yet, Mike. Walk with me." Paul was serious.

Mike looked at Steph, who smiled at him like she knew this would be a one-way conversation.

It started as soon as they set foot out of the apartment. "Have you got rocks for brains?"

"Paul, trust me. The nightclub is an opportunity," Mike answered defensively.

"Not the nightclub—Steph!"

"Oh, right."

"'Oh, right'? Is that all you can say? Tell me another woman out there who will ever live up to her?" Paul was shaking his head.

"She has to find her path, Paul."

"Her path is with you, Mike. She loves you."

"Maybe not. Maybe her path and my path aren't compatible."

"That's nonsense, and you know it. What the hell is driving you?" Paul looked at Mike. He could see he needed to back off a little. "What's going on inside your head?"

"I think I'll be able to tell you in a day or so. Remember, if I disappear, read the note on the USB. It may give you peace of mind."

"And Steph?"

"No. Steph has other demons to exorcise."

Paul hugged Mike. "You and Steph could make something of this. You're made for each other. I love you both too much to witness the car crash that will inevitably happen."

"Thanks, Paul."

"Gave you a hard time, did he?" Steph offered Mike a drink straight after he returned to the apartment. "I'm sorry," she added.

"Why are you sorry?"

"That I am not fitting too well into this plan of yours, Mike Sharpe. I understand what you're trying to do to a point, but I really need to get away for a while. I wanted to get away with you."

"Where would we go?"

"To the Caribbean. My father has a house that fronts onto an exclusive private beach club." Steph smiled.

"Tempting."

"If that's not enough, the house has its own staff when we're in residence, supplied by the club. We don't have to do anything except drink, eat, sunbathe, and be naked." Steph winked at him.

"I do have rocks for brains," said Mike.

"Pardon?"

"Something Paul said."

Steph smiled at him. "I assume you don't fancy going for a massage. I can cancel my appointment if you like."

"No, you go ahead. I'll take a quick shower and then go for a walk and grab a few things for dinner."

Steph grinned. "Sounds good."

As Mike walked up the street toward a small enclave of more reasonably priced shops, distinct from those within the apartment complex, he pondered over his intricate situation. His attraction to Steph was nothing like he'd felt in any other relationship. He knew they were still in the honeymoon phase, but being with someone who knew what it was like to be in combat, be in the military, and know how military people think made all the difference.

Then he had his team—all good people whom he was about to get involved in something legit. But also, deep down, he knew Paul was right about John Tort and the connection to the club.

Then there was Bec Reed and her clear suspicion that Mike and the team were involved in the incident at The Eagle. Would she pull in more members of the team or leave it alone for now? He wasn't worried about the team; he knew they were too well trained to talk. But he was concerned about any ongoing surveillance or inquiries. *Who is Steph turning to in all this? She came to me; she would have talked to Skippy,* he thought. *Wow, Skippy would be an interesting sounding board.* He smiled as he thought of Skippy telling Steph that Mike had probably gotten a head injury in Afghanistan.

Mike continued to walk up the road, taking in the Georgian architecture of yet another street that was clearly steeped in history. It was getting busy as he got closer to the shops. He loved the familiar things in London, the red postboxes, even the occasional red telephone kiosk—they were what he thought about on operations. Funny how it was the smallest of things that made him yearn for home.

He looked up the road and noticed for the first time a blue van parked there. Had he missed it while deep in thought? There were no windows on the back of the van and no obvious rear entry point. *Keep walking,* he thought. *But stay vigilant.* Was there anything else out of place? A foot—he could see a foot, a homeless guy on the footpath opposite to the van. *Fuck, this is it,* he thought. His hunch was about to be proven. *Relax, don't resist.* He was getting tense. *Good guys or bad guys? Good guys or bad guys? Fifteen meters. Come on, calm down,* he thought. He could feel his heart beating faster, and he tried to breathe deeply. He could feel the adrenaline rocketing through his body. Five meters, two meters . . .

The homeless guy launched at him. Two others sprang from the side door of the van and picked him up like a rag doll. *Relax,* he thought. *Relax.* He could just see a Land Rover screech to a halt in front of the van. *Good guys,* he thought. It took less than a second. When Mike was in the van, a sack was placed over his head, and he was cuffed. He didn't move but waited for someone to speak. First, it was a radio message: "Bravo Oscar, Bravo 10: target acquired."

The next message was telling in the way it was asked: "Bravo 10, Bravo Oscar: Resistance?"

"Bravo 10: Nil. Out."

Then the first words spoken to him: "Don't resist. Keep behaving, and all will be good. Reply *okay* if you're all right."

"Okay," said Mike.

The way he'd been handled, Mike knew he was with a Special Forces snatch team that was employed in London to support antiterrorist operations. They would have probably been briefed on who he was but not why he was wanted. This was SF doing the dirty work for another agency—well, at least, Mike hoped it was. Was his hunch actually playing out?

He tried his hardest to determine where he was being taken, but it was proving difficult with a lot of ambient noise. He wondered if he was getting a blue-light escort from the Land Rover, as they weren't stopping often in the usual London traffic. The snatch team was professional, no chatter among themselves, and a hand rested on Mike's shoulder to prevent him from trying to get up quickly. Mike decided that he would be the model prisoner— unless, of course, things went bad.

The van suddenly stopped, and Mike heard what he thought was a guard or someone else giving directions to the driver. The van moved forward slightly and then stopped again. Mike had determined that wherever they were, it was very secure. The second stop was for further checks. He could hear the sound of something being passed under the vehicle, probably checking for an IED.

They then drove forward again into what must have been a tunnel or an underground car park, as Mike heard the familiar echo of the engine noise bouncing off the wall. The van stopped.

"Right, we're going to slowly get you out of the vehicle. You'll kneel down while one of my colleagues searches you.

Do not try to slip out of the plastic cuffs, and do not make any sudden movements. If you do, it will become painful for you very quickly. Understood?"

"Yes," said Mike.

Mike had been searched many times in his career, but this was a truly professional job; everything was checked. It was thorough. "Okay, we're going to take down your trousers. Your groin will be searched. We also want you to bend over."

Mike couldn't help himself. "I might enjoy this bit." It was an old gag he'd used many times before.

"I'm sure we fucking won't," came the response from someone who, if he hadn't known Mike was military, probably did now.

After he was searched, someone called out, "One mobile and a credit card only."

"Okay, take him to the room."

The room was cleverly located within ten meters of where Mike was searched and where the blue van had dropped him off. The closeness made it so much easier for the snatch squads to get someone into a holding room, especially if they were being uncooperative. Mike was placed in a comfortable chair. He had also noticed that the floor was carpeted. This didn't seem like an interrogation cell. Where was he?

A door opened. "Oh hell, get the sack off his head and remove the cuffs." The voice was familiar to Mike, but he couldn't place it.

The cuffs were removed, and the sack was taken off Mike's head. He blinked many times as his eyes adjusted to the light in the room. There, next to him, he saw a fully kitted Special Forces soldier.

"Sorry, mate. It was orders," he said.

"Thanks for touching my dick," said Mike.

The guy laughed. "Not me, fortunately."

"That's all," came the voice again. "Thank you, gentlemen."

As the soldier moved away, Mike saw someone whom he knew instantly. "Oli?"

"Hi, Mike. Sorry about all the drama, but we had to get you off the street in the most convincing way."

Oli Turnball was an MI6 operative who had worked in Afghanistan. Mike had crossed paths with him as the Skirmishers' reputation grew. Oli had spent some time getting to know the team and would provide advice to them on the intelligence picture as well as what he needed from an intelligence perspective. Oxbridge educated, Oli looked out of place in Afghanistan—in his own words, it was pretty hard to blend in when you have the Oxbridge twang, are six feet tall, and have red hair. He was very smart, spoke six languages, and always seemed to be a step ahead of those around him.

"Coffee, tea, water?" said Oli.

"Water will be fine, thanks."

Oli handed Mike a bottle from a fridge that was in the corner of the room. *This is definitely an office or some sort of breakout area,* thought Mike, as he began to take in his surroundings.

"The room," said Oli. "You were probably expecting something different, I'd guess?"

"What the hell is going on, Oli? Why am I in front of an MI6 operative?"

"All will become clear in good time, old boy." There was a little sarcasm in his voice. "You knew we were coming?" Half question, half statement.

"I had a hunch," said Mike.

"Care to share?" Oli was smiling.

Mike smiled too. "All in good time, old boy."

Oli laughed. "I knew we should have got some whiskey for this. Mike, I'm going to be straight with you: You need to tell us everything you've done since Tuesday morning, including the pub. No bullshit, no Terry Patrick alibi, no denying what the Skirmishers did to the Clover brothers—and also tell us about the job offer at the Red Zone."

"Seems like you already have it all. Why do you need me to fill in the gaps when you have Andy?"

Oli sat back on a low cabinet. Mike's statement about Andy confirmed he was already switched on to the situation.

"Yes, of course you knew—that explains a lot. We thought you did, but it's good to hear it from the horse's mouth, so to speak. Mike, I'd like to take you upstairs. In fact, it was always the plan, but I want to warn you that you'll need to keep an open mind and your emotions in check."

"Oli, you should know me by now—nothing surprises me anymore. I'd like Andy present, though. I take it he's up there?" Mike made the statement like it was fact.

"He is." Oli seemed to be lost in thought.

"I take it I don't need to be blindfolded?" Mike smiled.

"No, but the snatch team is on standby. You're seen as some sort of *Lethal Weapon*." Oli smirked.

"Maybe you should be looking for Officer Riggs."

Mike was taken up two flights of stairs and then through a corridor that reminded him of just about every army HQ that he had ever been to in the military—the sort of corridor where each person's titles were posted like street signs outside of every door.

At the end of the corridor was a door that clearly led to an office of the person in charge. It was that similar to an army HQ that Mike thought he could have found his own way there. Oli knocked diligently and then entered. In the room was Andy, already looking sheepish, and a woman whom Mike didn't know. The office was fitting for whoever was using it; clearly, the individual must be important.

"Mike, this is Stacey Simpson. She'll explain her role to you when the boss turns up."

"Boss," said Andy as he looked at Mike.

"Andy." Mike embraced him, which not only caught Andy off guard but also came as a welcome relief. In fact, the whole room was relieved.

"Take a seat, Mike. The boss will be through shortly."

"He's been taken!" Steph was careful to restrict her words on the phone to Paul.

"Say nothing. Meet me at Location Delta," said Paul. "Cover your movements as well."

"Roger. Out." Steph still used military radio procedure in everyday conversation.

Paul took the USB that Mike had given him and opened it using a USB cable that he'd had converted for his phone. He was impressed with his own discipline that he hadn't opened it earlier. He read the small note that Mike had compiled in bullet point form. As Paul read down the list, his hand went to his mouth in disbelief.

He memorized each bullet point and then deleted the encrypted file as instructed. He sat down to think. *Fuck me, what are we getting ourselves into?*

10

Mike was seated comfortably, a coffee and biscuit accepted in a setting hardly resembling an interrogation. An awkward silence dominated the room, everyone anticipating the arrival of "the boss."

"Shouldn't be much longer," said Oli.

Mike looked at Andy, sensing unresolved tension. Mike knew his secret, and Andy knew Mike had already guessed it—but what else was going on? If Mike's hunch was right, then Andy would come out of this okay, but there would be a lingering question of trust.

The door to the office swung open. Mike looked up. He could feel the adrenaline start to pulse through his veins. His hands went clammy and his throat became dry. Although he'd an idea of who the boss might be, he was still taken aback as the reality unfolded.

"What's the matter, Sharpie? Looks like you've seen a ghost." Colonel Tom Sawyer had entered the room with a commanding presence.

Mike controlled his breathing. He was trying to play it cool. He looked at Oli. "You called the army in?"

"Not exactly, Mike." Oli now realized how much Mike knew and, more importantly, how much he didn't know.

Tom took the seat behind the desk.

"No way," said Mike. "You're still with the intelligence services, Tom? Don't answer—it already makes fucking sense."

"Don't be hard on yourself, Mike. You guessed about Andy, didn't you?"

"Rather than interrogating me, can someone please tell me what the fuck is going on?" Mike was genuinely perplexed.

Tom looked at Oli. "I'm happy to go with that approach if you are, Oli."

"Yes, sir."

"Mike, you need to agree to fill in the gaps on our side," said Tom.

"I'm not going to compromise the team, Tom." Mike was firm but polite.

"Just fill in the gaps. We're here to protect you," Tom said directly.

"Protect me? You've been spying on me and the team." Mike was on the attack. "Andy working for an intelligence agency was one thing, but your involvement . . . How on earth does that come into it?" Mike knew he needed to calm himself.

Tom looked at Mike. It was hard for him to tell whether Mike was putting on a show or if he knew more than he was letting on.

"I could remind you that you're still in the army, Mike. The SIB would have a field day with you." Tom knew this would put Mike on the back foot. It reminded Tom of the day he'd approached Mike to lead the Skirmishers; it had been an easy decision for him to make but a painful one to get through the army's top brass.

Mike looked at Tom. He knew the boss had just backed him into a corner. Colonel Tom Sawyer was an imposing figure. Standing around six four, he was built like a long-distance runner. Mike knew that Tom had been around awhile, but nobody ever asked about Tom's career in the army—it was always an off-limits question. Mike had concluded that those who knew Tom well, especially in an army uniform, were also confused by the fact he had disappeared for months—or even years—at a time.

"Sorry," said Mike, now realizing that he needed to play the game. "Please fill me in, Oli, and I'll help with the gaps."

Tom smiled. A few years ago, Mike would never have backed down.

Oli looked at Tom. "Everything, sir?"

"Everything. Get him to sign, though."

"Sign what?" Mike was confused.

"Mike, you're cleared to top secret, but we need to reinforce that before briefing you. What you're about to hear is a question of national security, will put lives at risk, and has the potential to fell a government."

"Okay." Mike was handed a form, a single piece of A4 paper, barely a paragraph on it, and worded to remind him of his obligations under the Official Secrets Act.

"Thanks," said Oli after Mike returned the signed form.

"Mike, let's get started with Andy. He was an MI6 field operative while with the Skirmishers. He was one of Tom's picks for your team because he was ex-army, resourceful, and moved in and out of intelligence his entire career. Giving him the rank of corporal was important because he had full access to you as part of your leadership team. When did you realize he was working for an agency?"

Mike smiled. "I guess I should have known all along about Andy, but it really only came to me during this op, when he placed the listening device detector in the apartment. My suspicion was further confirmed when we received the secure comms for the Red Zone recce."

"How, sir?" Andy was genuinely puzzled.

"The army, Andy, and its desire to mark everything with its own serial number system. Also, I guess Bec Reed mentioned that the comms equipment could only be from the intelligence services or the military. Her words sort of solidified my thoughts."

"So you took a look at the equipment after I fitted it? You would have seen no serial number and concluded it wasn't army—that's brilliant." Andy was being genuine. "That's when you interfered with the microphone."

"Yes. I didn't want you to become some sort of voyeur."

Andy laughed.

Colonel Sawyer also smiled.

"I didn't really see you being part of this, Tom, except my lingering doubt about our discussion in Afghanistan. I guess it makes sense that you chose Andy for the Skirmishers, but he wasn't the only one you hand-selected for the team."

"No, Mike, you're correct, of course—my rank of colonel in the army has always been a little distracting, as my career has always crossed between the intelligence community and the military. I actually outrank myself in the civilian world, if that makes sense."

"So you've always been MI6?"

"It's complicated, and I can't provide the details, I'm afraid."

"But you're clearly in charge. How high up are we talking here?" Mike looked at Stacey, who was sitting quietly, blending in, taking notes.

Tom nodded to her as if to let her know that it was time.

"Mike, apologies—I've been too silent, but I'm head of D section at MI5," said Stacey. "Andy and Oli reached out to us when they first realized you were going to—how shall I word it—settle a score with the Clover brothers."

"I don't get it. I understand Andy might have asked for help, but you didn't stop us. In fact, it would appear you helped us." Mike had been thinking about this scenario in every decision he made.

"Yes," said Stacey. "This is the bit that's going to take some getting your head around. D section looks for threats to our nation through organized crime, normally at the strategic level. Our job would be to gather intelligence, process what we need, and then pass it on to the police."

"What do you mean, what you need?" It wasn't clear to Mike.

"Once upon a time, organized crime in London was almost a familial tradition, passed down from father to sons. In those days, the police could easily identify each family, keep tabs on them, and make arrests as appropriate. The only people getting killed on the streets of London were the main members of the opposing crime families. Each family adhered to a code of sorts. John Tort is the last of the old-school kingpins; there are no successors. Nowadays, organized crime in London comes from overseas or from UK citizens who have based themselves overseas to shortcut supply chains. It gets complicated. For example, we have Albanian gang members in prison in the UK still running large portions of London's drug scene. These guys have been given hero status among kids in their country, so there's plenty more fresh blood coming in. They're also highly adaptable at using technology, such as encryption or other agile methods; they are, in fact, just like any legit business. I've pointed out Albanians as an example, but you can replace that country with many others, including the UK. There is no family code, though, and now innocent people are getting seduced by the quick buck, drugs are hitting communities all over the country, and most of it is coming through London. Below the high-level gangs, you have lower-level gangs that have produced a knife culture in London. We're talking about kids as young as ten and eleven being hired as drug mules. That's just drugs, Mike. The list extends to weapons, human trafficking, money laundering, and more. The illicit networks are sprawling and increasingly arduous to police, with those at the helm masquerading as regular entrepreneurs, shielded within the guise of legitimate enterprises."

"Okay, why do I feel like something is coming at me?" said Mike.

"You and your team took out the main players of a gang in about five minutes. For the police to do that, it would take weeks, but you upset the balance and put Tort under pressure, and we already know of a gang looking to pick up the pieces." Stacey was serious but changed her tone suddenly. "Then, Mike Sharpe, we reviewed what you had done. We sat down and evaluated the entire situation. The recce, you changing the plan during the raid, and then the one that really made us open our eyes: you had the balls to talk with Terry Patrick and then meet with John Tort."

Stacey looked at Oli to pass the baton.

"This is now your turn, Mike," Oli said as he adjusted his notepad. "Before we go on, we need you to answer a couple of questions. The recce—what made you come away from that with a clear picture of the Clover brothers' dynamic and, more importantly, the role Terry Patrick had in the organization? Where did Tort come into it for you?"

"Terry Patrick was agitated that night. I'm sure Andy has already debriefed you. At first, I thought it had to do with Tommy taking that beating and Terry guessing he was a professional. I knew that it would take one to know one, if that makes sense. I recognized that the Clover brothers were deferring to Tort, so the power dynamic was clear. To be honest, it wasn't until the operation at the pub that I confirmed that Terry was probably not working for the Clover brothers but for Tort or someone else. Terry and Tibbsy could have made it more difficult for us, but they held back. They wouldn't have done that if it had been Tort."

Oli nodded. "As we expected, good work. Genuinely good work. Why meet with Tort after the incident with the Clover brothers? Actually, answer that second. Why did you go off script in the pub?"

"'Off script'?"

"Sorry. You changed the plan?" said Oli.

"Simple—I suspected Andy was working for you lot and wanted to confirm it."

"Bit of a risk, Mike," said Tom.

"Only if you think I was following the planned brief."

Tom nodded.

"Cause and effect," said Mike. "I always had that plan up my sleeve."

"Sorry, Mike, I don't understand," said Oli.

"I do," said Stacey. "It could be a segue into what you'd like to propose, sir." She looked at Tom.

Tom smiled. "Okay, Stacey, it would be a good test to see if you're really in the mind of Sharpie.

Mike, this could be presumptuous of me, but I think you and I are worried about the same thing. Taking out the Clover brothers is one thing, but who will replace them was your major concern, and that was the reason you went to Tort. It wasn't just about what band of thugs took over but what that meant for the area, the locals, and those paying for protection. That's why you went to see Tort."

"Impressive," said Mike. "There was just one more thing, though, and it was the most significant from my perspective. I wanted to know what it meant for the team long term—could they walk away, would there be repercussions, that type of thing."

"And then he offered you a job . . ."

"Yes, a little unexpected but not surprising when I started piecing the story together. I did my research; the club is legit, and it could be an opportunity to get the team some well-paid work." Mike wasn't sure this would sit well with anyone in the room.

Stacey said, "Yes, it could."

"So I have a question for you," said Mike.

"Go ahead," said Stacey.

"Not for you, Stacey—for Tom." Mike turned to face his boss, and the laser eyes flickered on.

Tom smiled. "You want to get to it quickly, Mike. Some things don't change."

"How long have you had this plan in place, sir? When did you decide to sanction the Skirmishers to proceed with the Clover brothers and the pub? What are you planning now?" Mike wasn't keen on small talk, and although he was very direct, he remained polite.

Tom stood up, his tall stature making him look down on them all like a giant would look down on little people. "Very astute, and rather than let Stacey explain, I'll get right to the point. I visited Tommy in hospital because I was contacted by the army compassionate cell. I realized quickly that it was unlikely the Skirmishers would be able to walk away from Tommy's beating. Then the girl was gunned down. I called Stacey and Oli and put them together to form a small task force. I chose Oli because you know him, and Stacey because she's the head of the MI5 D section, as we already explained. We were already working together, though, on an idea." Tom rubbed his chin.

"I'll be honest—this has been a long-term issue, and I saw an opportunity to accelerate the idea and work to change the course of organized crime in London and potentially give an element of bite back to the authorities. The crime syndicates in London and throughout the UK are too sophisticated and too well organized, and the people pulling the strings are untouchable. While they remain untouchable, the expendable criminals at the lower end of these organizations are easily replaced and basically become cannon fodder. The problem is that these people are unscrupulous, and without a code, we now have a situation where, more often than not, the general public is being caught up in the mess that ensues."

"How on earth does this involve me and the team?" Mike was concerned. He knew the answer, but he also needed to hear the gravity of what he thought would be briefed.

"You and the team could make a difference, Mike. If you take the offer of working at the nightclub, the roles will naturally expand beyond the club. Tort is dead in the water at the moment, and he stands to lose Shoreditch. Go to work for him under our authority. Go be our eyes and ears. Go clean up the streets of London with official approval."

"'Official approval'?" Mike's jaw would have hit the floor had he not heard it straight from Tom.

"Yes. Any wage you're given from the club will be yours, but anytime we ask you to do something, it will be under the guise of army intelligence through MI5." Tom knew those words would take some time to sink in.

"You're telling me that an elite army unit working for a kingpin crime boss—but actually for British intelligence—is sanctioned to operate on the streets of London? I'm sorry, Tom, but that sounds like total bullshit, and we'll be hung out to dry at the first sign of something going wrong."

"Mike, this is at the highest level and sanctioned with the home secretary and select members of the Joint Intelligence Committee. The police, the London mayor, and most members of parliament will have no idea. This is a need-to-know operation."

There was a minute's silence as Mike thought about it.

"Fuck me, they're going to do this—the army policing London?"

"Let's not go there, Mike. You won't be policing, exactly," said Oli.

"*Cleaning* is the word," Stacey added.

"What guarantees can you give me that we won't end up doing time? I mean, what happens if people find out that the home secretary sanctioned this?"

"They won't. This is a national security issue. It won't be spoken about until long after we're gone," Tom said, trying to convince Mike.

"It sounds fucking off, Tom."

Stacey stood up. "Mike, I can only give you a little in the way of a guarantee that you wouldn't challenge. You'll find a hole in anything I try to say around guarantees for the team. But every time we sanction an operation, you'll be paid an army reserve SF rate that would be gold dust should you ever find yourself in court. Although you won't be in court."

"You're right—I could challenge that." Mike rubbed his forehead, his brain buzzing.

"You had a hunch about this before we snatched you. You didn't react when the squad took you. What did you think we were bringing you here for?" Stacey asked.

"I don't know, maybe to pass intelligence on or to be an informant." Mike was half telling the truth. He had guessed that the Clover brothers incident had been sanctioned. He also didn't want to talk about the conversation he and Tom had had in Afghanistan.

"Well, that's what we're asking you to do, Mike. Among other things," said Oli.

"You won't stop there; you've already said it—sanctioned missions," Mike responded, almost with an air of resignation.

"True, and it is brutal out there. I wouldn't underestimate what we're asking," Oli said seriously. "You and the team will constantly be at risk from people who have no morals or ethics. They will torture, maim, and terrify anyone who gets in their way. But you'll have a discreet intelligence unit monitoring everything to give you an edge."

Mike continued to shake his head. "For Christ's sake, how do I get the team on board with this?"

Andy stood up. "They'll do what you tell them to do, like always. They need jobs, and they'll agree to work at the club, and they also know that could be close to the line. We can both convince them that this extra work keeps them firmly on the line."

"And totally in danger. Andy, do you really believe that about the line? You know the line will disappear under this arrangement." Mike was clearly still coming to terms with what he was hearing.

"Three members of your team are already on board, Mike." Tom had switched back on with the presence of a commander.

"Who?"

"Jon, Timi, and Andy," said the colonel.

"All your picks, of course," said Mike.

"Jon and Timi have worked logistics, among other things, for me for a long time. Don't be hard on them. If Paul comes on board, the rest will follow."

"Except Steph."

Tom looked at Mike. "Ah, the burgeoning relationship."

"It's not the relationship, Tom—she wants a break from the violence. She certainly doesn't need the money." Mike was also thinking about just how much the team had been under surveillance by the people in front of him.

"Steph's family is incredibly wealthy. It was always going to happen one day, once she had got whatever it was out of her system. You can't persuade her to stay?"

"No, I really don't think so. Maybe she'll stick around for a couple of weeks at best," Mike said forlornly.

"Fuck, that's a problem, boss. Steph is the best NCO I've ever worked with," said Andy.

"She also has a business brain, which would be perfect for the club," added Oli.

Tom was staring off into space. "I'll brief the team—all of them, including Steph."

Mike looked confused.

"I started this journey with you, and I'm your commander. Having you ask them to do this is unfair. I'm sorry. I should have realized that earlier, but things have been moving quickly. Go home, Mike. Spend some time with Steph. But I need an answer from you by noon tomorrow. And I need you in the club on Friday, ready for your first mission, which perhaps will be the most important of all. I'll speak to the team this evening." It was impressive the way Tom had suddenly taken total control.

"This evening? How will you get them together so quickly?" Mike knew the colonel would move fast.

"I was on the phone to Paul before I arrived here; that's why I was late. He told me about the USB you gave him. Mike Sharpe: one step ahead of everyone." Tom smiled.

"Seems you were one step ahead of me. You knew Paul would call you."

Tom wanted to end it there. "Any questions, Mike?"

"Fucking hundreds," said Mike. "Just need to get my head around this. But what about John Tort?"

Tom smiled. "Mr. Tort is now a pawn in our game, Mike. Just a pawn."

Mike got up. "Who will be controlling us?"

"Joint Operations MI5 and MI6. Unusual, this one," said Oli.

"Where is the headquarters?"

"We'll advise you on everything once the team is ready, including the rules of engagement. And we'll spend some time with you on how to maintain a discreet presence in the London crime scene," Stacey answered.

"What?"

"You need to think like them and act like them, Mike. We'll also be providing you and the team with a regime of regular SF and intelligence training." Stacey looked at her notes to see if she had missed anything.

"Oh, and one more thing: What about DS Bec Reed? She's coming for me." Mike looked at Tom.

"If you choose to board this train, Mike, she won't be able to get near you. She'll become another pawn in the game."

Mike shook his head. *Just how high up is Tom in this organization?* he wondered.

"Get some rest, Mike. It's been a long day." It was almost an order from Tom.

Mike left the room, leaving Tom, Stacey, Andy, and Oli alone.

"He looks like he has the weight of the world on his shoulders," said Stacey.

"Agreed," added Andy.

"He's already on board," said Tom.

Oli was confused. "How did you work that one out, sir?"

"With Mike, it's about what he didn't ask. Sometimes with people, Oli, it's about what's not said rather than what's said. Clear as mud?"

Oli nodded.

"He already knew about all this, Oli. He was just waiting for our confirmation, and he's still holding back. His entire concern to date has been about cause and effect, and he now knows the answer. He was dismissive of Steph being a problem, and most importantly he wasn't inquisitive about the first mission. Had Mike been thinking about walking away, he would have asked about the first mission just to satisfy a curiosity that would have burned him up for months afterward. He also didn't challenge me when I said I would brief the team." To the others in the room, it was clear that Tom really did know Mike well.

"So we're on. Mike will send a message to Tort as soon as I've briefed the team this evening; therefore, I want the HQ fully functioning within twenty-four hours. Mike and the team are now our assets. Stacey, get in touch with Jack Holby at the Joint Intelligence Committee and tell him Op Archangel is now a go. Jack will make the necessary arrangements with the army. I'll make arrangements with our executive."

"Isn't that you?" asked Andy.

Tom smiled.

"Oh, one thing: Mike and Steph are to be left alone tonight. Keep the police off their backs."

Mike was on the balcony in his apartment, looking over London's evening skyline. He had gone for a workout in the gym, followed by a swim and a warm shower. It was now late. He was sipping a whiskey, contemplating everything that had happened in the last few hours. The missing piece of the jigsaw: Tom Sawyer, the only piece he hadn't fully understood. Not the fact he was behind it but the fact he was still in the intelligence community. Mike smiled to himself. Tom had contacted him an hour before to tell him he had briefed the team, and they were in. Mike had already been in touch with John Tort; there was no doubt the team would be on board. John was over the moon and was going to visit Mike at the club at lunchtime tomorrow to make introductions.

"There you are." Steph walked through the open patio doors onto the balcony. "Why didn't you tell me?" she asked quietly.

"I suppose I didn't really believe it myself, Steph."

"I understand the implications of what's being sanctioned are huge," she added. "Tom Sawyer is a sneaky bastard."

"To be honest, I'm slightly bewildered by it all."

"What's your greatest fear?"

"The first time we're asked to kill someone on the streets of London, how will it all hold up?"

"You mean, if there's trouble, do they throw us under the bus?" Steph already knew the answer.

"Yes."

"Two weeks," said Steph.

"Sorry?"

"I agreed to two weeks with Tom and then three months' break to get my head straight."

Mike gently held Steph's hand. "I really want to be with you, Steph . . ."

Steph put a finger to his lips and stopped him from talking. She took the whiskey and drank a mouthful. She then gently kissed him.

"Is there something wrong with the computers?" DS Bec Reed walked into the middle of the operations center at the OCD. It had been a very long day.

"No, ma'am, all fine here," came the response.

She looked at Detective Grimmer. "Can you access the files on Mike Sharpe?"

"Yes, ma'am—I mean, no, ma'am." Grimmer looked confused. He'd had them open a moment ago.

Bec raced to the office of Inspector Miles. The PA had long since gone home, but Bec dutifully knocked on the door.

"Come in," called the inspector.

Bec entered and was about to talk but noticed that the inspector was on the phone. He put a finger to his lips.

"Yes, sir, I understand," he said. "I understand, sir. We'll back off, sir. Yes, sir. Thank you, sir, and good night, sir."

He hung up.

"Wow, that must be someone of importance," said Bec. She could tell the inspector was distracted.

"Er, yes, yes. What is it, Detective Sergeant?"

Bec was surprised by the formal nature of the response. The phone call had clearly gotten to him.

"Inspector, I was just wondering whether you had cleared the warrant for me to search Mike Sharpe's apartment? Something strange has happened. All the related files have disappeared from our system."

"No, Bec," said the inspector.

"No, you mean you haven't got the warrant?"

"No, no further action on Mike Sharpe." James Miles realized that was not going to go down well.

"'No further action'?" Bec felt the hair stand up on her neck.

"It seems he and his team are now a matter of interest to national security."

"We're a special branch, sir; we should have that information," said Bec.

"Not in this case, it would seem." The inspector was firm in his response but didn't really understand himself.

"Well, at least let's request full disclosure, if required through a judge. We're supposed to be working together with these agencies, aren't we?" Bec was genuinely taken aback. "It was that phone call, wasn't it?"

"Bec, you don't understand. That wasn't just someone at the Special Intelligence Service who called me. This came from the very top."

Bec had known James Miles for years and had never seen him react this way.

"I've been working in this special branch and the OCD for many years, as you know, and I honestly thought that there couldn't be much more that would surprise me. I have no idea what your man Sharpe is into, but whatever it is, he's to be kept at arm's length for now."

"They wiped our records, sir."

Inspector Miles nodded. "I honestly don't know what to say, Bec."

Mike lay on the bed, exhausted. First, the interview with the police and then the intelligence services, all in one day. He had a new job, which had more bells and whistles attached to it than your normal everyday position. The team was now signed up to join him and would be told they were effectively back in the army reserve as well. Most concerning to Mike, though, was the world they were about to enter, of which they knew very little. He looked at the clock. It was half past midnight on Thursday morning. The last forty-eight hours had been brutal. Today was probably going to be an easier day, but tomorrow—Friday—Tom had mentioned a first mission.

"Okay, mister, you need to get some sleep." Steph gently kissed him.

"How long were you at the meeting yesterday, Steph?"

"I don't know, three or four hours of briefings. I've been told not to talk about it with you until you've seen Tort."

"Tom Sawyer playing the *authentic* line again?"

"He wants you to appear naive when you talk to Tort. Mike, these people are fucking brutal, you know."

"What do you mean?"

"Tom made the whole team aware of what life could look like in the future. These gangs are as bad as anything we've seen. Today, I was shown pictures of what some of them do when things go wrong. Images that I can't get out of my head. Torture using drills; hammers; pliers; fucking machetes, for crying out loud— and of course, knives, the most common weapon. They're also illegally moving everything that you could imagine, including humans, and then using the money in legit businesses."

"Steph, stop."

She looked at Mike and could see how exhausted he was.

"I'm sorry. I forgot what a day you had."

"My brain is buzzing."

"Back to basics it is, then." Steph smiled and got out of her clothes in the blink of an eye.

Mike smiled. "That's your answer for everything."

"You're not complaining, are you?"

He laughed. "No."

His brain did switch, though. He suddenly realized how much he would miss Steph. *Damn,* he thought. *How did Steph creep up on me?*

11

John Tort was sitting in the exact same chair he had occupied during his last visit to the Red Zone nightclub with the Clover brothers. The main difference this time was that he had Mike Sharpe and Terry Patrick flanking him, and his lawyer, Wayne Simmonds, sat opposite him. He had given Mike a tour of the club and ensured that each of the new employees was introduced to and looked after by the regular nightclub staff. Mike also met the club manager, Chris Tomlinson, who clearly had worked in the industry for many years. It was quite apparent to Mike that Chris understood the implications when a new team was suddenly brought in. It was also a no-brainer that he wanted to be involved only in the running of the nightclub and to keep his distance from Tort.

"Welcome, Mike," said Wayne as he took the last of the contracts and put them into his briefcase. "I think you'll do really well here, and the investors are pleased to have you and the team on board."

Tort laughed. "Don't worry about all that bullshit, Mike. You'll come up to speed quickly. Okay, Wayne, go get yourself a drink; I need a word with Mike."

"So, only the girl has decided not to stick around, then, Mike?" said Tort.

"Two weeks, and then she's off to travel." Mike tried not to give away his emotions.

"Sorry to hear that. She's a beautiful woman, perfect for this business. We'll keep her contract open for when she returns." Tort said this in a way that suggested he knew she meant a great deal to Mike.

"That's very kind. I'll let Steph know."

"The other girl—now I like her. The Aussie, really feisty. She's going to keep all of us on our toes."

Mike laughed. "Skippy. She'll do that."

"Now you mentioned you got pulled in by DS Reed. Everything go to plan?" Tort knew the answer but thought he should check anyway.

"Shortest interview ever. They had nothing, really." Mike knew honesty remained the best policy.

"We thought as much. I'm sure they won't follow up on their inquiries unless they find something concrete. Did you tell them about the job offer?" Tort smiled.

"Yes. They warned me off. I told them it was a legit business backed by city investors."

Tort smiled again. "Good."

Tort thought for a moment and seemed to drift off somewhere, as though he was testing himself.

"Mike, I want Terry and his small team to be your eyes and ears inside and outside the club. Although the nightclub is legit, it is under threat from scumbags who wish to move in. They won't come here, though; they'll go to the pub first. I need a favor, if you don't mind."

Mike nodded. He was surprised by how quickly the first favor had been asked. With what Tort was paying him and the team, he knew it was inevitable.

"Not at all," said Mike. "What do you need us to do?"

"Simple—go to the pub once a week. I don't care what day or days, but have a presence there. People need to know we're back in business."

"What's the threat?" Mike looked at Tort.

Tort smiled. "Clever boy. I'm not sure yet, but they'll make a move at the pub, not the club. This place might get cased, but with your people and the existing security staff, they won't risk it. They also know that any action here will impact the reward if they drove us out. Punters are fickle, Mike: they'll be gone at any sign of trouble that can't be handled."

"Where do we get our intel from?" said Mike.

Tort nodded at Terry.

"A bit like the military, Mike—from the streets. Mr. Tort is very well established on that front, and he has people on his payroll who provide intelligence. It may surprise you, but we get it from everywhere."

"Not here," said Tort, cautioning Terry not to say too much. "In time, Mike, we'll let you know how things work. That's why Terry needs to be close to you."

"Terry, I'm guessing most of these gangs are armed," said Mike.

"Some, not all. But treat everyone like they are, especially here. The pub is extremely exposed, but it's still rare for someone to use, say, a gun in broad daylight."

"Okay—my rules, though," Mike insisted.

"What do you mean?" asked Tort.

"Security, everything in relation to my team—I'm in charge."

Terry smiled. "I told you he was going to be good, sir."

Tort nodded. "We've been lacking leadership in this area for far too long. All I want to see is profit and no threat from scumbags. Do that, and the rewards are huge for you and your team. But don't underestimate what these scumbags are capable of. I'll see you soon, Mike. You have a lot to learn." Tort was abrupt but had clearly satisfied himself on what he needed.

The last thing Mike heard was Tort roaring with laughter as he was leaving. He had bumped into Skippy and they had seemed to hit it off.

"He likes you, Mike, and the team," said Terry.

"Terry, can I trust you?" Mike looked at him, eyes piercing like a laser.

"You can to a point, but remember who's paying my wages."

"I appreciate the honesty."

Mike did a final walk around the club to check on the team and then jumped into a taxi and made his way into Central London. He got on a bus for one stop and then went on to the underground. He got off one stop later and walked around the maze of the underground station. A little way up one of the corridors, he turned into a "No Entry" area, which led to a small service tunnel. He waited in the dark for five minutes to confirm he wasn't being followed and then opened a service door. In front of him was a lift, and he pressed the button for the first level. The doors closed, and he waited for thirty seconds before it moved down, not up. The doors opened, and he was met by a security officer, who took him through an area that resembled airport security. Following the secure area, he was given a pass and told to proceed to an opening within a glass tube. He got inside the tube, and it spun to seal him in and then spun again to let him out the other side.

"Mike," Stacey called out to him. "Welcome to operations."

The operations center was impressive. Mike had seen a few, and there was no doubt this was on another level. Clusters of desks that comprised different teams made up of intelligence gatherers and operators. They in turn would fit into a larger group that contained other support elements. Finally, if the field operators were about to execute a mission, there was the ability for a commander to display important aspects of the mission on a large screen that formed the focal point for the entire room, similar to the way a big screen at the movie theater immediately draws you in.

Stacey beckoned Mike away from the operations center and up a flight of stairs to a main office, which looked out over the entire room. She knocked on the door and walked in.

"Mike, come over and join us." Tom Sawyer motioned him to a seat in the middle of the table. "Team, this is Major Mike Sharpe. He and his team are our assets. To most people outside of this room, they're seen as persons of interest. Right. Let's make some introductions. Mike, you know Oli and Stacey." Mike nodded at them both. "Meet Felix Wright; he's head of operations, a former operator himself, and the person who will control your overwatch. I'll come back to that later."

Mike could tell Felix was an operator just by looking at him. Every line on his face had been etched by a moment in the field. Years of living under the sun had aged him.

"Everything in this operations center is geared toward monitoring organized crime in London and your team." Felix had a very confident tone and a crisp, clear accent. "Your team will be monitored twenty-four/seven, with eyes on them the moment they leave their apartments."

"Karina Williams wears multiple hats; she is a lawyer, a political adviser, and an MI6 operative with field experience. She will outline the rules of engagement and have direct liaison through Tom to the home secretary and our allies within the Joint Intelligence Committee."

Mike studied Karina. She looked like a businesswoman in her sharp suit, but he could tell from her build that she was capable of holding her own in a fight. Her brown eyes were mesmerizing, and she had flawless dark skin.

She smiled at Mike. "What are you thinking, Mike?" Her accent was a blend of British and African.

"Sorry, it's a habit—assessing how much of a fight you would give me if it ever came to it."

"Let's hope we don't need to find out." Karina gave him another flash of a smile and a stare that confirmed she'd seen action.

Finally, he was introduced to Rupert Brown, the technical wizard. "Rupert will support everything Andy does in the field.

He has access to every camera in London—every traffic light—and can hack most systems."

Mike looked at Rupert: long hair, reasonably fit, but clearly sat behind a desk all day. "I'm normally called Cookie," said Rupert.

Mike laughed. "With your first name, you would have been the perfect army officer, but I guess someone decided Brownie was too obvious a nickname?"

Rupert laughed. "Something like that. Original, huh?"

Tom chimed in, "Mike, we monitored your communications with John Tort; well done on that front. Do you have any questions or concerns before we proceed with the initial briefing and the first mission?"

"Just one for now: John Tort has appointed Terry Patrick as the eyes and ears for the team in terms of intelligence. I can see a couple of potential issues—one, that Terry will realize we're being monitored by you, and two, that if our team puts surveillance on him, he'll spot it."

"Terry Patrick is an important pawn in this game, Mike. He's spent enough time in the underworld for you to learn from him. He'll be an ally, as long as you don't give him any reason to get suspicious of you. In terms of him providing outside surveillance, he's smart enough to know that the police are likely to keep monitoring you. That will be your story should he pick up on it," said Stacey.

Tom looked at Mike. "We briefed your team on the world you're all entering. It's unforgiving and often brutal. Don't get taken in by Tort and his code. If he needs to, he'll pull fingernails out himself or break bones. Don't underestimate what any of these people can do. We need you to play the naive part, though. It will bolster your cover. You should appear to be learning as you go. We'll spend the next hour briefing you on Tort, his network, and his role in the overall organized crime ring in London."

Mike spent the next hour learning about John Tort's background, how he worked his way up from very little to being one of the most feared men in London. How that fear dissipated with the arrival of new, more ambitious, and, at times, brutal regimes. What really stood out for Mike, though, was that on a daily basis, a lot of unsuspecting people wouldn't know that their investments were also being backed by the profits of crime.

Stacey began the mission briefing. "So, Mike, your first mission is straightforward. We'll refer to it as Holding the Ground. You may have displaced the Clover brothers, but the vacuum you've left is attracting attention from the underworld's lower rungs. You've appeared on the radar, but as usual, within these groups, they puff themselves up before worrying about newcomers. You'll be targeted by an East End crew called the East Street Gang. This gang occasionally gets support from gangs in Kingston, Jamaica, or Eastern Europe. They're very low level, though their main focus is the distribution of drugs—and on the whole, any action you take will be considered just a blip on the radar by the larger organization. The East Street Gang will see this as an opportunity to get some proper skin in the game and impress the kingpins.

"Now, don't get me wrong: I don't want to play down the risk to you and your team. This gang will be desperate to impress and will do anything to gain the pub or the club. Both locations, as well as the extortion racket, will put them on the map. Don't forget: in your case, it's John Tort who remains the kingpin; therefore, you're still below the radar."

"How many should we expect?" Mike asked, assessing the potential threat.

"Maximum of ten," said Oli.

"And then your second mission will need to be a retaliatory strike. We'll brief you on that after the first mission. The second mission actually carries the most risk." Both Stacey and Oli emphasized this point distinctly.

"There will be around fifteen to twenty operatives on their turf," Stacey pointed out. "Your mission, Mike, is to fend them off at the pub, give them a bloody nose on their own patch, and then make sure they know who you're working for."

"They'll know Tort is behind this rather than focus on the team?" said Mike.

"Yes, they'll know Tort is behind it, but they'll need to understand where you fit in from now on," Stacey said.

"Won't this operation piss Tort off?"

"On the contrary—he'll appreciate not having to deal with the pond scum in your area."

Several pictures were highlighted on the screen before Mike, depicting the diverse members of the gang.

"Pretty diverse backgrounds," commented Mike.

"There's no time for racism or sexism out there when they're taking the risks they do each day."

"So how far do we take it?" said Mike.

"These members"—Tom pointed to five pictures—"are low level. Give them something to remember you by. These three here, I'd like you to hospitalize two of them and let this guy get away. He's influential in the community and will likely spin a story of how dangerous you are. These two are the leaders. This guy is Dom Hammond and this one is Darren Chester. Dom is the main contact with the major firms; he needs to be hospitalized but be able to talk."

Mike shook his head. "All very matter-of-fact. Tom, you really want me to decide who goes to hospital and who doesn't?"

"You're painting a picture for the future, Mike. You just need to provide the effect." Tom's tone didn't change. "Now, this guy, Darren Chester, is a total head case and a complete loose cannon. He's modeling himself on the type of gangsters you see in movies but with a total psychopathic tendency." Tom pulled up a picture on the screen of what looked like a body. Mike could hardly make out what was in the image.

"What is that?" said Mike.

"Glad you asked," said Stacey. "This is what Darren Chester did to a man who he thought had cooperated with the police on an ABH charge involving Darren. He tortured him and his wife for about an hour until he realized they knew nothing; he kept them alive, though, as a reminder to anyone who would cross him."

"He recovered?" said Mike.

"Yes, but he's suffering mentally and physically. Darren cut of his balls and tried to feed them to his wife." Stacey's emotion didn't change, as if she had briefed this many times before.

"What, are you joking? That's guerilla warfare tactics." Mike was shocked.

"No, that's the act of a psychopath, and there are plenty of them in this game," Oli said emphatically, wanting to hammer that point home.

"Holy shit. And you briefed the team on this?" Mike looked concerned.

"Yes," Tom confirmed. "You're to kill him, Mike."

Still reeling from the torture picture, it took Mike a moment to realize what Tom had just said.

"Pardon? Did you just say 'kill him'?" Mike felt his stomach turn.

"Yes. Do you have a problem with that?"

"Of course, I fucking do. Are you mad?"

"No, I'm deadly serious." Tom looked Mike straight in the eye. "Did you think this was going to be all clean, straightforward, not-get-your-hands-dirty work while living the lavish lifestyle of a TV gangster?"

"No—but state-sponsored execution, Tom?" It was Mike's turn to get serious.

"It's authorized under your rules of engagement. It was signed off on this morning by the Joint Intelligence Committee subgroup." Karina Williams's words didn't disappoint; she spoke like a military-style lawyer.

"That makes it okay, then, Karina, I guess," Mike replied sarcastically.

"Mike, the strategy for this entire operation is that you'll be a below-radar enforcer or even an above-radar kingpin. You can't get there by staying clean." Oli was also being deadly serious.

"Wait a minute—a fucking kingpin? When was that decided?" Mike asked, trying to remain calm.

Oli raised his eyebrows. "When you said yes."

"We don't care who kills Darren, but he's not to walk out alive. He's a danger to the public, and we're now operating within a sanctioned mission." It was Tom's turn to ram the point home.

"Can you hear yourself? I need to get out of here," said Mike.

"The attack on you will occur at the pub tomorrow morning at eleven a.m. It's a good job that Tort decided to renovate the pub after the attack on the Clover brothers. Rupert and Andy will equip the team; brief them over secure comms tonight. You're then to be at the club tomorrow night as promised to Tort." Tom paused to give Mike a moment to think.

"How will they know we'll be at the pub? We haven't planned that," said Mike.

"We told them you'd be there," said Stacey.

"Of course, you did." Mike stood. "Sir," he said half sarcastically to Tom.

"Good man, Sharpie." Tom gave a half grin.

After Mike left, Stacey looked at Tom, Oli, Rupert, and then Felix, who had been quiet throughout the meeting. "Thoughts?" she said.

"Felix, you wily old bastard—you managed not to say much, as usual. What do you think?" said Tom.

"I don't know where you dragged him in from, but he's perfect. A maverick with a conscience." Felix smiled.

"Agreed. That's exactly what he is," said Oli.

"We need to watch over him—all of us, no matter what," said Tom.

Tom looked them all in the eye. "Whether Mike Sharpe likes it or not, he's probably the most important asset the SIS has ever had in the field."

"Valuable, but certainly risky, considering what we're doing," Karina reminded them.

"If we succeed, we'll keep the support," Tom countered.

"A change in government would be interesting," Oli added.

Felix chuckled. "I've seen it all before. This is top priority national security—the press would be wary of reporting it, and the public would find it unbelievable. It would be suppressed before gaining any traction."

"Well, let's see what we can do to help London. It's now in our hands." Tom stood up.

Karina looked at Tom. "When we talked all those months ago, I never would have thought you'd get approval for the army to carry out sanctioned killing on the streets of London."

"The army?" Tom replied. "It's a new modern army, Karina."

Paul lay in bed next to his sleeping wife, Sarah, wide awake, his mind abuzz from the brief Mike had given the team thirty minutes earlier. Their new apartment in London, provided by Tort, was a dream compared to their past residences and income. The Secret Intelligence Service had also begun a complete security assessment of each apartment as part of the team's overwatch program. Even though the program gave them a sense of security, Paul remained concerned for their safety. He had phoned Tom Sawyer to seek reassurance and got as much as he could have hoped for, considering the circumstances.

Paul was deeply contemplating the sanctioned killing of Darren Chester. He knew what that meant in the long run and could see how this could spiral out of control. The word *pawn* had been used to describe the many members of the London underworld, but it was evident that the Skirmishers were also pawns in this grand scheme. Another concern was Mike taking the team with him while the one person who could hold him together, Steph Holgate, was leaving after the weekend. *Where the hell would that leave Mike?* he thought.

As much as his brain was buzzing, Paul compartmentalized the issues, controlled his breathing, and tried to drift into sleep.

"Your briefing tonight was concise and to the point." Steph was looking deeply into Mike's blue eyes as they lay side by side.

To Mike, the situation was straightforward: bad guys would storm the pub, there'd be a confrontation, the team would take out key gang members, Darren Chester would be eliminated, and they'd walk away, no witnesses. At the end of the day, the message to his team was not to underestimate the East Street Gang and especially not Darren Chester.

"What would you have briefed?" Mike replied.

"How the fuck are we going to get away with the assassination of a civilian?"

She had a point.

"It's the biggest test we've ever faced, Steph. But to be fair, this guy is a psycho."

"Mike, stop insulting my intelligence. It's not that low-level shit I'm worried about or even taking him off the streets—I'm more concerned about the politicians or public servants who are authorizing this. They'll throw us under the bus before any of them take the fall."

"You're right, of course, but I'm trying to put that out of my mind for now."

"There's also a real danger that we become more like Darren Chester as time goes on. If the people we work for feel they're losing control of the situation, then we're also at risk. That's why I'm walking away after this. I need to get this right in my mind. I wish you would come with me, but I realize this has given you and the team a new purpose."

"I don't want you to leave." Mike gently touched her face and traced his finger across her body.

"I know you don't, but it's what I need."

"I know. That's why I won't make it difficult for you," he reluctantly responded.

"You'll visit, though; I want you to."

"Of course. When I can."

"That's good, really good." She smiled.

"Steph, you know I've fallen for you, and letting you go will be the hardest thing I've ever done." Mike was trying to open the box marked "Emotion."

Steph took a deep breath, slightly taken aback by his confession. She was happy to hear it, but it also made her feel torn between what she wanted for herself and the potential of this relationship. She looked at Mike and kissed him. She was unsure how else to respond.

"If you want to be with me, I'll try to wait for you. I want to be with you as well."

Neither used the term *love*, but it was what they meant. Mike was torn—the first person he really had feelings for would walk out of his life in the next couple of days. It was the first real open conversation they'd had that didn't end up trailing off into nothing.

His mind momentarily drifted away from their relationship to the concerns Steph had voiced. Although only a few higher-ups knew about their unit, the potential backlash for them was enormous. Mike recognized the need to establish contingency or exit plans for the team.

"What are you thinking?" Steph asked as she looked at Mike.

"Just planning something."

Steph smiled. "Just remember who truly matters in your life, Mike, and what awaits you if you join me." She pulled back the sheet, revealing herself.

"How the hell can I forget?" he said with a smile.

<h1 style="text-align:center">12</h1>

The Eagle was undergoing renovations sanctioned by Tort, but progress was minimal. Most of the internal fittings and fixtures had been ripped out, except for the bar and the elevated area in which Mike was now sitting with Paul, Mark, and Tommy. Paul and Mike had earlier followed their tradition of sharing a nip of whiskey with a local priest to ensure the mission was blessed.

The pub's interior was concealed with thick plastic, typically used by painters and decorators, but today, it served a more clandestine purpose. The workers, informed to take a paid break, were delighted, especially after Mike's encouragement to spend time with their families.

Terry Patrick and Tibbsy had positioned themselves in their usual spot, prepared for rearguard action. Terry had alerted Mike about a potential threat to the pub. His intel matched the security service's. Mike briefed him on the procedures when the East Street Gang arrived, insisting Terry leave serious matters to the team. "If it escalates, let us handle it." Mike didn't want Terry's connection to Tort to overshadow the message being sent by him and the team.

Mike liked that Terry was a professional. He didn't question things unless he needed to and then offered an idea of how he could quietly remove two of the East Street Gang from the rear without the others being aware initially. He mentioned to Mike that if there were seven of them, they would quickly become five. Terry also cautioned Mike on Darren Chester. "He's brutal, Mike. I've heard things about him that are truly fucked up."

The team had a simple comms network in place so as not make Terry or Tibbsy suspicious. Andy had secured some electronics with Rupert that would stop any outside eavesdropping and enable Mike to hear and talk to HQ.

"You have incoming." Andy's voice buzzed over the comms.

"Sierra Alpha, this is Magic Circle: overwatch in place." Felix lit up the network.

"Roger. Out." Mike didn't know how it really worked with the discreet earpiece he had on, but he could be fed direct communications from HQ—otherwise known as Magic Circle—and it was the new but familiar voice of Felix within the ops room that was informing Mike that an overwatch team was in place.

Although the pub was closed, the front door was unlocked so that the contractors could enter and exit freely during the refurbishment. The East Street Gang wouldn't bother to do much of an intelligence sweep before entering the pub anyway, probably just a cursory check that Mike and his team were in there. To any observer, it would look like there was a lock-in bar in place, a bunch of locals who had been invited to enjoy a drink despite the pub's closure.

The front door abruptly swung open, and seven men clumsily entered, almost tripping over one another. Mike instantly deemed them as dangerous amateurs. They failed to notice Terry or Tibbsy and nearly overlooked Steph and Skippy at the bar, focusing instead on the table where Mike, Paul, Mark, and Tommy were seated.

Darren was the first to speak. "Which one of you cunts is Mike Sharpe?"

Darren stood around six feet tall and a gym junkie— probably used steroids to get the bulk he had. He was huge, but Mike figured he was slow. He had several tattoos on his pasty-white hands, which Mike had guessed formed part of a larger piece of art that would go up his entire sleeved arm. Next to him was Dom Hammond, who could have passed for a male model, probably also six feet tall but with a dark, flawless complexion that wouldn't have been out of place in men's magazines. Both were wearing designer casual clothes, and Mike had already noticed that Darren had a hammer tucked down the front of his pants.

"Who's asking?" replied Mike in a cool, disarming tone. He knew he had already thrown Dom off with it and further annoyed Darren.

"What the fuck? What do you mean, who's asking? I'm Darren Chester; we're the fucking East Street Gang, and we're moving in."

"Never heard of you, and are you sure you want to take over this place?" said Mike, looking around at the mess caused by the renovation.

Mike sensed Darren's reliance on his size to instill fear; it seemed he was accustomed to people feeling intimidated by him. This time, however, he wasn't receiving the fearful responses he usually did.

"What the fuck does that mean, man?" Dom's first words, spoken more in hesitation than anger, broke his silence.

Dom wasn't stupid; he'd seen people like Mike before. They were at the top of organizations and had almost no fear, which meant they were usually dangerous. He had already sensed that all was not what they thought it was, and he was nervous.

"Who the fuck is Mike Sharpe?" Darren pulled out the hammer.

"You're talking to him, friend," said Mike. Still seated, Mike turned until he was square on with Darren.

"I'm taking over this fucking place, so you have two choices: leave now or leave in bits." Darren had shown his hand, and Mike knew that regardless of any answer he would give, Darren would now need to send a message, and Mike and the team would be attacked regardless.

"How the fuck are you going to do that, Darren? You're outnumbered," said Mike.

"What the fuck are you on about? There are seven of us and four of you."

"Are you sure? I mean, are you really sure?" Mike stood up. "There are only five of you."

Darren turned around, as did the rest of the gang, as two of their members were knocked unconscious by Terry and Tibbsy.

"Fucking hell, bro," said Dom. "I told you this was fucked. No one messes with Tort." He was looking at Darren.

"You better get used to knowing my name, mate," said Mike.

Dom looked back at Mike. Darren's short fuse exploded, and he swung the hammer backward. Mike knew it would be brought forward onto his body. The problem with most weapons was that they almost always have a tell, especially hammers, baseball bats, and any type of club. The person holding them will move the weapon back before driving it forward. As the hammer went back, Mike moved forward, as close to Darren as possible, which in turn meant Mike moved into an area that avoids the force of the hammer and put Mike on the inside of Darren's arms, leaving his body open. In the blink of an eye, Mike blocked Darren's arm, and he was quick to follow up with an elbow to the gang leader's jaw. Darren, being a big guy, stumbled backward.

While this ensued, Skippy broke the arm and nose of the guy standing next to her, and Mark began a carefully orchestrated attack on Dom. Dom fell backward onto the floor, unsure of what had hit him. Steve Kenny then quickly dispatched the guy next to him, and Terry and Tibbsy carefully brought them toward the door. Jon and Timi took over and started moving them toward the back door, where a van was waiting.

Two of the younger guys had seen enough and made a run for it. "Let them go."

"Knife!" Paul shouted to Mike as Darren, from out of nowhere, produced a blade and slashed at Mike. Mike felt the knife gently scrape his shoulder as he moved away from Darren's reach. It was only a nick but enough to draw blood.

Darren launched again at Mike, but this time he lost the knife as another hand skillfully disarmed him and threw him slightly off-balance. Darren, in a state of rage and completely out of control, made another grab for Mike, but this time he was hit by a sledgehammer of a punch from Paul that smashed his nose across his face.

Darren's rage subsided a little. He was stunned by the blow and struggling to breathe. He felt an arm around his neck, small but tight—really tight. He then felt another blow to his stomach as Skippy delivered a roundhouse kick, removing the remaining air from his lungs. The grip around his neck tightened, and the strength in his body began to disappear.

"You're going to fucking kill him, bro." Although semi concussed, Dom's concern for his partner was urgent.

"Get him the fuck out of here," said Mike.

Jon and Timi marched Dom out the back and told him to run.

Mike looked at Steph and shook his head. She didn't need to be the one to kill Darren.

"I think he's had enough, Mike," Terry said with worry in his voice.

"You told me we need to send a message."

"Fuck me, Mike, really?" said Terry.

"They'll come back if we show leniency, and this monster needs to be off the streets."

Terry was confused; he didn't think Mike or the team would have the stomach for getting blood on their hands. "Think it through, Mike. Are you sure?"

Mike looked at Steph again. She had a tear in her eye.

"You don't have to do this, Steph."

"This is for that poor fucking guy and his wife," she whispered into Darren's ear.

Darren relaxed and began to twitch as the life ebbed out of him.

Steph released him, and he slumped to the floor.

"He's dead," said Terry, after checking for a pulse.

"We need a cleanup, Terry, quickly," Mike said with a sense of urgency.

"We can do that, Mike. We have people who can get rid of the evidence." Terry was still aghast at what just happened. "I need to tell Tort."

"It's not over, Terry," said Mike. "We'll hit them tonight on their patch."

"You guys get out of here. Let our guys take the van to the hospital." Terry was slightly in shock.

"Thanks, Terry."

"Sierra Alpha, this is Magic Circle: you're clear to leave."

Mike moved away from everyone. "Roger. Out."

A little while later, Mike received a call from Terry telling him that all was fine at the pub but that Tort would be coming to the Red Zone for a meeting that evening. He told Mike not to worry but said it had taken Tort by surprise that Chester had been killed. Mike's immediate worry wasn't Tort—or anyone else, for that matter—but Steph. He raced back to the apartment to be with her. Paul had put a couple of stitches in Mike's shoulder, which meant he was always going to arrive later than Steph. The car he was driving was given to him because of his role in the nightclub, one of the many perks. Mike knew it was a high-end BMW but had no idea what type; he just wasn't that interested in cars. He threw the keys at the valet, who greeted him with a smile. Mike told him he was in a rush and to leave the receipt with the concierge. He raced upstairs to the apartment and let himself in. He could hear the shower running.

He walked into the bathroom, which was pretty steamed up, the extraction fan fighting to remove the moisture from the air. Mike saw Steph sitting on the shower floor, legs drawn up to her chest. He joined her, fully clothed, put his arm around her, and pulled her in close. He didn't say anything but cradled her like a mother would her child.

After a little while, Steph looked at him. "The UK was my sanctuary away from the killing, Mike, and today those two worlds collided."

"You didn't have to do it, Steph. I would have done it."

"I was protecting you; he would have stabbed you had I not intervened. The anger coursing through my veins worries me."

"You were in control. You remained in control."

"I felt nothing for him, though. I just remembered the pictures from that torture scene. I felt nothing. Surely that's not right."

"He was an animal, and we took him off the streets. It doesn't matter if it's a land far away or our country—these people do not deserve to live."

"We shouldn't have the power to make that choice. That should be decided elsewhere."

"The government is fed up with dealing with these people with kid gloves, Steph. Now it's time for the gloves to come off."

Mike reached up and turned the shower off. He grabbed a towel, wrapped it around Steph, and dried her. He reached for one of the fluffy apartment gowns, put it on her, and walked her to the lounge. He picked up the phone and ordered two hot drinks to be sent up to the room.

Mike quickly got out of his wet clothes and put on a pair of jeans and a T-shirt. When he returned, he saw that Steph was on the phone. "See you tonight, darling." She hung up.

"Who was that?"

"Skippy."

"All okay?"

"She called, told me to stop sulking, complimented me on a hell of a move, and told me we would have a drink tonight at the club, in secret." Steph half smiled.

"You're okay with that?" Mike was slightly confused.

"Skippy knows me well," Steph said as she looked into the distance.

The mood had changed again suddenly. Mike felt it.

"Tomorrow is my last day, Mike. I need to leave." It was a statement of fact.

Mike said nothing and kissed her.

Tom Sawyer sat at the head of the ops room table. Like all meeting rooms, it had VIDCON capabilities but little else.

"Felix, what's the initial word from ops?"

"Textbook, clean mission. They're good; the ops team was impressed." Felix himself was impressed.

"And evidence?" Tom asked.

"No evidence. The body went within the hour," Felix said, like it was a normal occurrence.

"Oli, Stacey—intelligence?" Tom was methodical in his questions.

"Network chatter is high, considering we're talking about an event that's barely a few hours old. Starting with Tort, he's secretly impressed with Mike but will give him a dressing down for Chester's death. Terry Patrick remained balanced but seems a little concerned now that he's seen what the team is capable of . . ." Stacey's voice trailed off.

"What about within the wider underworld?" Tom pressed.

"Dom Hammond went straight to a middle-ranking Eastern European, Slovan Melick. Slovan has informed his bosses and sent a message to a low-level Jamaican gangster, Devon Smith. The reason he'd go to the Jamaicans is that they're distributing drugs through the East Street Gang—or rather, *were*." Oli had a keen interest in Jamaican influence.

"The news is spreading wider about the fact Tort appears to have gained a strong arm again. This will get back to other kingpins. A fortified Tort has its pros and cons for them, considering their aspirations to control Tort's London infrastructure..." Stacey emphasized.

"Rupert, anything from you?" said Tom.

"No, um—well, yes. I'm worried about the planned follow-up mission we're conducting on the estate out of which the East Street Gang operates. It's a maze and full of places that will put the team at risk."

"Noted, but it has to go down. Mike needs to put a stamp of authority on London." Tom was looking into the distance as he said the words; he was already thinking about the overall strategy. "These two first missions may be the most important in helping us achieving our overall goal."

"We're rushing them," said Rupert.

"After tonight we'll take a short break," Tom assured, his tone somewhat unconvincing.

"So you're really leaving us, Steph?" Skippy looked concerned as she gazed at her friend. Steph had been there throughout her tour with the Skirmishers. They prided themselves on serving in an elite unit that valued their capabilities over their gender. They had never had an issue with the team, only with outsiders looking in.

The subtle rhythm of the nightclub music permeated the meeting room they occupied in Mike's new office.

"I have to get out of this environment, Skippy. I need a break and to find some peace."

"I get it, but things are starting to look good for us— the job, Mike and you, Tommy and me."

"I know, I know. And Mike is trying his best to not make this difficult for me, but I can see it in his eyes that he wants me here with him."

"How long are you going to go for?" Skippy asked, always to the point.

"Indefinitely."

"You're not coming back?"

"I don't know, Skippy. I really don't know."

"Does Mike know this might be one-way?"

"I don't think so, but I'll let him know where I'm going and that he can visit anytime."

"Fuck, he'll take that hard, mate." Skippy knew her boss well.

"You need to keep an eye out for him. For me." Steph touched Skippy's arm.

"Of course." Skippy looked away.

Steph put an arm around her friend. "Glass of champagne?"

Skippy was still feeling sad but made sure she lit up for the invitation. "Fuck yeah."

John Tort studied Mike intently. "Why kill Chester?"

"We needed to send a strong message; otherwise every gang will try to challenge us," Mike said calmly.

"Dead bodies are a messy business, Mike. From now on, I sanction it unless you need to protect yourselves." Tort was serious.

"Okay. What about the estate this evening?"

"Ram home the message, but be careful. It's a dangerous place you're entering. This message needs to be verbal only, Mike—a show of force that you're not worried about going into other peoples' areas if they come into ours uninvited." Tort had seen it all before. "You and your team did well, but just remember that to keep you out of jail, the organization needs to know who and where, when it comes to dealing with people. I'll need to see you and Terry tomorrow for a debrief."

Mike shook his head. "I can't tomorrow, Mr. Tort."

"Oh, sorry, I forgot," replied Tort, genuinely concerned. "The young lady, Steph, is leaving?"

"Yes. I need to take her to the airport."

"No problem. Terry can debrief me."

Tort walked up to Mike and hugged him; Mike wasn't expecting the embrace, and it felt slightly awkward. "We support each other, Mike, just like any other business, and tomorrow will be a tough day for you. Just letting you know I'm here for you."

Knock, knock.

Steph and Skippy turned towards the meeting room door.

"Come in!" Skippy called out. "Busted!" She laughed when she recognized John Tort.

Tort smiled. "Young ladies, please don't worry. May I join you?"

"Of course," said Steph.

"I understand you're leaving us tomorrow—sorry, Steph, isn't it?"

Steph nodded. "Yes to both."

"Please forgive me, Lisa and Steph. I'm an old man from another generation, and what I'm about to say is likely not the right thing nowadays: two beautiful girls like you, and both as deadly as you are beautiful, it's something I don't think I'll ever get used to." Tort sighed. "And, Steph, you're leaving us tomorrow, after taking a monster off our streets today. The world should be thanking you, my dear. Anyway, I didn't want to leave tonight without seeing you again and letting you know that you have a place here as my business manager anytime you want it. Your credentials are impressive, and I'll keep my current manager in place until you return." Tort made sure that Steph realized the offer was genuine.

"I'm not sure that will ever happen," said Steph. "I have a lot to think about."

"Then go off and find yourself, but make sure you come back to us when the time is right." Tort gently touched Steph on the hand, as if to reassure her.

Steph smiled. "Thank you."

Tort held Steph's other hand as well. "Sheer beauty. I'm getting too old. Good luck, my dear."

He turned and looked at Skippy. "Are you going to be okay, young Lisa?"

"Yes, sir," said Skippy.

Tort laughed. "You're not in the army now. Maybe one day you can get used to calling me John."

"Or Dad." Skippy laughed nervously; it had slipped out.

Tort stopped in his tracks. He turned to look at Skippy and then roared with laughter. After he left the room, a member of his entourage approached Skippy. "Don't push it."

Steph looked him in the eyes. "Fuck off, or I'll break your nose."

Steph and Skippy both laughed.

"We're clear," Mike affirmed, standing with Paul atop the Red Zone nightclub.

A burst of radio static buzzed in their ears before being replaced by a crystal-clear tone. It was like activating the noise-canceling feature on high-end headphones.

"Clear," came Andy's response. "Connecting you now."

"Sierra Alpha, this is Magic 1: Radio check. Over," came Rupert's now-familiar voice.

"Loud and clear. Over," Mike responded.

"Loud and clear also. Stand by for Magic Circle."

"Roger. Over."

Felix immediately erupted onto the comms network. His first words were to tell Mike to ditch radio procedure for the briefing and treat it more like a conference call. This was alien to both Mike and Paul, who would keep slipping back into normal radio procedure.

Felix went on to explain the reason for the mission, the overall strategy, and the fact that it was all about the personal message they would send to the East Street Gang, which would also start a chain of events around London's organized crime syndicates.

The East Street Gang was on the lowest rung of the organized crime ladder but was ready to take a significant step up in the hierarchy, possibly backed by Jamaican or Eastern European gangs. The aim of the mission was simple: to send a warning to the East Street Gang that any aspirations they had in rising through the ranks would not be at John Tort's expense. More importantly, it also sent a message to those farther up the chain that Tort was still in control and still relevant. And it would serve as an introduction to Tort's new Shoreditch team.

Mike detected Felix's anxiety surrounding this mission; he described their adversaries as "amateurish," contrasting it with a palpable respect for the estate's chaotic structure and its youthful, knife-wielding inhabitants serving as sentries. Paul shared concerns about the hasty, seemingly improvised planning, and its implications on the team's safety. Mike, sharing the concern, appreciated Felix's candid insights.

Tom Sawyer soon interjected, "I understand your apprehensions, gentlemen, but unpredictability is inherent in your new environment. Let's not forget, we are poised to offer overwatch and aerial support should things deteriorate significantly. Paul, your concerns are duly noted, but we must advance undeterred and establish our intent firmly."

Mike looked at Paul and gave a wry smile.

Felix informed them that the SUVs, courtesy of Tort, were now equipped with military-grade gear. "Terry Patrick has delivered your weapons—all sanctioned by the home office. You have lightweight Kevlar capable of withstanding knife attacks and

9mm rounds from a distance. Avoid conspicuous gear; subtlety is paramount."

The briefing lasted about forty-five minutes, which gave Mike and Paul little time to brief in the team. Tibbsy and Timi would not be joining them, as they would continue to oversee the security teams working the nightclub. This was especially important, as the nightclub might be vulnerable without the team present for an hour or two. The club would also be used as the main alibi if anything went wrong during this mission; in effect, from a monitoring perspective, the team would be at the club.

Steph and Tommy would be the drivers for the evening, remaining with the vehicles at all times and acting as emergency backup if anything went wrong. Like most of the team, they had been trained in defensive driving, which could prove useful if they needed a quick escape. Because Tommy and Steph were staying with the vehicles, they would be obvious targets for the teenage gangs on the estate. They would need to keep their wits about them, as they could be quickly overrun.

Mike summed up the briefing to the team: Essentially, seven of them would enter the building and would need to remain close to one another. He further informed Terry that he had a couple of old mates providing some other cover for the team and that they could be trusted. It was the only way Mike could think of explaining away any support they may need from the overwatch without breaking cover.

Terry seemed to be relaxed about this but pointed out to Mike that Tort could have helped.

Terry then took over the last part of the briefing, explaining that the firm had its headquarters on the top floor of the building. Almost all the flats in that part of the estate were empty, and they had done a lot of work to create a safe environment there that reflected their status but that also provided them with a secure sanctuary. The fact that it was away from prying eyes might serve them well.

"Remember, our diversion on this one is simple: We're going to knock on the front door," said Mike, almost smiling. "We'll be invited up, but we need to ensure we can get out."

"Won't they just shoot us?" said Steve.

"You'd think so, but no. They'll want to know what we want first. Sounds strange, I know, but effectively this is a kingpin—Tort—visiting people after they overstepped the line. They'll have weapons drawn and be ready for a fight, but in reality, they'll also be licking their wounds over Darren Chester's killing," said Terry.

"Will they want revenge?" Tommy asked.

"They won't want bloodshed, if they can avoid it," said Terry. "They'll know the repercussions for messing with Tort."

"Okay, get kitted up. The pistols are all Glocks, seventeen rounds. The vests will stop a knife as well as a 9mm bullet at range. Close up, though, it won't stop a round," Paul said.

"Team," Mike said, "I know the prep for this is not ideal, and where we're going means that any plan will almost certainly change. I don't want any contact, if possible—react only if you're set upon or your life is in danger. Questions?"

13

London's night traffic was as bustling as ever, cars creating a ceaseless trail, each following the next as if sheep to a pen. The team split into two SUVs, with Mike, Terry, Mark, and Tommy in one, and Paul, Jon, Skippy, Steve, and Steph in the other. Tommy and Steph navigated efficiently through the traffic, and the stoplights seemed to favor them as they approached their destination.

The Cowling Estate was fast becoming a relic, hastily erected in the 1950s and 1960s to replace war-damaged housing. It was initially a short-term solution that morphed into a long-term one, lacking in design features that promoted safe and communal living. The initial families moved out, leaving a space that should have been bulldozed and rebuilt. Instead, it attracted nefarious landlords and individuals, making it a dangerous and despondent place, especially for the youth drawn into crime or addiction. It was a hard area to grow up in and a tough one to leave.

Some of the Skirmishers had experienced life on similar estates, opting for military careers as escapes from their environments. But the Cowling Estate was worse, a labyrinthine complex where every turn seemed identical and perilous, especially for outsiders.

Andy's familiar voice broke across the network. "Good evening, everyone. Your overwatch is in place." Andy had tried to dispense with radio protocol, but the team knew it wouldn't last long. He did it more for Terry than for the team.

"We can hear you," Mike replied.

"Lots of movement on the estate; groups of teens are about. They're called apprentices, otherwise known as foot soldiers, so be careful."

Terry took a deep breath. He, like the rest of the team, knew this mission could be fucked from the start. "I don't like this, Mike," he said.

"I know, Terry, but we really do need to send this message or we'll be dealing with this at the club or the pub. We need to restore the hierarchy. We need to ensure Tort is the main kingpin."

Terry's mobile burst to life. He answered. "What the fuck," he said. "Okay, we'll be there in five minutes."

"What's going on?" Mike was concerned.

"Tort is here. He's meeting with them."

Mike smiled. *Of course. I should have seen this coming,* he thought. Tort wanted to be there to deliver a message personally.

"Tort got intelligence some major players would be here tonight," Terry added.

"Surprised he didn't bring his enforcer along." Mike looked at Terry.

"He knows we're coming," responded Terry. "And besides, I'm not his only protection."

Mike sent a quick text message. All call signs: Tort is on the estate. I'm guessing we can expect more than the East Street Gang when we show up.

In the control center, Felix was rapidly briefing the ops team, as well as Tom, Stacey, and Karina.

"This was already a risky mission." Felix's briefing style was concise, direct, and calm. "How the fuck did we miss this?" He looked down, thought for a second, then looked up. "We need to activate the immediate reaction team, launch the air asset, and throw a net around the area—no police."

Felix's words were also being patched to Mike and Paul, who were both listening in.

"I would recommend that Sierra Alpha and Sierra 1 carry on the mission as planned. The likelihood is that Tort's presence was expected, and he took the risk, as he holds the upper hand because of his knowledge and ownership of the London supply chain. If there's an audacious attempt to overthrow him this evening, we can expect a massacre. Sierra Alpha and Sierra 1 need to be prepared and ready for a full-blown firefight."

Tom Sawyer stared into the distance. He was processing the situation and working through several potential outcomes. He looked at Felix. "Agreed. Move ahead as planned. This might actually work out better than I'd hoped."

Felix was slightly surprised by the optimism.

"Ensure the medivac team is on high alert." Tom wanted it ready to react to any issue.

He then turned to Karina. "Inform the home secretary that we need level five rules of engagement for this mission."

Karina looked at Tom. "So soon? It'll draw the crabs."

"Yes, it will, but this might just cement Tort's standing while accelerating Sierra Alpha's within the London organized crime community." Tom was still deep in thought.

"Okay, the home secretary is already awaiting my call." Karina looked at Tom.

"Sierra Alpha, we'll be switching to level five ROE. Switch camera on, and we'll identify targets as required," Tom said, letting Mike know he had their back.

Mike tapped his throat microphone once in response.

"Sierra Alpha," said Tom, "Operation Becker is a go—the one we spoke about previously."

Paul heard the final words from Tom. *What was that about?* he thought. *Operation Becker, that was the previous mission's name. What on earth are Sharpie and Tom up to?*

"Sierra Alpha, all call signs." Mike was now deadly focused. "We're clear to go. When we arrive, open the boot of the car and take an additional weapon. You're to follow my orders carefully, as I give them. If there are a loss of comms, we pull back. If I go down, Sierra 1 will resume command and pull you all back. If Sierra 1 goes down, you are to return to the vehicles and EVAC immediately."

As they entered the estate, Andy provided coordinates to a secluded, poorly lit area on the estate's perimeter. This would allow the team to exit the vehicles, grab the weapons, and enter the complex maze of corridors dotted with identical front doors, largely unseen. The vehicles would then relocate to a more illuminated rendezvous point where Tort's vehicles were stationed.

As the team exited the SUVs, they felt the cool night air hit them. Despite the unseasonably pleasant weather, the crispness of the night air was a harbinger of the approaching winter.

"MP7s," Paul remarked as he slung the weapon from the boot, pointing out the Heckler and Koch firearm. He was surprised that they were being given a submachine gun to conduct the mission.

"Terry, you need to stick to my orders," Mike said in a tone that made clear he was telling him, not asking him.

"Roger that," Terry responded, almost like he was back in the Foreign Legion.

Although their suits made them stand out, they entered the building without encountering anyone. Most of the estate's youth were drawn to Tort's SUVs, a distraction that benefitted Mike and the infiltration team during entry, but could pose complications during exfiltration. This would especially trouble Steph and Tommy, who were to stay with the vehicles.

"We have clear passage," whispered Terry to Mike. "Tort has forewarned them we're coming."

"Roger that. Stay sharp, Terry. We've been dicked already." Mike looked up. Terry followed Mike's gaze and spotted a shadow trying to move stealthily through a corridor above them.

"Nice catch," Terry said.

"I hope this isn't a fucking trap," Paul whispered into the mic.

"If I were them, I'd be the one worried," Mike said, trying to reassure Paul.

They continued to make their way up the staircase to the seventh floor. Andy was guiding them in, and Terry was confirming each direction from memory, having been there before.

"Okay, it's now a turn to the right and then the last door facing us at the end of the corridor," said Terry. "There's a security camera at the start of the corridor. They'll invite us down or ambush us. As we proceed, any door on the right could burst open."

"Sitting ducks," said Mike. He looked at Paul and then Mark. "Change of plan—Mark, you take command of the team while Paul, Terry, and I go inside. We want to limit the potential for all of us being taken out. Mark, I want a potential distraction or distractions."

Mark nodded. "Roger that, boss."

"If you hear 'Becker,' create chaos." Mike winked.

Steve smirked. "Bring the storm."

Back in the ops room, Felix looked at Tom. Tom didn't have to say anything; he just nodded.

Felix got onto the network and informed overwatch of the change in plans. "Watch and observe. Do not engage."

Mike heard the message and took it that all was okay with the plan.

Terry looked at Mike. "One final suggestion: We need to get rid of the HKs. The three of us will look like we're intent on bloodshed if we walk in with these."

Mike pondered for a moment, but it was Felix who made the decision. "Listen to him, Sierra Alpha. He can be trusted."

Mike looked up. "Agreed. Good point."

"Take these, Mark, as well." Mike handed over his weapon, and the others followed.

The three of them waited for the others to leave and then turned the corner.

Steph and Tommy had pulled up behind Tort's two vehicles, each guarded by two men.

A gang of kids had mostly surrounded the guards, who seemed undisturbed.

They both alighted and assumed positions by the driver's side doors, mirroring Tort's men.

"What the fuck do we have here?" one of the older boys said. He was about nineteen, which Steph thought probably made him the oldest.

Two of Tort's men walked over to Steph's vehicle; Tommy approached the rear of her SUV.

"You're with us, I take it," said one of the men.

"Sort of," said Steph.

"Well, darling, if these kids bother you, then let us know and we'll save your pretty little arse."

Tommy let out a sigh. He was wondering whether Steph was going to react.

"It's okay," Steph replied. "If I need saving, I'll be sure to ask you."

The older boy walked up to Steph; Tommy moved slightly farther forward.

"Think you might need saving from me, do you?"

"No," replied Steph.

"You should be fucking scared, lady," the boy said, trying to intimidate her.

Tommy moved closer still.

"It's okay, Tommy. Don't worry, this kid is just trying to impress his mates." Steph knew it might escalate the situation, but her aim was to defuse this quickly, one way or the other—and besides, the kid wasn't much younger than her.

"Fucking impress my mates—you need to have more respect, bitch."

"You need to earn that," said Steph as she worked to slow her heartbeat.

The other boys moved their attention away from Tort's men toward Steph.

"Fucking respect. You know how I get respect? This is how I get respect." He pulled out a knife.

"Put it away," said Steph, now slowing her breathing.

"Give me one reason why I shouldn't stick you."

"By the time that knife gets close to me, I will have broken your wrist and probably your nose." Steph was now calm but very focused.

"Are you fucking hearing this bitch?" He looked at the lads behind him but was slightly unsure of himself.

"Stick her, Lenny," said one of the boys.

"Yeah, fucking do it," said another.

Tort's men were slowly moving in. Tommy put his hand up as if to tell them to stand back.

Felix and Tom were listening in, as Andy had patched them through.

"Don't go too hard on him, Sierra 5," came Tom's familiar voice through Steph's earpiece.

Steph smiled at the kid called Lenny.

"Why the fuck are you smiling?" said Lenny.

"My boss doesn't want me to go hard on you." Steph saw fear creep into Lenny's eyes.

"Fucking stick the bitch!" one of the boys shouted loudly.

Lenny lunged. Before he realized, pain shot through his wrist, twisted and broken by Steph, followed by a painful blow to his face. He felt dizzy and fell to the ground.

Steph had hardly moved. She just stood there and put the knife in her pocket. The other group of lads were in shock. "Why don't you all go home and get to bed?" said Steph. "Take Lenny with you."

"Why the fuck should we listen to you?" said one of the braver boys.

"Defuse the situation. Show them a weapon or something," said Felix.

Tommy walked up to them. "Piss off, lads, or I'll get her to break all your arms."

"Who the fuck are you, jock twat?" said another of the boys.

"Now, now, boys," said Tommy. Steph almost smirked, as Tommy really didn't look that much older than them. "Don't make me introduce you to my German friend, Herr Koch."

Steph stifled a laugh, struggling to keep her composure.

"What fucking German? Who the fuck is Herr Koch?"

Tommy skillfully pulled around the HK MP7 submachine gun and pointed it at the group.

He could swear one of the lads pissed himself.

"Fuck, we don't want that sort of heat," one of the boys said.

"Go home, and don't fucking tell anyone, or we'll come after you," Tommy said with authority.

The lads began to disperse.

Steph looked at Tort's men. "Were you guys wanting to say something?"

"Er, no, no—er, sorry," replied the one who had walked up to Steph when they'd first arrived.

"Well done, Sierra 3." Tom sent a quick burst on the radio to Tommy. "You managed to make us all laugh."

Terry took point, Paul was in the middle, and Mike was watching the rear as they entered the corridor. They didn't have weapons drawn, but they were within very easy reach.

"Stop there." The voice came from a speaker above the camera at the very start of the hallway. "Are you armed?"

"What do you think?" replied Terry.

"We don't want any bloodshed. Mr. Tort is here, and you can speak to him."

"Terry, Mike, Paul—come on down. We're having a very interesting discussion in here. Come meet one of the other kingpins, Mike." It was Tort's familiar voice.

It all seemed relaxed, but the three highly trained men were hypervigilant as they made their way down the corridor. As they got closer to the door, it opened slowly, and a man in a suit walked out, unarmed. It was one of Tort's men, and Terry immediately recognized him. He nodded at Terry and walked toward him.

"You can go in. The tension is high; keep your fucking wits about you," he said. "They'll want your weapons."

"They're not fucking getting them," Paul and Mike said together, but they kept the Glocks holstered.

"Sierra Alpha, Sierra 6: we have company up here." Mark had led the team to the roof.

Mike whispered quietly, "On my mark, Sierra 6."

Mike, Paul, and Terry made their way into a large room. Mike was approached by a guy who was around six feet tall and sporting well-established dreadlocks. "Gimme your weapons, man." He sounded like he was of Caribbean descent.

Mike looked at Tort and shook his head.

"Mike won't do anything in this room without my approval; you have my guarantee. Let's not take their weapons away, considering your men are still carrying, Jimmy."

Jimmy smiled. "Still got the smarts, I see, John. It's so rare to see you in the field nowadays."

While the introductions were made, Felix was monitoring the miniature cameras hidden in the buttonholes of the teams' designer jackets.

Stacey recognized Jimmy first. "Fuck, that's Jimmy Grant. He's a kingpin—and the guy next to him, Uri Kiselyov, is Russian." She looked at Tom. "Priority targets, both of them.

Jimmy hasn't surfaced for years, and Uri is the right-hand man of Oliver Ivanov, another kingpin. This could be a takeover attempt. Sierra Alpha, be ready. The only reason those two would be seen on this estate is if something big needs to be discussed." Mike listened intently to Stacey but didn't say anything or even flinch.

"It's probably the reason Tort made a hasty decision to turn up," added Stacey.

"Looks like eight targets in the room in total," Felix said.

"Mike, Jimmy and Uri have made me a very interesting proposition following the events of the last few days and your run-in with Darren Chester this morning," said Tort. "They've offered to buy me out and let us walk away. *Retire* is the word they used."

"Why would they offer that without the other kingpins present?" said Mike.

"Smart boy," said Tort, his voice raised.

"Where are the other firms, Jimmy? Are they on board with this idea? Where is Oliver, Uri? Does he agree with this little coup?"

Mike looked at Jimmy and Uri; he didn't need to hear an answer. He knew that this was an opportunity for two firms to take over and move Tort aside, one way or another.

"It's time to move on, John," said Jimmy. "You're out of touch. Go and enjoy your retirement. We'll even let this cunt leave alive." Jimmy was looking at Mike.

"How will that arrangement go down with the other kingpins, Jimmy?" said Mike.

"Who said you could fucking talk to me? Your boss is the only one I'm talking to. You're lucky we didn't cut your throat when you walked in," said Jimmy.

"Answer the man," said Tort, much to Jimmy's disgust.

"We'll go to them after we take over. Everything will be the same, just different, more powerful owners."

"They're happy with that, I'm sure," said Mike sarcastically.

Jimmy was getting agitated; he wasn't used to being disrespected in front of his men. Tort looked at Mike and smiled as if he didn't have a care in the world. Mike realized quickly that Tort had lived in this world for most of his life, so everything was pretty circumspect in relation to the situation.

"You've convinced yourself that the other kingpins are going to be okay with a takeover? You'll start a war on the streets of London." Tort's voice was calm.

Uri looked up. "My boss is on board. He'll be pleased."

"Who said you could talk with me, Uri? Your boss is the only person I'll talk to," Tort said, repeating Jimmy's words to Mike, much to Jimmy and Uri's aggravation.

"I'll give him a call now," said Tort.

Uri looked at Jimmy like a deer caught in the headlights.

"No one is phoning anyone," said Jimmy. It was clear at this point that his boss, Oliver, wasn't aware of the situation.

Tort looked at Mike and Terry in such a way as to acknowledge that this was not exactly the best situation to be in. "So, gentlemen, where to from here?"

"Like I said, you give us what we want, you walk away—but he'll limp away." Jimmy looked at Mike.

"And if we don't obey, how will that go down? You'll need time to take over the London infrastructure and supply chain," Tort said, as if he was at a business meeting.

"We have our ways," said Jimmy.

"What if we decide to stay and fight?" said Mike.

"If you don't die in this room, you'll die on the estate. You're outnumbered," said Jimmy.

"The East Street Gang? C'mon," said Mike.

"No," said Jimmy. "My guys are on the estate, as are a few Russians."

"I see," said Mike, trying not to give anything away. He knew the ops room would light up at that news.

"For you, my friend, you'll have five minutes with Dom before walking out of the room."

Mike had spotted Dom Hammond from the East Street Gang on the way in.

"I don't think Dom has the stomach for that," said Mike.

Jimmy looked into Mike's eyes. He had seen the expression before; he knew the man in front of him was dangerous.

"This is getting tedious, Jimmy," said Tort. "I think it's time for us to go."

"You're not going anywhere, old man." Tort was forced into his seat by one of Jimmy's henchmen.

"Get your hands off me," Tort said but quickly waved off his two guards from doing anything.

"You're fucked, old man," said Jimmy. "We're taking over. I'm only letting you go out of respect for what you've done throughout the years."

"Hand over the plans to your operation, ensure a seamless transition, and retire, John," said Uri.

Mike chuckled.

"What are you laughing at?" Uri snapped.

"This is an interesting situation, possibly a stalemate—reminds me of something that happened a few years ago to a friend of mine," said Mike.

"What are you talking about?" Uri was even more agitated.

"Well, kill us, and you have three to six months of supply chain issues and possibly a gang war, and you may eventually get the spoils. Let us walk away, and you'll probably just have a gang war to contend with. Doesn't matter what you do—you'll struggle to have total control, and not being in control of a life-or-death situation sucks." Mike looked at Paul. "Reminds me of that five minutes when we had no control over the situation with Tony Becker."

Mark heard it, the name *Becker*, and his voice came on the radio. "Five minutes. Roger."

Paul looked at Mike. "Bit of a stalemate, that one: fucked if you do, fucked if you don't."

Terry looked at them both and could feel the adrenaline running in his veins. *Fuck,* he thought. *These two are going to do something.*

Tort shared a knowing look at Mike before addressing Jimmy. "It's okay, Mike. Remember the last conversation we had . . ." He paused. "It's all sanctioned." He continued to smile at Jimmy while talking to Mike.

"You're going to hand it all over to us?" said Jimmy, confused by the smile.

Tort stared into the distance. "I knew your mum, Jimmy," he said.

In the operations room, Felix and the team were working feverishly to ensure they had everything in place. Felix knew that, with the rising tension, this was about to get messy.

"Overwatch, await the distraction—minutes three." Felix was also feeling the adrenaline.

"Roger that."

"IRT, stand by." Felix remained calm as he issued the orders.

"Roger that."

"Sierra Alpha, this is Archangel." Tom was talking to Mike directly. "Operation Becker, stand by."

Tom looked at Karina. "Rules of engagement confirmed level five?"

"For the record, you have permission to engage using rules of engagement level five," Karina responded.

"Sierra Alpha, Archangel: in your own time, carry on; priority targets first." Tom was clear and concise.

"Sierra Alpha and Sierra 6, this is Sierra 7: we're at minutes one." Andy was now calling for Mike, who clearly could not give orders.

"Sierra 6: you have the call when needed." Andy had to hand over the final call to Mark, who would start the chain of events with Skippy, Steve and Jon.

Tort carried on, telling Jimmy the story of his mother.

"Are you stalling, John?" Jimmy was bemused.

"Sierra 6, Sierra 7: thirty seconds." Andy kept the countdown going for Mark.

Mike maneuvered slightly but not enough to cause alarm.

"Ten seconds." Andy knew Mark would soon take over.

On the roof, Mark looked at his watch and across at the men he was observing. Steve had one of them in his sights. He was a few meters ahead of Mark and hidden by a dark spot away from the lights but close enough to take him out.

Skippy was going to cause the main distraction, as she had found a gas cylinder that she was going to shoot at from a distance.

Mark had also positioned two small IEDs to ensure there would be a loud explosion.

Jon would take out everything else.

Mike looked at Jimmy and Uri. "What happened to respecting your fucking elders?" This took the whole room by surprise but was enough of a distraction to make everyone turn to Mike.

What followed would have been missed in the blink of an eye.

Mark's voice came on the radio: "All units, stand by. *Go, go, go.*" Mark's three simple words unleashed the team.

Skippy and Steve fired at the same time with single well-aimed shots. Steve watched his target fall, and Skippy watched the cylinder, which she decided must have been acetylene, explode like a bomb. It was a good thing she had sought cover, otherwise she would have been taken out. Jon opened up with a short burst as confusion reigned, killing at least two targets.

All the windows shattered around Tort and his two bodyguards as they fell to the floor in an almost intentional action.

Jimmy and Uri had shut their eyes and lowered their heads in a natural reaction to the blast. They had no time to look up; Mike had already pulled his pistol and double-tapped two rounds into their heads. Paul turned and instantly took out two of Jimmy's men. Terry was caught unaware of what was going on but quickly regained his senses. He ran to Tort and made sure he was protected and not in the line of sight.

"Sierra Alpha, Overwatch: You have incoming. Numbers: Twelve; all armed and two floors below you.

Sierra 6 is clearing upstairs."

Mark looked at Steve and Jon. "Get down there and try to hold them off. Skippy and I will finish up here."

Although Mike had heard the radio, he was dealing with the confusion in the room. In his mind, he knew four targets were down, but they had more to deal with. He looked around to get his bearings as the dust cloud that had formed from the windows started to disperse. He spotted one of the four remaining targets already on the floor—either Paul had shot him or he was unfortunate enough to be too close to the window when it blew in and had been cut down. Mike sensed another two shots in quick succession; Paul had emptied rounds into the body to make sure he was dead and then took another target out, which had appeared out of a darkened corner of the room. Mike then heard two more shots, this time from his side of the room. He responded with a double tap, hitting one target, and then shot toward where another muzzle flash suddenly lit the room. Dom Hammond felt a bullet rip through his shoulder and fell to the floor. He didn't want to die and so dropped the weapon. He did so in the knowledge that he was sure he had hit the big man who was covering John Tort.

Bec Reed was urging the armed response team to drive faster. She had been in the OCD ops room when the report of an explosion and gunfire on the Cowling Estate came through. She already had guessed it must be the East Street Gang, John Tort, and Mike Sharpe. She was slightly annoyed that her inspector had raced to join her in the vehicle. The blue lights were screaming with urgency as they got closer to the estate, and she could make out the glow of a small fire like a beacon on the roof of one of the apartment buildings in the distance.

"Roadblock ahead, ma'am," said the pursuit driver.

"What the fuck?" said Bec.

They came to a screeching halt.

"Who's in charge here?" shouted Reed, agitated.

A figure walked toward her. Bec realized she wasn't a police officer.

"I am," said the woman.

"I'm DS Bec Reed of the OCD. I have jurisdiction here. Let me through."

"Sorry, DS Reed. Orders have come down from on high. This is a covert operation."

Bec was about to argue when she heard Inspector Miles call out, "Bec, back in the car, please."

Bec quickly looked around, resigned to the fact that she had no other option.

"What the hell is going on, James?" Bec said, dropping his title.

"This is way too big, Bec. I honestly don't know, but I'm guessing that it's not a mission involving a police unit."

"Have we really just lost the streets to the military?"

"I'm sorry. I really don't know," replied James Miles, who was also concerned about what was happening.

"Man down!" Paul shouted to Mike.

Mike kicked Dom in the head, knocking him out instantly. He looked over at Paul, who was trying to treat Terry; he'd somehow taken a round through the Kevlar vest he was wearing that left an entry wound into his lung.

"Stabilize. I'll cover," said Mike.

"He needs medical help urgently," said Paul.

"Magic Circle, Sierra Alpha: I need a sitrep from the other call signs and a medivac. Room secure this location, one in custody."

Mike raced across to Dom and quickly put plastic cuffs on his hands and feet, then diligently covered the door.

Felix rapidly conducted an all-call signs check. Mark and Skippy had cleared the roof. Andy was still monitoring twelve targets two floors below who seemed to be hesitating, probably because of the sounds of sirens in the distance and the fact they had started taking some incoming from Steve and Jon.

"All call signs, this is Magic Circle: We have targets two floors below Sierra Alpha. We need them to disperse."

"What about an extract from the roof?" said Paul to Mike.

"We would have to leave Terry behind," answered Mike. "And it's risky. It's too far, and besides, we'd have trouble moving him. We'd leave the helicopter exposed. This all may come down to how willing they are to get arrested."

"What?" said Paul.

"Magic Circle, Sierra Alpha: let the police through to the inner cordon and tell them to have sirens on."

"Sierra Alpha, Archangel: stand by." Tom took over.

Mike looked at Paul, who was now working hard to stabilize Terry's chest wound.

They read each other's minds. *What is Tom up to?*

"Overwatch, this is Archangel: Targets, fifth-floor corridor. Take out two only."

"Roger that," came the response.

Jon heard the call, and he and Steve moved back into the cover of the stairwell.

"Overwatch, Archangel: targets down."

"Roger," Tom said.

Andy quickly came on the radio. "Sierra Alpha, Sierra 7: targets rapidly leaving."

"Just how much support do we have out here?" Paul said to Mike. "Snipers?"

"I think I've underestimated how big this operation is," said Mike. "Tom seems to have a lot of firepower at his disposal."

"All call signs, Magic Circle: Extract by vehicle. You'll be given ten minutes before the police get through the cordon."

"Sierra Alpha, Magic Circle: aeromed, minutes five, inbound."

"All call signs, Sierra Alpha: extract now," Mike said with urgency.

Mike looked at Paul. "That includes you and Tort."

"What about you?" said Paul.

"I'll be okay. Go, man, go," said Mike.

Tort was lying face down on the floor, as he'd been instructed to do. Paul grabbed him like a rag doll and bolted through the door.

Steph and Tommy were positioned beside their vehicles, engines running. They instructed Tort's men to leave, and surprisingly they obeyed, probably for fear of being arrested, but no doubt because they knew that Tom and Steph were professionals; they were ready to provide cover as the team moved to extract.

Slowly, the team began to emerge. Gunfire suddenly erupted from a lower-floor balcony. It wasn't well aimed but would eventually be on the team. Steph and Tommy opened up with the MP7 to provide covering fire. Figures slowly started to emerge from the shadows—first Mark and his team and then Paul and Tort a couple of minutes later. As the two drivers entered their vehicles, Tort and Paul provided covering fire from their SUVS. Before long, though, they exited the estate.

"All call signs: Vehicles exiting. Let them out of the inner cordon." Felix was watching the timing very carefully.

The team had been instructed to go north; the inner and outer cordon had been ordered to let them through.

Bec Reed was south of the estate, waiting in the rapid response vehicle by the inner cordon. She watched as the same woman she'd met before walked over to her vehicle.

"DS Reed, you may proceed to the estate. You have ten men in custody to collect."

"Ten men? On what charges?"

"I don't know. I'm sure you'll think of something," she replied.

Mike felt Terry's pulse; it was weak but okay. Terry had lost a lot of blood, but Paul had done a good job of patching the wound and making sure he was positioned in a way so that his good lung wouldn't fill with fluid. The door flew open. "Overwatch, Becker," came the call.

"Sierra Alpha," said Mike.

The first soldier took off his balaclava and smiled at Mike. It was one of the same men who had taken him off the street in London.

"Good to see you, Mike. Don't worry, we'll take care of him and get him extracted." With that, he grabbed Mike's arm and smiled at him, then proceeded to cuff him.

Mike smiled. "Not again."

"Boss's orders. DS Reed will be here soon, and you're to be one of those taken into custody. I'm guessing it'll look to the Russian and Jamaican mobs that you got lifted as well."

"Archangel, Overwatch: Sierra Alpha in custody."

"Roger. Strip him of weapons and comms. Take him out to the others," Tom said matter-of-factly.

"Sierra Alpha: Say nothing to the police. You will not be in custody for long," Tom reassured Mike.

"Roger. Out."

It wasn't long before Mike was taken down to the ground floor. He heard the helicopter lift off soon afterward and the approaching police sirens. He looked around at the ten men who were cuffed alongside him. He figured four were Russian and six were Jamaican. They all looked at him with little idea of the part he'd played in all this.

14

Felix was absorbed in coordinating the ops recovery. Knowing the building was secluded and largely isolated from the residents, he focused on ensuring minimal footage of the operation reached the press. Mobile phone signals in the area were jammed, and Wi-Fi was disabled. Door-to-door inquiries were being conducted by officers identifying themselves as police, seeking any mobile phone footage. Any found would be discreetly corrupted, and all network activity would be monitored once services were restored. While not foolproof, these measures were effective. Felix also instituted a no-fly zone to prevent press from approaching the explosion site. He estimated he had about an hour left to manage the situation before actual police inquiries began. Allowing DS Reed through first was strategic, as her attention would be occupied by the arrests.

"How confident are you that she'll realize that Mike's arrest is part of the show?" Felix said rather casually to Tom.

"She's a smart, ambitious woman. Reed will have far too many questions about what the hell went down but will know that the chances of Mike actually being charged are almost zero. She'll cotton on very quickly."

"And if she doesn't?" said Felix.

"Then we have James Miles." Tom smiled.

"The inspector knows?" Felix should have realized his boss would have it covered.

"He knows enough."

Bec Reed, surveying the scene, felt bewildered. She noticed they were the first on the scene and that all men in cuffs were known criminals, except for Mike Sharpe, who was deliberately avoiding eye contact. She walked over to where Inspector Miles was talking to a balaclava-clad soldier. Realizing he wasn't a police officer, she whispered, "Who authorized the military to operate in London?"

"We'll talk about it later, Bec," said Inspector Miles.

"Okay. So when can we bring our people in to take over?" Bec wanted to get control of the situation.

"We're almost done here," came the response from the soldier. "Be thorough in your inquiries, Inspector," he added.

With those words Bec knew that the police would find only what this unit wanted them to find.

The soldier looked at her. "Would you like to come with me? I have something to show you."

Bec was taken upstairs to the seventh-floor office of the East Street Gang. Even with all her years in the force, she hadn't witnessed a scene like it. The cool air from the broken windows created an ambiance that seemed out of place given the sheer carnage in the room. She looked at Inspector Miles, who had just joined her. Nothing was said; it was almost like they had both come to the same conclusion that answers would be a long way off, maybe never available.

Bec looked at the two bodies slumped across the table at the front of the room.

"Holy shit, that's Jimmy Grant and Uri Kiselov." She hadn't meant to say it out loud; it was a subconscious reaction.

She turned to Dom Hammond. "Who did this, Dom?"

"I ain't talking to anyone," Dom responded. In reality, he was still coming round from being unconscious. He also knew that his life was in danger now that Tort was showing his teeth again. No matter what happened, you never grassed on anyone—it was the code he had been brought up to follow.

Bec also knew that Dom, like the rest of them, wouldn't talk. They would either do their time or have some hotshot lawyers get them off on a technicality. Mike Sharpe, however, was going to be an interesting player in all this. She had already guessed that it was a complete charade that he was in cuffs with the others. Someone like Mike wouldn't get caught, and if his team was involved, they wouldn't leave him behind.

Exiting the room with Inspector Miles, she stayed clear of the escorting soldiers. She discreetly noted to Miles that another injured person had been in the room. "I'm guessing that was why a helicopter landed on the roof," Miles said.

"Once our people move in, I want to take Mike Sharpe with us, separately from the rest."

"They're going to take him, you know."

"I know, but I'll have a few minutes with him."

"Do you really think he'll say anything?"

"Who knows? Probably not." Bec sighed. "These past few days have been surreal."

In the ops room, Felix was briefing Tom. "The team is back at the club; all their gear has been taken away and is en route for disposal. The SUVs are now at another secure location. Terry is in a special wing of the Royal Hospital in London; our people are looking after him. He's stable and doing well. The final part of the mission is to ensure Mike never reaches a police station. We'll set up another roadblock." He hesitated for a second. "It's our driver in the police car." Felix had the look of a cat who had gotten the cream.

"He'll take a route that means they'll have to go through the roadblock, which is comprised of just a routine road maintenance crew. To the public it will appear to be like any other roadworks. The driver will play his part and pretend he knows nothing."

"What about the Cowling Estate? Any collateral?" said Tom.

"Not really. The East Street Gang chose the derelict part of the estate for a reason. It meant that you had to be really nosy to know what was going on in that particular block of flats. Aside from multiple 999 calls, there appears to be little knowledge of what happened. We've handed everything over to the police, and they're now dealing with the press using our headlines."

"Are they buying the gangland feud tagline?" Tom smiled.

"They're suspicious, but I guess, yes. At the end of the day, our story will sell newspapers or get them the social media clicks they're after." Felix hated modern journalism.

"Okay, Felix, after you spring Mike, leave Bec Reed and James Miles to me."

"Yes, sir."

"The team did well tonight, Felix, but let's ensure in the future we never conduct a mission on such short notice again."

Felix looked at Tom curiously. "Isn't that your call, sir?"

Tom gave him a smile and a wink. "Until next time, Felix."

Mike Sharpe was sitting in the rear seat of the SUV. Next to him was Bec Reed. He could sense she had arranged this, aiming to snatch a few off-the-record minutes with him.

"What the hell have you got yourself into, Mike?" she said. "By the looks of things, unless you have a guardian angel, you're up for a number of charges relating to organized crime."

Mike was tired and really didn't want to engage.

"Why have you been left behind?" Bec added, "Aren't you worried that you've been betrayed?"

To be fair to Bec, he did think for a second that he could be hung out to dry by being left behind. However, he knew the bigger picture, and he had to be taken from the scene in a police car, or suspicions would be raised with the rest of the gang.

"Fucking roadworks," said the driver.

"You have your blue lights on. Tell them to wave you through," Inspector Miles instructed.

"One of the workers is approaching us." The driver pressed the button on his door, and the window silently glided down. "You need to let us through, mate. Can't you see it's an emergency?"

"Sorry, we have a gas leak," came the response. "You drive through, and it may go off."

"But you just let those other vehicles through—"

The driver couldn't finish his sentence. He held his breath as he waited for the smoke canister to come through the window. As the commotion began, he unlocked the car doors, and suddenly they were all flung open from the outside.

Mike looked at Bec. "Guardian angel," he said.

Once Mike was safely away from the vehicle, the three police officers who now had sacks over their heads were stood up and walked back to the police car. "Keep those bags over your heads or we'll shoot you," said someone from outside the vehicle.

Inspector Miles, Bec Reed, and the driver sat in the vehicle for what felt like an age but was probably ten minutes. To add to the pretense, it was the driver who agitated first, and he knew ten minutes was considered a luxury by the soldiers. "I'm going to take this hood off," he said.

"No," said the inspector.

"It's awfully quiet out there," said Bec.

She removed the hood. "Fuck. Take your hoods off. They've all gone."

"Car's dead," said the driver.

Their radio burst into life. "Foxtrot Romeo, could you please get Tango Oscar to return to base? He has a visitor in his office."

Inspector Miles looked at Bec Reed. "Of course, I do."

It didn't take longer than thirty minutes for Miles and Reed to get the car working and then head back to the OCD HQ and into the inspector's office. Already waiting for them there were Stacey Simpson and Tom Sawyer.

"Can we help you—" Bec stopped midsentence. "MI5. I should have known."

Inspector Miles immediately showed deference to the man in the room. "Sir," he said.

Bec didn't know him but could tell immediately that he was obviously working well above their pay grade. Her boss rarely showed that much respect to one individual.

"Stacey," said Bec, holding out her hand as a courtesy. She turned to face Tom. "I don't think I know you."

"No, you don't," said Tom, not giving his name.

Tom looked at DS Reed and the inspector carefully. He knew that he was in a no-win situation, but he needed them to at least be partly onside.

"It seems we've witnessed the buildup and then the climax of an organized crime gang war in record time," said Tom.

"Or rather seen a potential drawn-out power struggle in the organized crime community snuffed out in record time," said Stacey.

"Cut the bullshit and spin," said Bec. "You orchestrated this."

"I don't see it that way," Tom explained. "We've all shared concerns over John Tort's waning influence in London, the surge in teenage gang-related fatalities, and the potential of such conflicts spilling over, risking innocent lives in the ensuing chaos."

Tom turned to Bec. "Wasn't it you who said to Mike Sharpe that these people are untouchable? Maybe the events of the last few days have put an element of doubt into their minds on that assumption."

"The police are here to protect the public; it's not the military's job. Military involvement on the streets of London is a dangerous precedent," said Bec.

Tom smiled. "The only military in London are those working with the counterterrorism teams." Tom knew he was telling a half-truth, but he wasn't prepared to open up any further.

"Mike Sharpe was leading a mission tonight," said Bec. "I had him in custody."

"No, you didn't," said Stacey.

Bec was smart enough to know that this was not a conversation that would end well for her.

"You have in custody the members of an organized crime syndicate, the protagonists are unknown, you arrested one of Tort's men, but he was released, as you had no evidence of his involvement. You think he may have been unlucky to have gotten caught up in it all as it was going down. The brave work by the OCD meant countless lives were saved, and London is a safer place. Sadly, though, despite the best efforts of the OCD, they couldn't get in quick enough to stop many members of the East Street Gang, and others, from being killed as the gang-related violence ensued. As a result of your excellent work, Bec, you will be promoted to inspector and lead a new OCD task force. Miles will be promoted to chief inspector." Stacey paused and waited for the dust to settle.

Bec was taken aback. *Wow, a promotion,* was her first thought, something she didn't think was going to happen. *Effectively being silenced,* was her second.

"I'm not comfortable with this," said Bec.

"Good," said Tom. "Remain uncomfortable. We're not asking you to do anything different."

"Except turn a blind eye."

"Or you can look at it like you, the OCD, might actually be able to have some teeth and make a change." Tom's tone was gentle.

"You have some control back, Bec," added Stacey.

Bec glanced at her boss. She knew he was already on board, a pawn in this game.

Inspector Miles—Chief Inspector Miles—looked at Bec. "We've never had this level of support sanctioned from the very top, Bec. We have a guarantee from now on that we'll have an element of notice if . . ." Miles thought for a second. "If whoever they are will be involved in anything that crosses into OCD territory."

"In fact, we fully expect that, in time, you'll be calling us," said Tom.

"But Mike Sharpe is destined to be a kingpin one day, after all this," said Bec.

Tom smiled. "Mike Sharpe runs a nightclub, Bec. He might think that we want him to be a kingpin, but we have other plans for his talents."

"God help him," said Bec.

"Maybe even he can't," replied Stacey. "So do you accept the promotion and a role that will see you head up a new OCD task force under the chief inspector?"

"I take it you won't give me time to think about it," said Bec.

"Actually, we'll need you to sign the contract now and sign the Official Secrets Act again," said Stacey.

Bec looked through the contract, which was exactly the same as her last one but with a new schedule on the end. "Wait a minute—are you sure?"

"Pardon?" said Stacey.

"The salary," said Bec, somewhat stunned.

"You're leading up a special task force, in a special role within the police. You and the chief inspector's taskmasters want you outside of police salary banding. Your role is unusual; therefore, it comes with unusual conditions." Stacey smiled.

After a short while, Bec signed.

"Good, and just remember, Bec, your day-to-day orders come through the chief inspector. But on the rare occasion when my people are involved, make sure you follow those orders to the letter." Tom made sure she understood.

"What about Mike Sharpe and the team? Do I investigate them?"

Tom smiled. "You have nothing to investigate. Why waste your time?"

Stacey looked at the OCD officers. "Just remember what you've both signed, too. It's all need to know. If you breach the Official Secrets Act, you'll never work again . . . if you're not in prison."

Tom once again used his most disarming smile. "Welcome, Bec."

"I didn't catch your name," said Bec.

Tom smiled. "No, you didn't. They call me Tom, but must people use my nickname."

"What's that?" said Bec.

Tom laughed. "Sir."

After Tom left, Bec turned to the newly appointed chief inspector. She was trying to reconcile in her mind what she had just signed up for.

"I know what you're thinking," said Miles.

"What have we done?" said Bec.

"Maybe you should look at it differently. The scales have always been balanced in the favor of those who commit crime. Maybe today things tipped just slightly in our favor."

"Or maybe today things got just a little more complicated," said Bec, still trying to reconcile the right and wrong of what this really meant. "Well, maybe it's better to be on the inside and have a voice than on the outside."

"Maybe," said Miles, deep in thought.

15

Mike surveyed the valley beneath him. The familiar landscape of the Brecon Beacons was totally visible today, a welcome anomaly for the season. Despite the chill, the morning was pleasant, although he was aware of the weather's fickleness. He traversed the ridgeline, relying on a traditional map and compass for navigation, until he reached his intended destination.

There, enjoying a coffee, was the familiar figure of Tom Sawyer. Mike smiled to himself, knowing Tom would have arrived early to observe those on the trail, just like him. Today, they seemed to be alone. There were a few hardened hikers on the route, but nothing like a busy weekend during the tourist months.

It had been two months since the events at the Cowling Estate, and Mike and Tom, as planned, had ensured that running a successful nightclub was the sole focus for the Skirmishers. Although there had been tit-for-tat reprisals in other parts of the gangland network, Tort had come out of the whole episode in a very strong position. Mike had played the plan to the letter, laying a solid foundation for success, and was more than ready for this meeting.

Tom looked up and smiled at his friend and colleague. Tom held up a metal box, and Mike dutifully took out his switched-off mobile phone and placed it in the box next to Tom's devices.

As soon as the box shut, Mike quickly joked with Tom about overhead satellites. Tom, in his deadpan way, said that coverage was at its worst for the next hour. Mike let out a whistle, unsure whether Tom was joking or not.

"You must have a few questions for me, Mike, but I'm guessing most were answered in Afghanistan?" Tom said, starting the discussion.

Mike thought back to that last day in Afghanistan when Tom had said, *"We have much to discuss over a drink later,"* words that had been spoken in front of Captain Stevens. If only Stevens had known where that conversation was going to go.

In Tom's office, Mike listened as Tom laid out potential futures for the Skirmishers, emphasizing the travesty of wasting young talents when numerous issues needed addressing, both at home and globally. Tom had been insistent that there would be roles for him and the team but urged patience and open-mindedness regarding opportunities. Mike had emphasized the need for financial stability, to which Tom had acknowledged, promising clarity on potential opportunities by Mike's army departure.

Mike was jolted back to the present, involuntarily shaking his head as he contemplated subsequent events.

"Did you really plan it this way?" Mike looked carefully at Tom.

"Yes and no. Honestly, we were struggling to understand how we were going to make it work, with risk being the biggest factor. Organized crime was one of the many priorities we thought you and the team could help with. The problem was deciding what objective had the highest priority, what we actually wanted you to do—and combining that with the overall risk of operating a unit like this, it started proving to be too much. I thought we were dead in the water before we began. Then Tommy walked into that pub."

"Please tell me you didn't arrange what happened to Tommy?" Mike's eyes tore like a laser through Tom.

"Give me some credit, Mike. No, of course not, but it was a hell of a trigger. The pub was under our surveillance." Tom seemed surprised by the coincidence.

"Terry?" said Mike.

"Very astute. I guess that must have been obvious after a while."

"He's very good—but yes, I also realized he called the ambulance, not the girl."

"He *is* very good, and he was wearing a wire that day for Tort while he was with the Clover brothers, which actually meant he was on a wire for us. I didn't want you to know about him, as I feared everything was already moving far too quickly, which could inadvertently lead to his cover being blown."

"Don't you think Tort already knows?" said Mike.

"Tort is a pawn. Let's just leave it at that."

"So, what went down in the pub triggered everything that followed. How did you get the go-ahead?"

"Terry was the one who called Emergency Services for Tommy. He took a huge risk and hit his panic button, which led to the activation of an incident response team. We intercepted the girl's call, but it played out as if she called Emergency Services. Tommy was still in danger, but Terry handled that situation well. You knew this, though." Tom felt he was going over old ground.

"Yes, I had guessed, but it's a hell of a coincidence that Tommy happened to set up a meeting through a dating app in a pub that was under your surveillance."

"You're one suspicious individual, Sharpie."

"So, when did you realize that this was the trigger for your Skirmishers option?" said Mike.

"As soon as I knew it was Tommy, it was simple from that point. I held a Joint Intelligence Committee meeting the next morning and warned them it might unfold whether we liked it or not. The Skirmishers would act, so why not with our blessing? I visited Tommy in hospital, and I knew he wasn't the first civilian to be caught up in the collateral of gang-related issues, and that was the impetus for the meeting. I also emphasized that, thanks to his advanced training, Tommy was fortunate to escape the encounter relatively unscathed."

"So you had pushback?"

"Yes, but not as you might imagine. I'll get to that later. Question for you, though, Mike: When did you start suspecting that this might be related to our discussions in Afghanistan?"

Mike sighed. "I nearly contacted you when it happened, but once I knew you had been to see Tommy, I left it alone. I knew you would be monitoring. It started with being frustrated that the police were unable to do anything—then, of course, Andy seemingly getting comms equipment that's difficult to obtain, if you know what I mean, and him acting strange. There were so many coincidences, and I soon realized that if it was you pulling the strings, you would need to take me off the streets—and you did. Though I still don't believe it, and at times you may think I was acting cool, noting the conversation we had in Afghanistan, but seriously, even I didn't realize the level you were working at."

"There's a reason you're leading this, Mike. You handle things well and are always prepared to challenge, to a point. You ask questions of people when they need asking or otherwise you keep your thoughts to yourself. For example, Terry, Tort, and so forth. This makes you stand out from the rest." Tom was genuine in his response.

"You didn't answer the question on pushback from the Joint Intelligence Committee," Mike prompted.

"This is the crux of this meeting, Mike, so listen carefully."

Tom explained that the idea around the Skirmishers was not a new one in the intelligence community. "The SAS were used regularly at the sharp end of a lot of covert operations that were above the normal type of work carried out by the police; however, they were an already overworked Special Forces unit that really couldn't be embedded undercover long term, and with that came limitations. So, the plan was to create a unit for discreet missions, determined by a list of priorities that were important to national security interests. The primary discussion, still ongoing among a select few in the Joint Intelligence Committee, was the concern that the unit might become mired exclusively in organized crime. The objective was to avoid annexing Tort's empire and sparking an inevitable gang war. The desire was to devise a strategy enabling us to deploy you across a variety of missions addressing a range of intelligence needs. We did start out with the plan for you to become a kingpin but have ended up being satisfied with you being a nightclub manager, where your external profile can be handled without raising your head too far above the parapet. That was the compromise we made, after you sealed a reputation in the organized crime community. Hence, the reason why you were all to go quiet and let rumors do the rest. It worked—no one has dared talk about Tort or the club for the last few weeks. The events are becoming a distant memory but also enough of an urban legend that people fear the consequences of challenging Tort again. The nightclub now provides effective cover, allowing discrete involvement in organized crime and availability for various missions as needed. Most importantly, we are fully operational and ready. I'm sorry that we were on the back foot most of the time during this mission, but we were still setting things up when the chain of events began. Hopefully that gives some reassurance about Tommy. If we had planned it, we would have been better prepared."

It seemed plausible to Mike, but he always had a healthy suspicion. "Did the girl, Rachel, need to die?"

Tom didn't answer and instead let one of his legendary pauses linger.

"So what's next?" said Mike, filling the silent void.

"Well, whatever comes next, you'll be briefed in a proper operational environment. Continue running the nightclub and keep your head down. Ensure the team meets their training objectives.

Keep them sharp, Sharpie." Tom chuckled. "You must be ready for anything, including short-notice immediate reaction missions. You have my permission to brief the team on this, and they must understand the consequences of any leaks." Tom's seriousness prompted Mike not to contest.

Tom pulled out a hip flask. "Quick nip, Mike?"

"Why not?"

The mood lightened as they recalled the number of times Tom had offered a whiskey to Mike over the years.

"So how do we keep a conversation like this going away from modern surveillance?" Mike asked, getting to more practical matters. "There will be times when we need to debrief separately from everyone else, noting this is a unique arrangement."

"Contact me through the recall process. It has the heaviest encryption I know."

"Are you sure?"

"Army intel is still penetration testing it, and so far they've been very unsuccessful," said Tom with a smile. "We'll use remote spots like this. I'm often invited out to watch military exercises."

"Selection?" said Mike.

Tom laughed. "Not today. Besides, it would be too nice a day for those looking to get into the regiment. No one has that sort of luck."

"I know that other military units and Special Forces are operating in nonmilitary settings. How do we avoid a blue-on-blue?" Mike asked.

"Great question. Our operations may be concealed, but we have precedence if it's our mission. Whatever we do, we'll establish an op code word that the team must use if challenged by someone else in authority. If they're on a mission, they'll have a code word that will enable them to be left alone. That said, they will also have a code word that they can use while not on a mission or if they need the authorities to carry out their normal duties." Tom looked at Mike, who had already understood the need for this approach.

Using a generic code word would allow entities like the police to continue their standard procedures, such as a stop and search, before releasing them. This would give the illusion of routine activity, as if they were ordinary civilians.

"Good plan," said Mike. "So, a generic password. . . just in case I get caught speeding on the way home." He smiled.

"Stick with *Becker.* The team will never forget that one."

"Roger that."

"Okay, that's time up. Sorry, Mike."

"I understand."

"You go back over Pen y Fan and down via the Storey Arms car park."

"Roger that."

Tom stood and faced Mike. "The girl, Rachel. Who said she was killed?"

Mike felt the hackles on his neck rise. One of the reasons the mission went ahead was because Rachel was presumed dead.

"You can call me a bastard if you want, but we had intel. I'm your archangel, Mike." Tom knew that Mike probably wanted to hit him.

Mike thought better of responding.

"Oh, and one more thing, Sharpie."

"Yes?" Mike was slightly annoyed.

"Take some time off." Tom's tone changed.

"Time off?" Mike looked puzzled.

"Go and see her."

"Steph?" Mike knew Tom had read him well.

"Who else?"

"She needs space." Mike looked genuine but knew Tom would see through it.

"No, she needs you, you fool. Sometimes I wonder if I've made the right choice." Tom raised his eyebrows and smiled. "And besides, you and the team need her more than you think."

Mike knew those words were true.

"She won't wait forever, Mike. Someone as attractive as Steph on a millionaire's resort in Jamaica is going to get a lot of attention."

"I'm concerned about leaving the team."

"Paul has got the team, Mike. What's holding you back?"

"I'm not sure."

"Then what have you got to lose? Speak soon, my friend," said Tom. "Remember, Jamaica."

As Mike walked toward his car, he heard the distant sound of a helicopter. *Don't tell me he flew in,* Mike thought.

Mike pondered the conversation carefully. He now realized how ad hoc everything had been and, more importantly, how slightly haphazard. It was good news for the team, though, as the nightclub meant legit work—and very well paying, at that—and the unit appeared to have the support to carry out other sanctioned missions. *This seemed to make it even more legitimate.* Mike smiled at his thoughts. *Legitimate. What does that even mean? What on earth will we be asked to do next?*

EPILOGUE

The sun was beating down on the pure white sand, which somehow added to the richness of the exclusive beach. The resort was an extension of a millionaires' row of houses that faced the private beachfront. Each home was allocated its own area of the beach, but it was encouraged by the resort that those worshipping the sun to get that all important tan chose the more communal sunbathing area. This would allow the endless stream of waiters and waitresses to fuel their clientele.

Steph Holgate was lying on her stomach, bikini top undone to achieve a line-free tan. She was reading a book and occasionally sipping from a bright-red cocktail placed at her side. She reached for the drink and grabbed her phone to check for messages. She looked up through her sunglasses into the glare of the sun, as someone had created a shadow across her body.

"May I join you?" came a European accent, one she recognized from the previous evening.

"I would rather be left alone, if that's okay," replied Steph, slightly frustrated by the guy's persistence.

"A woman of your beauty shouldn't be left alone."

It wasn't that Steph wasn't interested. From memory, he was an attractive older man. He'd made his money through a tech start-up and was loaded. He had invited her onto his yacht, but she had convinced herself that she wasn't looking for a relationship.

"That may be so, but you're out of luck, mister. I want to be left alone."

"Maybe I can rub some lotion on your back?"

"Touch me, and I'll break your fingers," said Steph, half joking.

He laughed. "If you change your mind, you know where to find me."

Fuck, Steph thought to herself. The downtime had been great—reading, sitting in the sun, and yoga. Then, over the last few weeks, she had added running, boxing, and martial arts as well as the tanning and drinking. Hitting the punching bag or working out with fellow martial artists had given her the greatest mental break. However, she also had other needs, and she was starting to think seriously about taking the guy up on his offer.

Steph looked at her phone again. She had a text message from Skippy. Call me soon or I'll put you over my knee x.

Steph laughed and dialed Skippy's number.

"Hello, beautiful." Steph smiled at the sound of Skippy's voice.

"Hello, gorgeous. How are you?"

"Fuck, Steph, you've been gone three months. I miss you. How do you think I am?"

"Stop it," said Steph. "You'll make me tear up. Besides, how is the gorgeous Scottish guy?"

"He's great. I'm training him well, but he's always like a dog in heat." Steph could hear an expletive being thrown back to Skippy by Tommy in the background.

"Stop swearing, you dag, or you're not getting any," Skippy shouted back at Tommy.

"So how is the club going?" said Steph.

"I can't say too much on the phone, but all is going well. The team is doing a great job. Paul is the king of security, and Steve is having a field day looking after VIPs. Who would have known that they all like his boyish charm? He's in his element."

"What about the others? Mr. Tort and all that?"

"You won't believe it, Steph. I'm like his long-lost daughter. I started calling him Dad. It was fucking hilarious the first time I said it, as you should have seen the look on his bodyguards' faces. One of them tried to have a quiet word with me, and I threatened to break his arm if he approached me again. The old man now hugs me like a daughter when I see him! Told me his family moved on years ago."

Steph roared with laughter. "I was there when that first happened. Sounds like you're enjoying it, mate."

"Jeez, so you were. I forgot about that. It seems like it was ages ago. This situation is great, Steph. It's sort of like being in the army again." Skippy kept up the pretense that they were out and not on technical reserve service.

"How's Mike?"

Skippy paused. She knew that question was coming.

"He's okay. He's taken to the club like a duck to water. Well, maybe not the business side. He needed you for that. But fucking hell, the guests are mesmerized by him, women throwing themselves at him." Skippy paused. "But he's not interested, you know."

"It's okay, Skippy. I've not heard from him much since I left."

"He's really busy. I can't say too much, but he had it coming at him from all quarters. It's settling down now, though."

"I said it's okay, Skippy," Steph reassured her again.

"I guess I just wanted to see you two to work out. Anyway, shagged any millionaires yet?" Skippy changed the subject and was as blunt as usual.

"Lisa Carter, you are incorrigible."

"Well?"

"Two minutes before you texted, I was talking with a guy who's been trying to shag me since I got here. He just offered to apply my suntan lotion." Steph laughed.

"What's holding you back?" Skippy joined in the laughter.

"I'm not that kind of girl, Skippy." She paused. "I guess Mike . . ." Steph was trying to be honest.

"I'm telling you, Steph, he's missing you. Why don't you come home? You know the job is waiting for you."

"I think I need more time, Skippy. I need more time." Steph was almost trying to convince herself.

"I'm here for you, girlfriend, anytime, and who knows what might happen in the future."

"I appreciate that, and I know you're there for me."

"Right, girlfriend. I gotta go. Need to keep this boy of mine in line and satisfied." Skippy laughed.

"Love you, Skippy."

"Love you, too, Steph."

Steph hung up, put the mobile down, and turned onto her back, removing her untied bikini top completely. She took a sip of the cocktail through the straw. Even though she was wearing sunglasses, she had to squint to protect her eyes from the strong rays. She could feel the sun on her chest and the cool breeze gently tickle her nipples.

She thought about how happy Skippy sounded and how the team appeared to be getting it all together. *Should I go back? Should I call Mike, maybe Paul? Fuck. Why is everything so confusing? Here I am, lying on one of the most beautiful beaches in the world, and I'm thinking about London.*

Steph felt the sudden cool air across her body as once again the sun seemed to disappear, like when the shadow cast by a cloud had made the sun's strength lessen. *Fuck, he's persistent,* she thought, as she realized that there hadn't been a cloud in the sky. She looked up to her right as she made out the shape of a man that was clearly not the guy who had been there earlier. This one was taller and broader but difficult to make out, as he had the sun almost behind him.

He threw the towel onto the lounger next to her. He was wearing a brimmed hat and sunglasses. *What the fuck?* she thought to herself.

"Excuse me, this is a private area. This chair is assigned to my family. There are loads of other places to sit on this beach." Steph felt a little privileged with that comment but wanted some privacy.

The man ignored her and carried on with what he was doing.

For fuck's sake, Steph thought to herself. *This is all I need.* She thought about covering up her exposed breasts.

"Oi, do you speak English?" said Steph, now irritated.

The guy looked over.

"I'm talking to you." Steph was firm and direct but knew it sounded rude. "I'm sorry, but this spot is taken," she said, trying to lower her tone.

"Nice tits," came the response.

Steph looked down at her breasts and then grabbed the towel and covered herself. "What the fuck did you just say? Getting a good view, are you?"

"Not really. I've seen them before."

"What are you doing, staring at—" Steph stopped. She felt her heart beat faster, and she could feel her body tingling, her breathing coming shallower. Her eyes adjusted.

"Mike?"

Mike Sharpe took off his oversized brimmed hat and sunglasses. "It was a shit disguise," he said.

"What the fuck are you doing here?" said Steph, almost laughing, almost crying.

"Well, I remember someone inviting me here and saying that I could eat, drink, and be naked with them all day."

"That was four months ago, Mike!" Steph was elated and excited.

"And I've thought about you every day we've been apart."

"But you didn't call much."

"I wanted to make sure you made a choice for yourself, Steph, not for me, and I knew you needed the space."

"Skippy said that you're busy with the club."

"I got Skippy to message you to get a position lock on your mobile." Mike smiled.

"She fucking knew you were here?"

"Yes."

Steph laughed. "I'll spank her when I see her."

"Steph, I came here on a complete whim. I don't know whether you've shacked up with someone or are leading your own life now, but I needed to see you to know for sure."

Steph's head was still spinning, but her body's reaction was giving away just how much she missed this guy, and it was now pretty clear he felt the same. Even though it had been four months, she guessed she could look beyond the lack of communication.

"Come with me, Mike," said Steph.

"Why?"

"You'll see."

Steph grabbed her things and walked with Mike about one hundred meters to the expansive house. Mike took Steph's hand, and she felt the excitement rise further in her body. This was a totally subconscious reaction to a very simple action.

They walked through the large glass-fronted patio doors and into the coolness of the air-conditioned house.

Mike let out a whistle as he saw how impressive the property was and how stunning Steph looked out of the sun.

Steph could now look at Mike properly. She saw his blue eyes shining as he took her in.

"Rosa," she called out.

"Yes, Miss Holgate?"

Rosa walked into the room to see a large muscular guy she instantly recognized from Steph's previous description.

"This is Mike Sharpe, the man I told you about," said Steph.

"About bloody time you came, Mr. Sharpe," said Rosa with a beaming smile.

Mike laughed. "Nice to meet you."

"Mike and I are going upstairs. We need some privacy."

Rosa smiled knowingly.

"Upstairs?" said Mike.

Steph smiled. "Mike, the moment I knew it was you, my body caught fire."

Rosa smiled. "You have a few months to make up for."

Steph removed her bikini bottoms and was naked before they got to the bedroom.

The next morning, Steph was awake before Mike. She jumped into the shower and washed off the night of lovemaking. Suddenly, things were falling into place, and her head was now absolutely clear. She knew exactly what she wanted. Steph walked out of the bathroom and into the bedroom. She looked at Mike peacefully asleep on the bed. She checked her phone. There was a message from Skippy.

If you two didn't fuck all night I will be pissed!

You are in fucking trouble when I see you, Steph responded.

She gazed at Mike again and smiled. He looked completely at rest, totally innocent in his slumber. She could see from the phone animation that Skippy was typing a response to her message.

You would have to come home to us all first, Skippy responded.

Steph smiled. Once again she looked at Mike and began to type a reply.

I am coming home Skippy. I'm coming home x.

The Skirmishers will return.